Some words in praise of this novel

Like a seed pod exploding, Fish's characters each go their own way, experimenting, and in reflection, catch that last bus to adulthood, with grit, tears, and aplomb. Bravo!"
— Robert McKean, *I'll Be Here for You: Diary of a Town*

Every page is a gift of wisdom and surprise, rendered in lush, poetic prose. It's a book of ideas with tremendous emotional power.
— Jonathan Vatner, *The Bridesmaids Union*

The characters in Fish's wonderfully funny, splendid novel twist and turn as they try to find themselves amid jealousy, longing, and trauma; these vibrant, riveting characters take their journeys through New York City, Finland, and New Orleans, creating a unique and compelling examination of self-reinvention at age 40.
— Karen E. Bender, National Book Award Finalist for *Refund*

Off the Yoga Mat is a delightful downtown romp about finding emotional balance when life unravels. Its authentic characters, compelling descriptions, and propulsive pace make for a heartfelt, joyful read.
— Amy Gottlieb, *The Beautiful Possible*

With a rip-roaring rotation of colorful characters, Fish's captivating novel weaves together the twists and turns of lives in search of renewal and purpose at the turn of a modern century.
— Pitchaya Sudbanthad, *Bangkok Deluge*

Three characters on the cusp of middle age search for emotional connection and meaningful work in this romp through dumpster-diving, Finnish saunas, yoga, toxic graduate school, erotic attraction, and the pursuit of family. Fish offers both a light touch and biting observations of self-reinvention, compromise, and creativity, as Lulu, Nora, and Nate try to figure out how to adult. A smart and funny read."

— Ellen Meeropol, *Her Sister's Tattoo*

Also by the author:

Poetry Chapbooks:
My City Flies By (E.G. Press)
Make it Funny, Make it Last (Belladonna #171)

Poetry Books:
Wing Span (Mellen Poetry Press)
Crater & Tower (Duck Lake Books)
The Sauna is Full of Maids, poems and photographs (Shanti Arts)

Non-Fiction Books:
A Stranger in the Village: Two Centuries of African-American Travel Writing, co-editor, with Farah J. Griffin (Beacon Press)
Black and White Women's Travel Narratives: Antebellum Explorations (University Press of Florida)

Off the Yoga Mat

Cheryl J. Fish

Livingston Press
The University of West Alabama

Copyright © 2022 Cheryl J. Fish
All rights reserved, including electronic text
ISBN 13: trade paper 978-1-60489-306-9
ISBN 13: hardcover 978-1-60489-307-6
ISBN 13: e-book 978-1-60489-308-3

Library of Congress Control Number 2022935864
Printed on acid-free paper
Printed in the United States of America by
Publishers Graphics

Hardcover binding by: HF Group
Typesetting and page layout: Joe Taylor
Proofreading: Cassidy Pedram, Joe Taylor, Brooke Barger

Cover Art: McKenna Darley

Cover design: Joe Taylor

short excerpts from this novel first appeared in:
Boog City (January 2022)
KGB Bar Lit (April 2022)

6 5 4 3 2 1

Off the Yoga Mat

For students and teachers

January, 1999

Chapter One
Inflexible

(Nate)

"When others achieve success, how does that diminish you?" Nathaniel Dart didn't care to consider this question from a talk-radio host. He was about to leave the apartment with a spasm in his back. His friend Gil, and his girlfriend Nora, had finally convinced him to take a trial yoga class in a studio a few blocks away. As he shuffled down Second Avenue, the success of others gnawed away at him. A cash bonus Nora received at the end-of-the-year—she deserved the money for a job well done—but he hadn't grabbed her around the waist or smiled in a swell of support. Nor had he taken her out to celebrate. And when Gil won a lottery for affordable housing nearby—which meant more space and rent stabilization—of course Gil rubbed it in his face, mentioning Nate's dark studio apartment with moths burrowing in the closet. Nate had no choice but to resent him. One other victory throbbed against his bony vertebrate.

His old study-group mate Monica Portman landed a teaching job in Boston, a position that Nate should have applied for, could have applied for...if only he'd finished his thesis. He struggled to accept Ralph Waldo Emerson's credo that "Envy is ignorance."

He stopped suddenly on the sidewalk to watch dumpster divers pick through garbage bins outside the supermarket. They'd cook what was still edible; someone shouted through a megaphone about the futility of waste in New York City. Determined to find freshness in what had been declared foul, the freegans sorted through packages past expiration dates and found perfectly decent bags of bagels, cookies and cut-up carrots. He heard them complain about tossing food when there were hungry and homeless folks everywhere. Nate felt disgusted by the vast inequalities in society; this topic mattered more than revising his thesis on jealousy as an evolutionary trait in humans.

Nate's research combined a trifecta of disciplines: science, literature and psychology. He knew it sounded loopy when he claimed a jealousy hormone benefited not only those species studied by Charles Darwin, like the blue-footed boobies of the Galapagos, but also Homo Sapiens. Envious rage might motivate men and women to loosen their desire for control, and the result could turn out for the better. Yet jealousy was no walk in the park—it caused primitive rage and destruction, something Nate witnessed everywhere. In his thesis, he proved his point by examining jealous characters in Shakespeare's *Othello* and *King Lear.*

How does their success diminish mine? He wished he could put that thought out of his mind. Nate spent countless hours in his swivel chair; one could say he lived where he sat.

In the yoga class, a tingling numbness ran down his legs: pain and trembling too. He stood in a darkish room; a teacher asked them to bend from their core towards the floor. He couldn't reach past his knees. I am not a yoga guy, he thought—I have more in common with the freegans. I should have never set foot in this dusty old hovel. He felt others staring at him.

Nate contemplated his future on all fours doing cow and cat, rounding his back like a feline. Or should he flatten it like a bovine? Who

Off the Yoga Mat

named these postures? The students stood in unison, placing a bent leg along their thigh for tree pose. He grabbed a beam.

"Focus on one point on the wall," said the teacher, a strikingly fit woman named Lulu Betancourt, who welcomed them warmly and insisted they obey their own bodies. "Take a three-part breath and be mindful. Let air seep out like a leaky balloon."

Nate smirked. He visualized a giant balloon emptying with farting sounds. He filled his lungs then exhaled, just as he was told. Relaxation could wash over him.

She soon introduced them to the series "Salute to the sun." A set of flowing movements that started with standing, progressed to rolling to the floor and rising into the cobra and plank positions with a rhythmic grace, and then ended with an upward curl, palms pressed together in gratitude. A subtle choreography he punctuated with jerking motions. If Nate could reach an inch nearer to his toes and roll down without collapsing, he felt like he would celebrate. His version might be called parody, not salute. But he was determined to modify his moves, like the barnacles, finches and beetles Darwin observed.

"Melt into the earth with a rushing sensation, rain drenching fields," Lulu said in a soft yet determined voice. She leaned against the wall, bowed her head.

Nate tried to experience rain. Instead, he thought about money. He benefited neither from the loopholes in capitalism that let the richest prosper, nor from a critique of its corruption. I am an academic serf living on rice and beans, he thought, and no one could care less. He was deep in debt from loans. He should apply for another fellowship or take an adjunct position at a City University campus. He wondered about the job mentioned by his advisor in his recent nasty note. Offendorf had scribbled dismissive comments on the pages it took Nate many months to write, and even more months to find the courage to mail to the university down in Maryland (with Nora's goading). Offendorf had the nerve to reply:

WAY TOO MUCH time spent on Darwin. It may be trendy to consider evolutionary theory, but I don't care for that approach. Take out feminism and limit psychoanalysis. You've inserted too many footnotes. Let's put this baby to bed. When are you coming to campus? Bring the revision—we'll talk defense date. Oh, and I might know of a teaching position."

As Nate considered whether the job was real or just another one of Offendorf's bluffs, he was instructed to twist his torso, knee cutting across his folded leg. This position evoked the twists and turns of Nora's desire.

"Let's conceive a millennial child," she said. Nineteen-ninety-nine high stepped like a marching band through her ovaries. Fear of her upcoming—their upcoming—fortieth birthdays felt like annihilation.

"Nora. I can't give you a baby now."

"I knew you'd say that," Nora said. "There's never going to be a perfect time."

"I'm not in the position to be a dad."

"You'd be very loving." She stroked his hand. "My salary can tide us over."

His inability to care for a child felt like a character deficiency. He needed to finish his degree before procreating—not focus on the milestone of age forty. When his mom visited from Long Island the other day, she slipped him a wad of cash.

"Don't say anything to your father."

"You don't have to keep doing this," he said, feeling sheepish and small.

***

Nate's spine cracked. Lulu headed over to his side during *dandasana*, a forward bend that segued into a seated, wide-angle pose. She crouched. "Breathe into your stretch." He noticed a beady-eyed frog tattoo near her shoulder—green and black, sinister. Lulu smelled of rose oil.

"What's wrong?" she whispered.

"I can't concentrate." What made her want to ink a frog into her skin?

"Observe your thoughts. They'll dissipate." She touched his head. "Probably."

How should he respond to Offendorf's reign of terror? Say, "I need Darwin like Shakespeare needed the source material for some of his plays, Holinshed's *Chronicles of England, Scotland, and Ireland?*"

While Nate rested in child's pose—head on mat, arms and legs compressed like a floating fetus—a surge of energy ran from the tips of his toes into his calves. So, what if Offendorf demanded he cut one-third of all he had written? How did their success diminish his? Disappointments acquired territory. One negative experience attracted others, expanding into new fiefdoms.

Monica Portman applied for everything. "I invented personal literary criticism," she said, convinced of her pioneering role. Wasn't she coming to town? As Nate struggled to pick himself up off the floor for the next posture, it occurred to him: send her the very same pages Offendorf trashed and ask for a second opinion. Monica's instincts resembled a baby sea turtle's—born in sand, hurdling towards the ocean. He should trust her to guide him to safety.

Then yogi Lulu announced to the room, "Return to downward-facing dog." He bent over, and placing his hands flat, stuck his butt in the air.

Chapter Two
Seva

(Lulu)

There may have been a connection between the yoga triangles Lulu Betancourt demonstrated and her tendency to form love triangles. She had reveled in her share of risqué encounters with men and women in the past decade. Now, Lulu thought, a brand-new year leading to the millennium. Slow down! She'd missed meaningful coupling, enduring love. Of her many relationships, including a brief marriage to Wendell, none had stuck. She visualized herself in a playful dance with one who twirled her, pressed her close. She could shimmy out of that person's grasp without breaking eye contact: solo and yet mutual. Then it would be her lover's turn to shine within her circle, a complete being all alone. She refused to dwell on recurring nightmares of a stout bald man taunting her in childhood.

Lulu walked from her apartment on Avenue A and 12th Street to 2 Squared, her studio in a red-brick building, on the corner of Second Avenue and Second Street. Teaching and assisting others in a trial hatha yoga class created a space to breathe out her nightmare. That man had known her mother in New Orleans when she was little, after her dad left. Lulu stared at the assortment of men and women in the room. They had all shown up to check out a free, sample class that she offered from time to time to attract new followers. She went easy, asked them to do a few standing poses. Then she worked on their cores, backs pressed into their mats. The chanting afterwards proved cathartic; the students, moved by harmonic vibrations, sounded like a string quartet in a glade of trees. The tone of voices in unison, low and deep, formed a protective shield around Lulu.

After folks cleared out, a guy named Jesse from the health food store stopped by—she forgot she had invited him over. They made small talk in the studio. Then he lifted her, kissing her non-tattooed shoulder. His lips on her skin tickled.

She expressed pleasure through non-Sanskrit chants and sighs. Lulu seldom planned such liaisons, but sex and yoga were mutual portals to her soul—the equipment in her playground. As Jesse spoke her name, Lulu thought, this feels rushed. It's not what I want. She heard the door to the vestibule open with a rattle outside the yoga room. Who was there?

"Hello." A deep voice echoed.

"Excuse me." She wriggled out of Jesse's embrace and adjusted her clothes. "Just a minute," she shouted. She walked into the small entrance.

She squinted through the dimness and recognized the tall, striking guy with unkempt dark hair, his pallor set off by facial stubble. He must have overheard giggles and kisses, might have glimpsed a quick embrace.

"Sorry I barged in," he said, offering his hand. "I'm Nate Dart. Sorry to disturb… whatever. I took your trial class. Forgot my backpack. Can I take a look?" He walked through the studio door without waiting for her answer. Then he reappeared. "Got it."

He was about to scoot away.

"Wait a second, Nate," Lulu said. "I am curious. What brought you to my class?"

He paused. "For starters, I've got lower back pain. And…I can't seem to write my thesis." His stomach growled. He rubbed his midsection. "I've decided…to try this yoga thing."

She noted wide dark eyes, long hair, tapered fingers. He was impossible to forget—wearing jeans in class, barely crossing his legs, and trying to duck out. Then he snored in bursts of intensity during *savasana*.

"Sorry to hear you're in pain." She pulled down her shirt. "If you saw or heard anything out of the ordinary...it's not in the curriculum."

"That's for the advanced class," he said, deadpan.

She laughed and whirled around. Handed him a pocket-sized schedule. "Yoga has great potential to release stress and increase calm—help you to cast off your demons. Everyone goes at their own pace. Come back! Don't let the others in class distract you."

"I know about distractions," Nate said. "I tend to avoid."

"Don't avoid me."

A powerful gust of wind blasted up the steps from outside through the doorway. She folded her arms and shivered.

"I'll close the door on my way out," he said. He flashed a crooked smile before turning his back to her.

This Nate—scruffy, cool as a cucumber. In class, she had helped him to his knees and into child's pose. She assisted in rocking him side to side, showed him how to form a spinal twist. He seemed embarrassed. "You've made me bend," he said. "I thought it was impossible."

She noted dark circles beneath his eyes, a dimple chin unaware of its sweetness. What was he writing about? Probably something unsavory.

After locking the studio door, Lulu found it impossible to focus on Jesse.

"I'm not into it," she said and led Jesse to her tiny office, where they drank hot water over tea leaves. After he left, Lulu, exhausted, stacked the stray mats and rounded up cushions and yoga blocks. Next, she concentrated on steady three-part breathing, then gathered her things to go.

She locked the door of the outer vestibule behind her and meandered down the long flight of steps. Outside she merged into the chaos of the East Village. A car blasted its staccato horn. A man rode a bike past her on the sidewalk, nearly grazing her toes. Someone yelled "muthafucka." Off to the side of the building, a tall skinny man with a mustache stood puffing on a cigarette.

"Ms. Betancourt? Glad I caught you," he said, exhaling. "Didn't you receive the notices? I'm from the building manager's office."

Shit. It must have been about those letters on behalf of the ginor-mous university. Why wouldn't they let her be? Did they have to keep migrating, taking over the West Village, and now the East, some kind of educational manifest destiny?

"You've got thirty days," he said. "The university is buying the building. Everyone out."

"I need time," Lulu said, composed. "I run a successful busi-ness."

"Don't we all," he said. "Fill out the papers. Agree to vacate. I have a feeling you can negotiate, see some cash. It's a win-win."

"I have to go," she said, breaking away.

She'd look them over later, maybe get some advice. No way would she let them toss her out. She had shoved earlier notices into a drawer.

As she walked north, a group of men and women climbed into and out of a dumpster in front of a supermarket. Others sat on the nearest stoop, sorting through fruits, vegetables and prepared cakes. A tall wom-an with a pom-pom hat gripped a megaphone. The participants, known as freegans, were mostly white children of the middle-class. Lulu had passed them many times before; she found their behavior perplexing. Why frolic in garbage to make a point? She preferred charity behind-the-scenes and to give back to women and communities of color who had it the worst. Those freegans? Privileged grandstanding.

Her recent New Year's resolution: focus on yoga away from the mat—*seva,* a term used by her teachers in the ashram to indicate a spir-itual presence directed to those in dire need. She considered developing a yoga class for distressed and angry children, kids who'd likely dismiss the practice but unwittingly find grace through it. Kids in the housing projects nearby who never had access to yoga. As an angry frightened child, racially mixed at a time it was rarely discussed, she could never be sure of peace. She was never certain of her parents' love. Her mother Rosa discovered yoga by following the moves of a TV guru; her lion posture cracked up Lulu as a child. On all fours, her mother stuck out her tongue and then roared. It marked a time before their lives spiraled away.

The freegan leader shouted into a megaphone on the middle of Second Avenue: "Who will join us? So much food in New York City is wasted while others go hungry. The world isn't going to end in the year 2000, but what if we could end hunger?"

Lulu stared at the scraggly dumpster divers. She planned to volunteer at The Bowery Mission or a nearby soup kitchen. So much begging on the sidewalks: ragged folks of all ages strewn across alleys and in Tompkins Square Park, runaway kids addicted to something and needing help they wouldn't seek. Could she ever find compassion for herself in this desolation? What if she was forced to relocate, thrown out of the humble studio she had built from nothing? She'd go back to zero. A term from Buddhism gave her perspective: *in the readiness of time. Embrace the one.* Nightmares disrupted her days, but relief came from consulting the Yoga Sutras of Patanjali, cryptic aphorisms by a yogi alive in the second century. She told herself to live in the now-and-here, even as she recalled dreaded fragments of her past. Sometimes she could not recognize the false from true, or find a plausible answer. She'd get to the bottom of her nightmares while serving those who needed it the most.

Let go of judging everyone, even myself, Lulu thought. Pedestrians sidestepped the rag-tag freegans clogging a patch of Second Avenue, as if their freshness long passed the expiration date. She dropped a five-dollar bill into the donation basket and prayed for patience and resolution.

Chapter Three
Like Peary, but With Panache

(Nora)

Nora Jane Lester hunched over her desk crafting biographies of cars for her firm Secanor's client, a car dealership. She had been asked to turn cars into characters, make them seem like beloved friends. She'd been assigned this project by Secanor's vice president, Rebecca Magum-Chin, now heavily pregnant, who acted fake-nice even when she was seething. RMC, the nickname they used for her, coddled demanding clients and expected Nora to follow her lead.

"You're my girl," Rebecca said. Nora smiled when her boss singled her out and promised her a cubicle with a window. "Real soon."

Fueled on caffeine and self-loathing, Nora wondered what to do about Nate. Far from perfect, but she knew him. *Fortieth birthday approaching* signaled to her monkey-mind. Go out there and find a grown-up partner. With any luck, she'd get a shot at becoming a wise, permissive parent. One recent night with Nate, a small gray moth flew out of the dark enclosure of his closet. It fluttered its gossamer wings in place and reminded her of time eaten away. "My eggs are drying out," she said, a stupid statement in hindsight, like hitting a panic button. "I don't want to gather dust, like those books." She surveyed rows bound to each other in bracketed sagging shelves above Nate's bed, next to his collection of vintage radios. Each time she slept over she anticipated a cave-in.

Nora envisioned Nate reclining on the open sea of his future, lighting up doobies, obsessing over Galapagos birds and bugs. Reading,

reading, clutching his back.

When she got bored of working on cars and considering how to break it off with Nate, Nora skimmed a book about attracting a beau who'd stick-to-your-ribs. The dating equivalent of oatmeal. She heard colleagues setting up a baby shower on her boss's final day before maternity leave. They were hanging balloons and streaming blue-and-pink banners inside the conference room. She watched delivery men carry plates of catered food. I should have taken a sick day, she realized; her head might burst, her stomach heave.

A few women accompanied Rebecca into the conference room. Nora overheard them sharing breast-feeding ordeals as if it was the stuff of legends. If only I could contribute to the conversation about latching and pumping, body-on-body demand. I am an animal, she thought, with instincts and receptivity and breasts ripe to nurse. Dropping the self-help manual, Nora dragged herself to the party.

"Nora's always making books and mock-ups, so she'll build the maternity hat," someone insisted. After downing two flutes of champagne and mingling a bit to be civil, Nora retreated to her desk, out-of-range of the squeals over baby outfits pulled from boxes. She mechanically glued ribbons and wrapping-paper scraps onto corrugated cardboard to design a ridiculous, yet stylish, hat. Nora penned "Mama Becca," in calligraphy on the front and went back to the conference room to crown her ebullient boss.

"Another stunning object d'art, Nora," said Magum-Chin, scratching her swollen stomach. "Wait till you see who's replacing me. A real hottie."

"Shall I keep writing about the cars?" Nora asked.

"Of course."

Nora often stayed late, creating copy to satisfy clients' inane demands. Her pitches passed muster with junior executives. Later, she'd recalibrate them for the senior VPs expecting more. She found it tedious to bite the hand that fed her; she disliked it when Nate criticized her fervor for complying. He'd called her "the consummate consumer." She earned a decent salary. Rebecca awarded her an unexpected bonus at

Christmas! Nora contributed to the gross national product, purchasing lacy tops, designer couture, shoes and kitchen gadgets at Century 21, her temple of a department store near the World Trade Center. Instead of investing in the stock market, Nora bought items she loved in bulk. When she realized she didn't want the identical blouse in three colors, she'd return most of them. Recently, she received a warning. "Ms. Lester, if you keeping buying and returning mountains of merchandise, we'll cut you off."

Nate advised Nora to change careers: from marketing to industrial design. She created home-made books, desk lamps, frames and ornamental pedestals for computer keyboards with a dedication he reserved for undecipherable theory books. Thoughtful advice, but she had no desire to return to school.

As Nora contemplated her future, Rebecca's belly sang an aria from its low protruding position. Everyone petted it. At the end of the baby shower, her boss stood at the head of the table. Called them to order. A handsome man stood by her side.

"Everyone, I'd like to introduce Mr. Jeremy Frankl. He'll occupy my position for three months, effective immediately. He comes from Secanor's downtown location...we are lucky to have him. But guess what, boys and girls. He's known for busting chops."

Hesitant applause. Some male colleagues pumped their fists. The women gazed upon Jeremy Frankl, shiny and bold as a new Ferrari. Nora's thumbnail impression: tall, graying fast, about forty-eight, European designer suit, classic nose, roving eyes, excessive testosterone. Oh no, she thought, as a warm rivulet of lust migrated from her belly button to her crotch. He's irresistible.

When the party broke up, Jeremy Frankl stormed her cubicle. "No-ra Jane Les-ter," he enunciated. "You're going to write a press kit and prepare a catalogue for a plastics designer. I'll go over the details in the morning." He handed her a fat stack of paper.

"Yes, sir," she said, smiling.

"What are you writing?" Jeremy craned his neck towards her screen.

"I'm finishing a project for Rebecca."

"You report to me."

"I still work for her."

"I come first." He placed his hands and hairy forearms on her desk. "Your output has been terrific. I checked." He winked. "Someone's having a great hair day."

Her heart pumped. She excused herself, walked briskly to the women's bathroom. Glanced at her hair in the mirror—it must have been that glaze they added at the salon. Then she leaned against the door of a stall. Jeremy Frankl combined masculinity and self-assurance. Sexy, powerful. Probably a dick.

The new boss favored neckties decorated with beer steins or The Oxford Debating Society's emblem of gavel and lion. He ran his first meeting at the end of his first week using a modified version of Robert's Rules; a staffer obtained the floor by rising and shouting "Mr. Chairman." When a debate took place on a strategy for the Drogan account, Jeremy made a motion, demanded a secret ballot and silenced all dissent. Lonnie, Nora's best friend, begged her to date men she'd usually rule out; Lonnie repeated, "Dump Nate Dart." Nora set aside the car profile of Bradford the BMW for her absent boss and prioritized Jeremy.

In the weeks that followed, Nora caught whiffs of his cologne and wondered what she should do. He flirted up and down the halls with women from secretaries to managers—Nate would have called it "marking his territory." She imagined Jeremy waiting for her down the aisle as she donned a Victorian bridal gown, heavily pregnant. But then Jeremy morphed into the Frankenstein monster. She smacked the side of her head. Woman, deny your base instincts. He's toxic.

She missed the deadline for the plastics catalogue. On the day it was due, she took the subway to All About Plastics on Canal Street, purchasing samples with her own money to create a plastics tome that would blow Jeremy's mind. Show him her way with objects and textures, her unique sense of style, her determined intensity and ambition. But when she turned over her finest work—pages bulging with samples of thick and colorful plastics, dense as a pane of glass, pure virtuosity—Jeremy threatened to dock her pay.

"Nora, I wanted it on time. I don't need fancy," he said. "Why are you messing with me?"

"It's unique," she said, struggling to meet his eyes. Glorious, complex: Nora at her best inside a binder. "I am not messing with you."

"Would you mess *around?*" he whispered under his breath.

She opened her mouth: nothing came out.

Back at her desk and unable to work, she thought about artistry. It required more than occasional inspiration, a glimmering evocation made real. Despite her obedience and her drive to display her finest creations, Nora wanted to run screaming from the place. She resolved with clarity to act as if it these were the end times. *Carpe diem.*

***

The next week, while Jeremy Frankl was attending a seminar in Princeton, Nora found his office door ajar. When the others on her team went to lunch, she entered Jeremy's cave to uncover his secrets. It reeked of hair gel and coffee. In his cushioned chair, she felt like Goldilocks. What else can I find out about him? She glanced at the pile of papers on his desk, material about the Drogan realtor/developer account...big snooze. His dog-eared copy of *Bleak House* sat on the credenza, next to a framed photo of Jeremy's son and ex-wife. Nora overheard Jeremy telling a colleague that he hardly saw his son. "I'd like to have another child," he said. On his desk she glimpsed a calendar page with the word "date" and a * symbol from the previous week. Was that some code?

Rising from his chair, Nora noticed a memo on the top of the inbox tray. Written on a yellow post-it: "Distribute to my team." From Rebecca Magum-Chin. He hadn't distributed it. Why not?

Nora picked it up. Subject line: **Nokia Opportunity**. She remembered collaborating on a project with that firm a couple of years back. She'd worked with Anita Willis, an executive who quit Secanor to become a freegan dumpster-diver and AIDS activist, shocking everyone. In the margin, Rebecca wrote "Jeremy, YOU cannot go abroad. Send someone." Nora ran to the copy machine, then put back the original. She sat at her desk and re-read it carefully.

Nokia, the cell phone leader in handsets, based in Espoo, Finland, has a five-month opportunity in its Tampere office for an American marketing professional. Finns stand to benefit from American expertise in product outreach to the United States, while the Nokia fellow will study Finnish strategies for technological innovation and serve on a Y2K committee. A course will be offered at the local university in Finnish history and culture. We hope to hear from you immediately. We anticipate your firm will see as much value in this exchange as we do.

Why couldn't it be a post in Paris or Rome? She had never traveled to Europe. What a gift. Finland couldn't be far from La Belle France. It rubbed against Russia, that behemoth of classical genius and former Communist scoundrels. SEND ME! Nora thought, laughing into the empty office. She could stomach working for Secanor as long as she got out of *here*. It would shock her into the necessity of separating from Nate, provide a blank slate.

Nora left a message on RMC's voicemail. "I hope you are relaxing before you give birth. Hear me out. Jeremy's at a seminar. He's been hyper critical. I heard about that assignment in Finland. I've never gone anywhere. Can you send me away? PLEASE."

RMC required more than selfish motives, so Nora thought fast: "I will bring back insider secrets. I'll promote our international reputation. Find out how to fix the Y2K bug. Call me back."

She held her breath. What had she done? Become her own fairy Godmother.

By the time Jeremy returned, Rebecca had granted her a get-out-of-jail-free card: a plane ticket to Helsinki enclosed inside an interoffice envelope—departure in *one week*. She could barely catch her breath! What about her dad's upcoming prostate surgery—they said "routine," but what if she lost him? Her dad loved her unconditionally; her stomach quaked at the thought of deserting him. Her plan had been to go to Maryland where her parents lived, squeeze his hand before they wheeled him into the OR. Wait until he came out. In one piece.

She phoned her parents. "Mother, they want me to take an assignment in Finland. I am sorry I won't be around for Dad's surgery...but

I promise to call you all the time. Oh, and one more thing. My relationship with Nate...on hold." There, she said it. Sounded better than "It's gone kaput."

Her mom sighed. "How are you going to settle down if you're unsettled?"

"No comment." Usually, her mom changed the subject when she brought up Nate. She met him once, underwhelmed.

"Why do you have to go so far away?"

"Congratulations!" her dad shouted from the other phone extension. "Have a wonderful time, darling. Isn't Finland where that code developer Linux comes from? Don't worry. I'll be fine."

"I love you daddy. I didn't know I'd be leaving right away. I am so sorry I won't be with you, but my prayers, my healing intentions... my love..."

"I know. You can't stand in more than one place at a time."

Nora would join a firm that had morphed from provincial rubber producer to global leader in cell phone handsets. She'd represent the North American consumer, informing managers how to penetrate the psyche of her fellow citizens as the new century approached. On the map, Finland poked out of the top of Europe, the Arctic Circle bisecting its upper third. A large land mass shaped like a tall, one-armed woman without a torch—Nora's version of Miss Liberty. Exile on ice would secure distance from her present life, let her make a name for herself. She imagined lumbering over the tundra in a fur parka, like the famous explorers Peary and Amundsen, but with panache.

"Watch me salute the sun," Nate shouted when she came in the door. On his frayed rug, he demonstrated how he rose with his arms flowing and then bended with labor onto the floor. He paused, out of breath, then moved snake-like to get back onto his feet. Nora applauded and felt sad; maybe she was crazy to go away. When they made love, Nora's heart pounded as if to say "stay home."

When she told Nate that Rebecca trusted her to do the company proud and urged her to go to Finland for this unique opportunity, Nate's eyes moistened. His face turned sallow.

"Five months…it's a long time," he said, shifting in bed to face the wall.

"Maybe you can visit," Nora said, thinking that he must at least feel relieved the baby conversation is leaving the room. Neither of them uttered the term "break up." The sensation of separating, of winter's darkness, hovered. He's shedding tears, Nora thought. Am I sure of this move? No, but not going would be worse.

Hasty preparation for Finland kept her busy. In the few days before her flight, she shopped for warm clothes amid spring-oriented racks at Century 21. No one had heard of Tampere, the second largest Finnish city. It was located inland and formerly known as the Manchester of Finland for its factories and working-class sympathies. Nora recalled that Nate's mother Audrey was half Finnish. And it turned out, Lonnie had known a woman named Bethany Mayles from her high school days in Minnesota. Bethany married a Finnish exchange student and lived with him and her kids in the suburbs outside Tampere. She helped settle recent refugees and asylum seekers. Lonnie gave Nora her email address.

"Pack light," Bethany wrote back. "We'll head to the thrift shops. Get everything from pots and pans to skis. Finns know how to recycle."

"I don't ever pack light," Nora replied.

At the Mid-Manhattan branch of the public library, Nora paged through books about Finland. She took out a movie by the Finnish director Aki Kaurismäki: *The Match Factory Girl*, a darkly humorous story of thwarted expectations featuring a young woman in a dead-end job in a match factory who gets pregnant by a man she picked up in a bar. Nora wondered what that foretold about her prospects. Full of adrenaline and focused on possibility, Nora spoke it out loud: SU-OM-EE. *Suomi, the name of Finland in Finnish.*

She stuffed two large suitcases with enough clothing, shoes and cosmetics to last a year. When it came to deciding between fur-lined boots and fashionable ones, she packed both. On a whim, she purchased a batch of beloved Dr. Seuss books and a frilly party dress for Bethany's children. She took two tiny onesie outfits perfect for a newborn baby. She was not giving up on a vision of a gorgeous baby bump.

In the far north, the heavens shine with light from sunspots, as particles escaping the sun send a revelation of solar wind to earth. Nora would ride that glorious aurora wind.

February, 1999

Chapter Four
The Darker Strata

(Nate)

Where was Monica Portman? Nate tapped his foot to no particular beat in a Hell's Kitchen tavern decorated with suits of armor, coat-of-arms insignia and large metallic steins full of beer. As the one in his dissertation group who always backed him and refused to kiss Offendorf's ring, Monica was Nate's golden girl. Finally, the door like an entrance to a castle swung open. She rushed over.

"So sorry. My fiancé and I sat forever in traffic," said Monica, sitting down.

Fiancé? In grad school she had rarely gone out. "Thanks for reading my chapters on short notice." Waiting to hear her thoughts had blocked the reality of Nora's departure.

"Any time," Monica said, out of breath. "First, the good news. You've integrated *Lear* with Darwin and Freud. Claiming jealousy as a death wish in family drama—so good. To quote Lear, 'allow not nature more than nature needs.' Offendorf must hate it! But that's not the biggie," she said. "Guess what. I'm here to advise you to write a *different* book."

"Huh?" he asked. "Write *what*?"

"No emotion in these pages." She flapped them. "They're flat, Nate. Jealousy should torture us! I am taken by the confessional approach. The personal angle." She removed her jacket. "Scholars should include honest realizations."

He was flummoxed, unaware that personal narrative could be blended with research—a form of psychological transference. It sounded disastrous. He just needed to remind Monica that he didn't dwell on envy. It made everything worse. Look at the sickness that inflamed Lear's eldest daughters, as well as the brothers Edgar and Edmund. In Shakespeare's time, jealousy was considered restless melancholy that transformed men into beasts. Nate recoiled from opening those gates. Monica had landed an impressive job. She flashed an engagement ring. He didn't burn with envy.

"Monica. You forget. I'm not the jealous type."

"Horseshit, Nate. Haven't you been deceived? Cheated on? At some point, you must have fallen for the same woman as a friend. Competed for a prize and lost. Own those emotions! I've been envious. It fueled my desire to win."

He laughed. "You get jealous. Why would I take the dissertation in a new direction now? It's been way too long."

"I know," Monica said. "Sometimes a new angle gets us cooking. This could lead to a fabulous job. Turn you into a star." She motioned to the waiter.

"Monica, I'm flattered. But…." In fact, he had imagined himself as a go-to critic, ivory tower pin-up boy. "I drove Nora crazy denying I was jealous," he said. "When she had drinks with a bunch of guys from work, I didn't mind. I didn't question it when she stayed out late and came back tipsy. She expected me to give her a hard time."

"It would indicate you wanted her."

"That ship has sailed," he said. "She's left for some job in Finland."

"Finland? Sorry to hear it. She was good for you."

"Anyways…Offendorf asked for specific edits. He wants something else."

"Convince him to see it *my* way. But don't name me."

"Hm. I'll think about it," he said. "Treat jealousy as some kind of social experiment that I'm part of?"

"That's the spirit. Go out on a limb. Set up a test case. Record the results. If your thesis is visceral, it will generate buzz. Who reads a typical dissertation except librarians and specialists? This can be something fabulous!"

He needed his book to make a splash, considering all the years he struggled to perfect it. Imagine attracting critical praise from *Rolling Stone* ("The Darwinian Case for Iago's Twisted Mind"); *The New Yorker* (*Talk of the Town*: "An Unfit Professor Who Thrived"). A profile in the *New York Times Magazine* and an appearance on the late show, wearing an Italian suit, maybe growing a small beard. Nate's insights gleaned from Darwin and Shakespeare would unnerve everyone. They'd be forced to admit the uncanny foundation of all language, thought and action. How does their success light a fire under our sorry asses? We are primitive, petty grifters. But academic fiefdoms being what they were, he couldn't branch out until he received his Ph.D.

"Haven't I ever told you, Nate, about that time I fell for a genius dweeb?" Monica said, sipping wine from a goblet featuring rhinestones. "I shopped, decorated his apartment, built him up, slept with him. Then he tutored a red-headed ESL student with a bird-like laugh, brought her books. She stole my beau from under my nose! I managed to get her fired from her job. She couldn't prove a thing. When I entered grad school, I made my mark."

"And now you have *your* romantic happy ending." Nate was surprised to learn his school pal was not merely ambitious, but vicious. "Who is your fellow?"

"I met Paulo at the narrative conference. We're hoping he can get a job in the Boston area. But back to you. These chapters need to pack a wallop. Fight for what you deserve, Nate. As my Italian lover says, if another guy eyeballs me, he's gonna break his head open. Court *gelosia.*" Her voice trembled. "Remember what William James said about the darker strata? In our darkest places, we catch the *facts*."

Darker strata. Nate guarded his vulnerability, obscured it with intellect and passivity. In truth, he often experienced bitter envy, hopeless defeat. So much so that he shied away from opening up or loving deeply, limiting his involvement with anyone who might shatter his fragile heart. He cowered, lied to himself, deceived others, and with his friend Gil, behaved like a permanent adolescent. That's why Nora could leave him in a flash.

Nate peered into his empty glass. "Monica, I hate you for making me confess this. When I was 16 or 17, my cousin Daniel arrived in Florida a couple of days after the rest of our family for a vacation. I had already befriended a wonderful girl named Ceci; we hung on each other's every word. Daniel challenged her to a tennis match while I swatted balls into the net and chased them over the fence. My insecurities dictated I do everything to make her like me…talking about music, complimenting her, making it worse. She smelled desperation. Daniel and Ceci were necking in the grass behind the condo, screwing behind a locked door. I prayed for an alligator to devour them in the canal. I flogged myself, picked my acne…my mother drove me to Cape Canaveral as a distraction. Jealous indeed. A long time ago."

Nate peered at the floor. "Now that kind of thing doesn't faze me. When Daniel and I were almost thirty, he was in law school. I considered graduate school. At a party on Long Island, a woman who flirted with me all afternoon chose to sleep with him. In Darwinian terms, unacknowledged competition. He eradicated me." He laughed nervously, never having shared this anecdote. "She wasn't my type."

He raised his head. Looked Monica in the eye. Shame pulsed through his limbs like a rich dye.

"Nate," Monica reached across the table, patted his hand. "It's normal. You coveted what Daniel stole. Of course, you'd get jealous… angry too. Anyone would! Change the names. Use that material," she released his hand. "Feel your fury. Your time is coming!"

He raised his head. "All right. I'll tell my friend Gil about your idea. See what he cooks up." Gil thrived on showy provocation and games. Now Nate had to get Monica out of his hair. He motioned to the waiter to bring the check.

"Do what it takes," said Monica.

"I'll try."

As Nate and Monica left the tavern, they embraced and promised to stay in touch. Nate made his way towards the 50th Street subway station. He took a three-part breath to dissipate a creeping sense of panic, his spine throbbing. Nora gone, his dissertation down the drain. He decided to run the entire perimeter of Central Park.

Chapter Five
Vulnerable and Cracked

(Lulu)

The shrill ringing of the phone pulled Lulu from deep sleep. A man chased her in their backyard. She heard his feet, listened to sharp gasps of his breath. She hid behind a Palmetto. Her doll kept on talking: "Let's play house. Let's…"

Lulu groped for the receiver. She mumbled into it, "Hello?"

"It's me," said Rosa.

"Mama…I told you not to call me after 10 p.m. You caught me…in a nightmare. I'm back in New Orleans." Lulu's voice cracked. "There's this man, stocky, bald."

"What you talking about?" Rosa said. "Say, 'good evening? How are things down at the shore?' Don't gallop headlong into the past."

.   "Mama. You know that man."

"You wanted to hear from me. I'm in Ocean Grove."

"I thought you had to get out of Mary's place. Why not move in with Uncle Monroe? He has room." Lulu shook off her sleepy haze. "Then you don't have to keep worrying about where to live."

"I like the shore," her mother said. "Got me a tiny closet of a room in Mary's guesthouse for a few more weeks. A Victorian in need of a paint job. Leaking and noisy, like me. Come see."

Dealing with Rosa required delicacy, patience. Lulu remembered a few days ago when she kept her New Year's resolution and had worked a shift at The Lord is My Shepherd soup kitchen, wearing gloves and a hairnet to serve meals. A U2 song blasted.

A woman named Ginny called her "dear." While Lulu collected plates and refilled water glasses, Ginny said, "I hear your southern drawl." Lulu hadn't lived in Louisiana since she was small; that was when she still went by her given name, Luanne. Ginny asked her to sit down as she described how she endured shock treatment. That reminded Lulu of Rosa's wailing about Maximilian. "Your daddy and his drinking made me consider getting shocked with probes," Rosa had said. Instead, she took a long walk out by Lake Pontchartrain, not far from their house. Walking along the water's edge, day or night.

As her mother clambered into her ear, Lulu realized Rosa was an aging queen without land or followers. As ever, vulnerable and cracked.

"Go to sleep, Mama, and let me try too. I *will* come see you. I want to know about that man. I have to get up early and teach."

***

That morning Lulu gazed at Nate in baggy sweats. A gentle soul, serious about yoga. She had a hunch he masked libertine behavior behind insecurity. He hadn't teased her over the near-tryst with Jesse, hadn't come on to her. Tired of men's assumptions, and worn out by their insistence and her own lack of willpower, Lulu's hormones would not quit. Could self-control and mindfulness haul her over the mountain of sex? If she developed patience, desire would simmer on the stove.

"Melt like a stick of butter in a warming pan," Lulu instructed. She smiled when pose inspired prose.

It looked like Nate softened on his mat. He attended her class twice a week—unshaven with deep-set brown eyes, limited in movement yet persevering. She relished his potential as an unlikely gift. Despite a tendency to drop out in the middle of a posture, he held his own in cobra and fish. Showed up without showing off. She'd encouraged him to do a shoulder stand, demonstrated the locust pose because that *asana* relieved sciatica. He'd raised his arms, stretched his torso and formed a straight line. With a subtler back he'd appreciate life, claim his radiance.

Lulu took the class from *tadasana*, mountain pose—a centering of the self in stillness—into Warrior II. "Jump your feet out sideways—take an elephant stance. Turn the right leg and foot inward, the left leg and foot to 90 degrees." She demonstrated. Her black leggings and dark tee-shirt became one with subdued light.

"Bend your left knee and rotate your upper arms…align shoulder with feet. Notice energy tingling from your spine to your fingers. Visualize a line running through your torso. Summon the courage to forgive."

Warrior poses evoked the stillness and acceptance of Buddha, who said loving-kindness and freedom are our birthright. She asked everyone to concentrate on their breath. Taut, outstretched limbs resembled a bow and arrow. They channeled Eros and cosmos—cleansing and restoring. Feet planted. The dharma of awakening.

"Summon strength and forbearance," she said. "Grasp what transpired during warrior." She perspired somewhere inside her shirt. Maybe they were tired of listening. Maybe they were bored. Lulu walked the rows, glanced at Nate. He seemed frustrated, yet willful and intelligent. Why didn't he hang around after class like the others? What was he writing about? How did yoga affect his story?

As she stood on her toes to lengthen her torso, Lulu decided to catch the train to see her mother. Discover missing pieces about that man in the nightmares and then vanquish him.

Her parents had torn each other apart when she was growing up. Maximilian cheated on Rosa, but he had doted on Lulu when he wasn't berating his daughter or threatening to punch out her lights. After she had hung up the phone with Rosa and fallen asleep, Lulu dreamed she lay buried beneath sand. Heavy and suffocating, the grains pressed into her unconscious. Near death beneath the weight, a coughing fit brought her back. When she awoke, she recalled a lengthy disappearance by her father long ago. That was the time when that other man kept company with her mother and had started pestering Luanne: grabbing her, telling her he'd buy her a new doll if she was a nice girl. To defy him, she became Lulu and invented a story where she lived alone on a floating island in the sea. She didn't feel scared or want for anything among the abundant trees and bushes—swimming in a steady rhythm, sleeping on shore.

As she watched Nate attempt each posture, she tried to experience his triumphs, brown hair spread across the mat. She placed her hands behind her back instead of ripping off another fingernail. Suffering is part of life, as Buddha acknowledged. But so is compassion. "Time for *Savasana*," she announced. She wished she could lie down, too.

After class, Lulu appeased the faithful students that stuck around, explaining in detail whatever they asked about a pose. Nate came to say thank you, but he quickly sped off. When the studio emptied, she walked home and packed a small bag to take on the New Jersey Transit coastal line.

***

Up and down the Jersey shore Rosa had traveled the previous summer and fall, painting portraits and character studies of clichéd landscapes, ocean and dune. When Lulu last visited, she watched her mother joke with customers, compliment their little ones and pet their dogs. The cops chased her for painting without a permit. In Ocean Grove, an alcohol-free community, Rosa set up outside the church and tents of the Methodists who ran the town and held camp meetings. They may have reminded Rosa of her half-brother Monroe, who loved his church and allowed no digs against religion. Ever since Lulu's father's reckless ways with money and his alcoholism forced them to give up their place in Maryland, Lulu had urged Rosa to settle down somewhere. They had fled to Maryland after the storm in New Orleans destroyed their home. Lulu had been nearly grown. Since then, Rosa kept on moving. An elderly lady needed a nest, Lulu believed.

"Make your home with Monroe," Lulu repeated, believing in a healthier alternative to itinerancy. The one constancy in Rosa's life: tending to her plants, crowding among them with a hoe and watering can, reveling in dirt and generative seeds. The growing season lasted a long time in Louisiana, but this hadn't convinced Rosa to move back.

During Lulu's last visit to the shore, Rosa ordered her daughter to steal someone's yoga students. "Teach here," she urged, an oddball attempt at closeness. "There's an old guru that holds a class on the pier.

He doesn't bend down. Makes the girls demonstrate. Run your class on the sand, or in one of the guest houses."

Rosa acted surprised when Lulu declined.

Now, Lulu walked from the train station to meet her mother at a cafe that stayed open year-round. A salty current attached itself to the wind. Gray waves pounded the nearly empty beach. Lulu watched Rosa stroll down the street in her direction. She wore a faded orange dress with slacks underneath, two woolen shawls wrapped around her coat and had a pink feather poking out of her hat. She looked small, her complexion light brown, her nose angular, and a dark mole prominent. Rosa greeted Lulu with French-style kisses on both cheeks. When they entered the cafe, she did the same to the waiter, Charles, who brought them a pot of Earl Gray tea.

"You made it, cher. Later, we'll go to Asbury Park. Only a few blocks from here, but so different. Some criminal element. Retains a touch of its former glory. There's this great mural of a mermaid."

"I'd like to see it," Lulu said.

They drank tea and ate cookies. Lulu met her mother's gaze.

"Your beauty's been wasted. You could have acted on stage, or modeled, or married a rich man. When you going to remove that tattoo? No one admires a frog catching a fly."

Rosa often spoke of the tattoo as an insult to artistry. The large mole on Rosa's right cheek, a splotch she would never remove, was an exception. "I was born with this," she'd say, claiming it as a "symbol of a dark and violent history." Lulu's mark was pin-pricked beneath the skin, a choice she made to mark her body. The mole and tattoo wrote interconnected, yet disparate, myths of hard living and survival.

Lulu stood up, about to walk off, then hesitated: "Mama. These nightmares have been tormenting me. I want to know about that stocky bald, white man you brought home when daddy went on a bender. Tell me."

"Sit down," said Rosa, sipping tea. "Don't know what you're saying. There were a few different men. I wasn't serious with 'em. Forget those times."

"Believe me, I try."

"See a shrink," Rosa said.

"I did a few years ago." Lulu took a deep breath. Anger lived in her throat. She pushed in her chair. "Why do you bring up acting and modeling? I've never given it a thought," said Lulu.

"I couldn't have put you in acting. Your father didn't come home 'til you fetched him from the bar. After Hurricane Betsey, what could I do? All these years in New York. You might have tried. Your stage name could have been Luanne Butler."

"Your fantasy." Lulu sighed. Her daddy, a mean and unpredictable drunk who once plucked a bunch of flowers, showed up at her school play and came on stage wasted. This man in her nightmares did more than that. Made young Lulu panic in the garden, take refuge under her bed. He brought her a Hershey bar and asked her to touch him. A knife-like pressure built inside her head.

"All I'm saying is you might have made more of your beauty," Rosa mumbled. "You never gave me a grandchild neither. Everything I ever wanted."

"Oh really? Why would I have a baby after such a troubled childhood?"

"I did what I could." Rosa spit some tea into the cup, frowning. "Not ideal. Neither was my life. Anyway, I can use some help. Got any extra cash?"

Lulu blinked, feeling woozy. "You invited me here to insult me? And ask for cash?"

"I don't need your money," Rosa grinned. "But you do fine." Rosa nabbed the remaining cookie, shoveled it into her mouth.

"I have enough." Lulu had to struggle to keep from screaming. "I just received notice. They're kicking me out of my studio." Rosa found people to put her up. She worked odd jobs. Lulu had a feeling sometimes Rosa barely managed to stay off the streets.

"How much do you need?"

"I don't know. Five hundred? A couple grand? What can you spare? I may be goin' down South. Not to live with Monroe. I was think-

Off the Yoga Mat

ing maybe Florida? That's where most old folks go. I'm not like most old folks."

For both their sakes, Lulu wished her mother settled somewhere. Then Lulu wouldn't always be wondering where she'd turn up and whether she'd get mugged or murdered. Out the window of the café, she watched as one family marched towards the beach, pulling their kids in a red wagon. Last summer she helped Rosa set up her easel on the boardwalk. Unbearable, watching her mother paint tacky, exaggerated caricatures in broad strokes; Rosa, a caricature herself, all nose, stringy gray locks and varicose veins edging from her shorts' cuffs, lighting up a thin cigar. She even wore a tiara! Rosa adjusted the price of her portraits depending on mood and need, a lightning-quick decision based on the rumbling in her belly and the glint in her client's eye.

"Mama, I'll mail you a check," Lulu said weakly. "Don't insult me. And try to remember something about that man."

Rosa poured out the rest of the tea. "I love you. You know?"

Lulu nodded, but she couldn't say those words. She needed to rest in Rosa's tiny room.

That evening they walked the short distance down the boardwalk to Asbury Park's dilapidated casino and convention center. It was quiet except for the wind. Lulu let every gust peel off a strand of anguish. Float it over the ocean. They passed the skeleton of a stone-and-wood casino, felt the fraying planks of wood beneath their feet. Lulu rested her eye against a peep hole, staring at debris and a scurrying rat.

"There's the mermaid," Rosa pointed to the mural of a squid-limbed creature, half woman, half fish, stretching the length of a concrete wall. She evoked frivolity with her smile and beckoning eyes.

My little sister, Lulu thought. A mermaid returns to the water after she's visited land. Like my peaceful floating island.

Lulu and Rosa passed Bruce Springsteen's hotspots: descendants of Madame Marie, the fortune teller, kept a tiny palm reading booth by appointment only. The Stone Pony nightclub posted a line-up of rock and alternative acts. In her teenage years, Lulu had related to the Boss's lyrics in "Born to Run" about getting out while we're young.

They climbed a staircase off the boardwalk to check out a reno-vated restaurant and lounge. The place attracted dedicated surfers in wet suits. They toasted each other, leaning their boards against the bar. Lulu spotted a tousle-haired fellow as she and Rosa drank piña coladas and munched on dumplings. Lulu shivered in her thin jacket, facing the sea.

Rosa grinned. "You brought me luck. Mary just mentioned I can stay."

"That's a relief. Do you know for how long?"

"Cannot appear desperate," said Rosa. "And I got an offer to transfer interest from one credit card to another. The river keeps aflow-in'."

Lulu straightened the wilted flower Rosa had pinned into her hair, worrying about the next time cops might chase her for painting and panhandling, or someone might attack her. Lulu imagined an ancient lady with shriveled skin and a rusty walker crossing a vacant plain. Can't become like her, ever.

The young surfer at the bar threw back his head. His friends clanged beer bottles. Lulu didn't care to spend the night in Rosa's de-pressing alcove.

"Mama, you look tired. Why don't you go back to Mary's? I'll see you later."

"I am fading," Rosa said. "You're staying? Promise me you'll be careful."

"I will. You get home safe." She kissed Rosa on the cheek and walked her to the stairs. When Rosa finished her slow descent to the boardwalk, Lulu imagined her mother's saunter to Ocean Grove. The Methodists' droll hymns might play inside her head. The family with the red wagon must be making their way back to where they came from. Everyone made preparations for promises in the dark.

As Lulu returned to her stool, the surfer approached. "Lovely evening," he said, extending his hand.

"I'm watching the full moon rise," she said. After a period of silence, she turned her voluptuous body his way. He frisked her with his eyes. Without thinking much about it, she pressed her palm against the zipper of his wetsuit where a tuft of curls emerged.

Lulu traced the surfer's chiseled biceps. When he put his arm around her, the background faded: white caps and sand, her mother's put-downs and request for cash, the threat of eviction and that unthinkable violation. One of the yoga sutra states that the restlessness of the body arises from distraction. At that moment, she sought passion, wild and free.

Chapter Six
Suomi

(Nora)

Before Nora knew it, her red-eye flight touched down at Vantaa Airport outside Helsinki.

On a bleak, late-February evening, Nora was whisked to a dinner at a small *ravintola* on *Mannerheimintie,* a busy sloping street in the center of Helsinki by two young men from Nokia, who came to fetch her. They ordered wine by the milliliter and pizza topped with ham and pineapple, then they sat in silence. The long flight had disoriented her, but after dinner the guys insisted on playing tour guide. They waited for Streetcar 3B, which circled the dark city with determinacy. It was dubbed the "drunk's tram line" because anyone could find their way home on that route. Nora boarded and rode through the misty, dark winter in a haze. Long, unpronounceable street names with strings of a's and n's. Finnish and Swedish, the official languages of Finland—Finnish streets end in *katu* and Swedish in *gatan*. Nora attempted to pronounce "*Aleksanterinkatu*"and "*Kaisaniemenkatu,*" after her guides enunciated them several times, but her tongue could not form such sounds. Luckily almost everyone spoke English in SU-OM-EE.

"I've been sheltered," she told her hosts after the tram ride. Her only previous trips abroad had been to Canada and Club Med in the Bahamas. They checked her into a chain hotel, *Sokos,* where she slept covered by a pod-like sheet with a blanket inside. She woke early and went downstairs to devour several servings from a buffet of herring, porridge, meats, cheeses and rye crackers. Nora's hosts walked her to the harbor on the Gulf of Finland, where cruise ships docked and islands dotted the coast. They guided her to an austere white cathedral rising from Senate Square, near government buildings and the university. In the short period of early February daylight, Nora made out yellow and pink pastel-colored buildings on slanted cobblestone streets. By the train station, people glided on an ice rink. Nora envisioned Jeremy's arm across her back, the two of them skating like Kitty and Levin in the opening pages of *Anna Karenina*. She imagined Nate sitting on the ice, an angry child who took a spill. Caught in the ether between North America and Northern Europe, Nora tried to shake off her past.

Exhilaration outweighed jet lag as she wrapped her scarf around her neck. What was the Fahrenheit equivalent of -10 Celsius? I'll be in another office in another day, away from the cubicle world of Midtown Manhattan. What will befall me? I'll discover Nokia's genius for technology, tap new contacts, find glorious romance...I hope I'll get pregnant. She had heard that the Finns loved children. They worked reasonable hours and made time for family; the welfare state ensured mothers received fully-paid leave for a year or two. Celebrated for honesty in business and in personal affairs, the Finns were a people Nora couldn't wait to experience.

Later, alone, her greeters gone, she entered an unusual church—known as *Temppeliaukion Kirkko*—church in the rocks. The roof was a burrow with slats through which light entered, gentle and meditative. The angle of the weak winter sun created stripes along the walls, filling her with optimism. Rows of wooden benches and dark ceiling beams transported the outside in. No one to be accountable to. Nothing left to prove. She found herself praying for the health of her dad and for herself. I can be selfish, she thought.

She used a phone card early the next day to call her parents before she checked out of her hotel. "I wanted to let you know I'm safe," Nora said. "Guess what? It's dark here. At 2:30 in the afternoon."

She boarded the train to Tampere, about 90 minutes northwest of Helsinki, and took a taxi to Nokia's branch. They escorted her to an office, all hers. "Thank you," she said. "It's not an open cubicle." A door she could lock, a small closet, a new computer and a phone. No booming voices or competitive drivel. No Jeremy in his dark suit, sparking drama and ogling multiple women. After she nearly nodded off in her chair, she watched as a tidy, short man approached her open door with his hand out. She stood and stretched.

"Hello. I'm Winn—actually Winchester," he said with a firm handshake. "My parents were partial to that famous cathedral in England, but I grew up in Wales. Here for an interlude, like you. To give the Finns advice on marketing and to steal their secrets. Welcome."

She believed she wouldn't have a thing for him. He was about 5'4," with a beard and a receding hairline. Nora preferred taller, more hirsute men. She hadn't internalized her singleness.

"I am Nora Jane Lester. Call me Nora," she said. "From Maryland, but after some years in the city, morphed into a New Yorker. It's my first time outside of North America. I'm shocked by the darkness, the quiet."

Later, she met her Finnish supervisors. Aino, from marketing, a white-blonde with glasses and a short leather skirt. Alto, a technical specialist, thin with small rectangular glasses and a long-striped tie. They piled on reading material about marketing plans and Y2K precautions for the anticipated meltdown. Alto took her downtown to acquire a bus pass and open a bank account. He walked her to her apartment in the Tammela neighborhood, carrying her two heavy suitcases without complaint. He contacted someone on the phone to arrange her weekly sauna session in the basement of her apartment building.

"I'm already sweating," Nora said, attempting humor. Alto didn't smile or make eye contact; in fact, he stepped back. In New York, density overruled manners: life so loud and fast you became your impulses. You could wait for a table with the pretension of the nonplussed. Finland turned out to be a big country with a minuscule population. Finns spread out, creating barriers inside buffer zones, seeking nature in the countryside to soothe their gentle souls. How would she fare amid these introverted, earthy folks?

"I'm so sorry," she said to Alto. "I didn't mean to talk you to death."

"It's not a problem," he said.

She cried the first few nights in her small apartment as heat bled from the radiator. A release of tension and welled up expectations. There was a small bedroom, one desk and chair, a pleather couch and a small bathroom. The kitchen cabinet had slats where you could line up washed plates. The excess water dripped through the bottom into the sink as they dried. What an ingenious invention, Nora thought. The shower-head nozzle came propped on top of a tube; no curtain or stall surrounded it. There was only a bare, tiled floor that required a squeegee to push water down the drain. It was clean and unadorned. She fiddled with a red button on the nozzle to control the water temperature until it was just right. Hot pellets of water took the edge off. Tears, warm and salty, came as she thought of telling her dad all about this place. He'd listen.

When Nora brought home her first bag of groceries, she couldn't locate a freezer component to the small fridge. She had nowhere to store certain items. At work she spoke to Alto, but he seemed unsure of what to do. No one had ever complained.

"Most visitors don't require a freezer," he explained. "They place their items on the windowsill. I suppose they use the microwave or eat out. There are many grocery stores, like K Kauppa and V Market."

"I know. But I like to freeze my leftovers, make ice cubes, eat ice pops...I don't mean to be difficult," Nora said.

Perturbed by her request, but out of niceness, he promised to order a freezer.

On the third night in her apartment, she found a guestbook sitting on a low table. In it were the names, the dates of stays and some chirpy comments from previous short-term residents. They recommended restaurants and bars, gave thank yous to various hosts and suggested day trips from Tampere. She wondered what words of wisdom she'd enter after her time had elapsed. Sleep descended on her as she thumbed through the log. She snoozed on the carpet and began to dream.

She was surrounded by Finnish schoolchildren wearing red snowsuits. This one-piece garment defined them for most of the year. A popular joke in Finland was that parents could easily take home the wrong child because they are practically interchangeable clones in padded coveralls. The children in her dream had an air like the Munchkins of Oz, except they were crying and dancing, snot trickling down their noses. They demanded assistance, but Nora ignored them and they began to smack her. Jet lag blockaded internal time; her clock failed to reset. She awakened with a stiffness in her back and a sensation of fear.

That first week at Nokia, she read manuals and went to meetings to get acclimated. There was grave concern about Russian nuclear plants melting down in the year 2000—that it would be worse than Chernobyl. On the positive side, Winn invited her out.

She partook of the tradition of drinking several pints of Karhu beer (*karhu* meant bear)—the Finnish Budweiser, or maybe the Finnish Coors. People sat outside, wrapped in fur blankets. Their tables were surrounded with lit torches or heat lamps. They might sing or scream; a few rowdies broke bottles or picked fights. Nora noticed a man passed out in the street.

"That's letting off steam," said Winn.

"From one extreme to the other," Nora said, drinking another bear beer.

"Wait until you see this." They ducked into a karaoke bar beneath the train tracks. Couples swayed drunkenly as the singer took the stage, pouring raw emotion into her ballad. Winn and Nora lacked the gumption to get up and sing, but they proved to be devoted bystanders. Nora followed Winn, since he had been in town for two months and knew what was what. He was easy to talk to and well-mannered.

Nora's anguish eased every time a singer gripped the mike and let loose. She ordered a refill and listened to a melancholy crooner with dark, tangled hair. It didn't matter what she was saying in Finnish. Nora knew from that voice she had been wronged in love, yet the singer maintained her dignity as mascara and pancake foundation ran down her face.

"Don't go getting pissed, love," Winn said. "You've an early meeting."

Chapter Seven
A Yoga Uproar

(Nate)

By the end of his first month and a half in yoga, Nate placed his mat in the middle row, no longer content in a corner way in back. As he lunged, his pants drooped; for the first time, he felt self-conscious about what he wore and how he behaved, part of a growing awareness of his body.

When Lulu approached, Nate inhaled coconut. He floated in the tropics as she adjusted his forward bend, easing a crick in his spine by placing two fingers on a pressure point. If only his vertebrae could spring with elasticity, like a spry beetle Darwin observed on his *Beagle* voyage. Lulu eased a kink in his outstretched legs, and as her hand moved, he studied the amphibian tattoo. Never before had he appreciated a collarbone. The British literary critic F.R. Leavis once wrote "a poem is not a frog." What impulses lay beneath the surface? She looked tired. Something was off.

When Nate met Gil later that evening and spoke about his class, Gil said, "I spy with my little eye—Nate's got a crush on Ms. Betancourt."

"She's attractive. Not my type, though," said Nate. He was used to Nora, with her blunt haircut, wide hips, small breasts and child-like enthusiasm. She was sexy when depressed or furious.

Lulu's attention became like an optical illusion. He took in the image. His brain processed it and misconstrued his perception. A trick of the eye…a lapse in the brain. She would never consider an out-of-shape underachiever like him.

"You make assumptions," Nate said to Gil. "You're way off base."

"Am I? It's amusing to watch you flinch every time I mention her," Gil said as they entered the Tower Records store on lower Broadway.

"Take her class. See how patient and supportive she can be." As soon as Nate uttered those words, they scalded his tongue. He wished he could withdraw them.

The next day, Gil strutted into Lulu's studio, holding a purple sticky mat under his arm. Nate did a double take when Gil seated himself in the first row, among the die-hard regulars.

He claimed the spot that belonged to Bina, a fiercely loyal student. When Gil went to find a cushion, Bina moved his mat. He returned and confronted her.

"Since when do you own that spot?"

"We've been coming here for years," said one of Bina's friends. "You're new."

"True," Gil said, "but what about humility?"

"You'll see it if you respect us," Bina said.

Nate thought he saw Gil shove Bina's friend, but maybe Gil merely lost his balance. Bina picked up his cushion and dropkicked it with her bare foot. The cushion sailed through the air and hit another student meditating in lotus position. Startled by the blow to his chest, he cried out.

Lulu rushed over.

"You," she said to Gil, "get over there." She pointed to a spot of exile, in front of and to the right of Nate. The buzz in class wouldn't die. Then a nasal voice announced over the loudspeaker that the building was conducting a test of the fire alarm system. A series of mind-numbing beeps emitted throughout the room on-and-off for ten minutes.

"Let's work through these distractions," Lulu said. "Pause for

Off the Yoga Mat

stillness."

Nate kept his eye on Gil when class resumed. His friend's sun salute was halting and partial. Gil's cobra barely lifted off the ground. So that braggart had minimal flexibility in his upper body, but he moved with more agility. Comparisons: totally against Lulu's philosophy.

Gil attempted to raise his legs way above his head and do some sort of a headstand. He lost control and collapsed with a *thwack*. Serves him right, Nate thought as he struggled to contain his laughter. Once again, all eyes turned towards Gil, who was receiving the attention he craved but did not deserve. Nate liked being the one assisted, even if it was due to his ineptness; Lulu encouraged him in a way he found addictive.

Lulu came around to check on Gil. He must have felt singled out when her hands rested upon him.

After class, Nate hung back, witnessing Gil's charming levity and apologies to Lulu as he put on a clean tie-dye shirt. He gestured broadly as if to ward off other suitors, flashing the equivalent of colorful plumage. Nate could have decked him. As Gil revved up his antics, Nate's temple throbbed.

Finally, Lulu broke from Gil. She checked in silently with Nate through angry eyes, inquiring, as if to say, why'd you bring *him*?

"I'm so sorry, Lulu," Nate said. "It's my fault."

As they walked out, Gil celebrated his rank ogling. "You should have warned me. She's a peaceful pinup in thong underwear and décolletage, a chanting enchantress with a twisted soul."

"She's an enabler," Nate said. "You're depraved."

"She's from N'awlins—part African-American, part Jewish, part Creole. I bet there's voodoo in her background."

"Did you hit on her?"

"Indirectly, my friend. I have to see her again."

As far as Nate knew, Gil hadn't had a girlfriend in years. He subsisted on one-night stands, musician-privilege seductions, strip club visits and burlesque performance art. He spoke of women alternatively as prey and as his albatross to bear. When Nate and Nora had been a pair, Gil invoked the principles of feng shui to warn Nate that he wouldn't finish his dissertation until he increased his *chi,* or vital force. He had advised him to remove the books from his bed and place his mirror elsewhere. Adding a small altar with rocks and water wouldn't hurt. Gil had urged Nora to rearrange her furniture to face southwest in order to hold onto Nate; she required earthy elements like wood. She had thrown her sandal at Gil, but he ducked. He said, "Your breakup is preordained."

As Nate and Gil headed towards their apartments, they passed the supermarket dumpster on 6th Street and Second Avenue where the freegans congregated. The woman with a red bandanna—the one he had noticed before—groped a garbage bag as she spoke to a couple of rapt listeners.

"Feel the bag from the sides. There are often discarded bagels. They can't be kept overnight. Never randomly stick your hand inside."

"Isn't she seeking feng shui on the pavement," Nate asked Gil, "finding the spirit of the still edible bagel?"

"No. She's foraging in trash," said Gil.

"Care to join us?" the Bandanna Woman asked. "We have plenty of bagels."

"Give them to the homeless," Gil barked.

"Some businesses donate, but many food banks can't take non-packaged food. We salvage the remains," she said. "There's nothing wrong with them."

Nate was hungry, so he accepted one. She said her name was Mariel Day. She studied modern dance.

"Can't take ballet for free," Gil said.

She pulled off her bandanna, releasing her curly red-gold hair; it complemented her blue eyes and musical voice. She smiled at Nate. Before he knew it, he had agreed to meet her at a free swap at St. Mark's Church in a few days to get rid of some of his junk. That seemed fortuitous. He chewed his bagel, rehashing the incident where Gil had fought with one of the regulars in yoga. Mariel cracked up.

"I hope to see you soon," she said, smiling.

When they walked away, Nate folded over to stretch. He swore he could reach an additional half-inch closer to his toes.

Off the Yoga Mat

"You interested in Ms. Pig Pen?" Gil asked as they reached the church's iron front gates. "Isn't she a bit young for you? As for me, I'm making a play for Ms. Betancourt."

How dare Gil disrupt the class, brazenly go after Lulu? As if acting on its own accord, Nate's fist erupted and landed as a punch on Gil's upper arm, jabbing hard.

"Ouch!" Gil said. "You have a problem? Want to fight?"

Nate's stretching and planks had firmed some muscle. On the yoga path, Nate felt gratified to pummel Gil.

"I don't have a problem," Nate said. "Let's keep it that way."

As soon as they parted, Nate's spirit soared.

Then he entered his apartment: spotted the manuscript pages piled on the table. He forced himself to re-examine the comments penned along the margins, the expletives, the question marks and the struck-out paragraphs. He thought about how Nora had read Offendorf's remarks. Then his mind flashed to a moment he and Nora made out in his bed. He had lit up that joint—couldn't curb his impulse even though she loathed it.

On his own now, with a decision to make. How could he improve the writing yet retain the project's integrity? Why not march down to Maryland, tell Offendorof he refused to cut Darwin? Punch out his professor's lights? Violent self-preservation had its benefits. Gil believed that neither Monica nor Offendorf actually wanted Nate to succeed. Instead, Gil claimed that professional jealousy, unconscious, deadly, drove their engines. Could that be true?

"The professors' agendas are the real subjects of your research," his father had often stated. Nate usually compared his old man's notions to those held by right-wing pundits in the culture wars. After forcing himself to go over Offendorf's blotchy red authority, etched in screaming NOs and XXX8*^%$))#? FORGODSAKES SLASH THIS NONSENSE GET RID OF THIS TRIPE, Nate accepted that his father was right. He had to face Offendorf, insist on a certain amount of leeway and assert his position boldly. *Kapalabhati pranayama* was the answer for now. Short quick breaths from his nostrils down to his tummy, concentrating on that compressed, whisper-like sensation.

March, 1999

Chapter Eight
A Nasty, Good Thing

(Lulu)

Lulu noted Nate's absence. He had stopped showing up in mid-February; now it was already the second week of March. Was he avoiding her because Gil stuck around, begging her to go for a drink or to attend a gig? She stood in front of the room imagining Nate in the middle row, with his tangled hair, struggling. The others awaited her instruction.

"Bear with me," she spoke tensely. "Move into plank. Shoulders should align with your wrists," she said. "Like you're hovering over a large puddle."

Nate had failed to handle this *asana*. Before he stopped attending, he had even tried sideways plank (also difficult): your weight rests on one side and your legs and feet are stacked. He hadn't succeeded, but he twisted and turned and switched hands to stay up. "I'm willfully collapsing," he said. Lulu had smiled at his admission of weakness, tinged with humor. Then he had whispered, "You seem far away."

"I'm having nightmares," she said. "It's not easy to push them aside."

"I'm sorry," he said while she crouched down.

She thought his eyes mirrored her sadness.

Lulu neglected to signal the class to release their planks, leaving them trembling. Bina shouted "RELEASE PLANKS, CLASS." There was whispering among the group. I am losing them, Lulu thought. I'm spacing out.

When class was over, Gil headed to the front.

"I need your assistance," he said. "It involves Mr. Dart and his dissertation research."

"What is he writing about?"

"Come with me, and I'll tell you." He put one hand on Lulu's waist.

She removed it.

Curious about Nate's project, she agreed to join Gil for tea. Over lemon zinger, Gil explained Nate's jealousy thesis. It was too academic, he said. Nate's friend and mentor Monica had challenged him to experience envy first-hand. At first, Gil spoke diplomatically.

"Please don't take offense or think me a hound for what I am about to say. Nate needs to get jealous. For real. Sexually jealous." He paused. Blew on his tea. "Let's help him. If we fool around, he'll get roaring jealous." He looked into her eyes. "His writing will improve, or he'll figure out something. It sounds bizarre, I know. But consider it. If he writes what he knows—if he faces emotions long denied—he'll end up with a decent book."

"It's twisted." Lulu sipped her tea.

"He claims he never gets jealous. That's got to affect his research. Let's wake him up."

"You can't predict what he'd feel."

"I've seen how he responds…he punched me for talking about you."

She felt uneasy. That didn't sound like Nate.

"It's not like I don't want you…anyway," Gil said. "But there's the extra bonus that I would be helping…*we* would be helping him. He's the Menelaus to my Paris."

"In that scenario…I'm Helen of Troy," she said without missing a beat. Greek and Roman mythology intrigued Lulu; in her living room she kept a framed poster of Botticelli's "The Birth of Venus," depicting the woman in the half-shell. There were times Lulu saw herself as a pagan courtesan. Sometimes she chose sexual partners that hurt her.

She wondered if Nate had feelings for her. If so, he probably *would* grow crazy jealous if his buddy slept with her. She had seen men in various states of hysteria when they failed to seal the deal and someone else did—a primal reaction evoking possessiveness. She struggled against such sexual shenanigans now; she imagined something with Nate based on friendship and respect. Yet any recollection of abuse by the stout bald man could lower her guard. *I am lost at sea, groping for a life preserver; I want to be held by someone who does not pressure me.* Sex with Gil? Degrading. But what if Nate never returned to her studio?

"We can hint that we slept together," she blurted. "It's an old tradition for a woman to come between friends. He'll buy it."

Gil put down cash on the table. "It lacks the juice of…doing the deed." Gil covered her hand with his. "I know how to make a woman come," he said. "Any way you want…I promise."

"Shut up," she said. She pulled her hand away.

"Nate needs to compete…feel the sting, live with resentment. Instead of starting a war with the opposing male, he'll write about it in his thesis."

"Where is Nate?" Lulu asked. "He hasn't shown up at my studio. Has something happened?" They put on their coats. Gil held open the door.

"Dropping his practice just like that…I worry."

"I haven't seen him. Probably in his cocoon, writing or avoiding it. You and me, darling, we will shock that monkey. He's going to thank us." Gil moved closer, but Lulu stepped back.

Feeling disgusted, she quickened her pace on the dark avenue.

Off the Yoga Mat

Chapter Nine
Bob Dylan of the Finnish Academy

(Nora)

Nora read the name of a Ph.D. candidate, Jussi Mulaantu, on the office door across from one they had assigned her at Tampere Technical University. An office all to herself, cozy. Nora exchanged her fur-lined boots for slippers and hung her coat on the hook. If geography is destiny, then a nation of 5.5 million people surrounded by thousands of lakes begets patience and enchantment. Nora felt insulated, like Tampere, an inland city between two glistening bodies, Lakes *Pyhäjärvi* and *Näsijärvi*.

A door slammed in the corridor. She hoped to encounter Jussi. The other day he had sauntered by with his long blonde hair and a serious expression. In the hallway, Nora had perused the posters hung by his office: one of the Moomins and another of Bob Dylan.

"Tell me about the Moomins." Nora had emailed Bethany, as part of her effort to figure out the sexy Finn.

"Adorable hippo-like animated characters, the subject of books, comics and merchandise—from soup to nuts," she responded. The Moomins were creatures bestowed with profound insights by the artist and writer Tove Jansson, a Swedish-speaking Finn. They were a loving family with a small entourage of friends, independent thinkers and dreamers, bound to nature. Moomins donned the colorful ceramic Arabia of Finland coffee mugs Nora noticed in everyone's office. She planned to purchase a set. Jussi must have a sentimental streak if he adored them.

Exiting the WC, she spotted him. "Excuse me," Nora called before he entered his room. "Hello…I am Nora…from New York. I'm working here for a few months, and taking a class. I like your posters." She smiled.

He shook her hand. "Welcome to Tampere, Nora. I am busy now. If you are free, join me for lunch around 1300. Come into the center of town. Let's meet in front of Stockmann's."

"I'll be there," she said, not certain where or what that was.

Based on first impressions, Nora considered Jussi the epitome of Nordic male perfection: slim and fair with piercing blue eyes. A beautiful man with sparkling rings on most of his fingers. She blushed down her neck, seeking her version of Valhalla—from the Norse mythology (not Finnish). Nora would be a Valkyrie, waiting upon Jussi and granting him life in the underworld to face his next battle: comrades in arms.

When she found him downtown, Nora's gloved hand skimmed Jussi's bare one. He wore his hair twisted and pinned up. She met his steely eyes with lightheadedness. They stood in front of Stockmann's Department Store, on *Hämeenkatu,* the main street in the town center. She donned a Russian fox hat she'd purchased in a local flea market. The temperature registered minus 15 Celsius. "I could kiss him right there and die," she thought, a cliché evoking Joan Baez's song "Diamonds and Rust." Nora also recalled a scene in the film *Doctor Zhivago,* with Julie Christie and Omar Sharif.

Jussi took her to a *ravintola* that was nearly deserted—most Finns ate lunch earlier in the day. She was glad for a break from the corporate cafeteria. She slid into the spotless padded booth. Time to delve into his secrets. However, he wanted to hear about New York City.

"There are more than eight million people in the metropolitan area, but you don't think about the numbers, only jay walk around them. Tampere feels more like a town than a city," Nora said.

Jussi spoke softly. "Tampere is a place to concentrate. Or become distracted. I'm working on two books. Not my dissertation." He cut his vegetables with a fork and knife.

"What do you write about?"

"Music and nature in Finnish literature," he said, after he chewed and swallowed his food, "and some nights I go out to boogie."

"You dance?"

"No."

"Then what does it mean to boogie?"

He flashed a sinister grin. "I cannot explain."

She must boogie with this sly, bejeweled scholar.

"You are a big fan of Bob Dylan," she said. "I saw the posters."

"I follow Dylan across Europe. I never tire of his shows."

In fact, Jussi fashioned himself the Bob Dylan of the Finnish academy, a master of disguise and providing minimal explanation. He wrote obscure academic essays, wore long coats and silver rings, and, when he had the funds, could out drink everyone to the toast of "*kippis.*"

"What are you studying in your Finnish culture class?" Jussi asked as they sipped their coffee, served in small white cups and accompanied by a wrapped chocolate truffle.

"The Winter War. The loss of life and land."

"Yes. Because of what we gave up in that war and the one after, we distrust the Russians."

"Americans have had our share of grief with Russia," she said.

Nora was getting up to speed on international affairs. At work, she attended a meeting about the Nokia handset, engineered to exude existential truth. All products combine desire and clarity; Nokia's phones were easy to use (they provided numerous samples to Nora). The firm wanted to expand into Canada and the Americas. Could she entice her compatriots to purchase and love Nokia products with unflagging loyalty? The competition was heating up. They racked Nora's brain to find out what she knew about the American consumer's aptitude, resistance and disposable income. They imagined that she, a mid-level copywriter for Secanor, had fingers on the pulse of her nation. She lacked that authority, but she pretended to be an expert anyways. She spoke of how the U.S. planned to spend billions to prevent the Y2K bug because they couldn't afford to lose all that data and replace hardware. She sounded confident as she absorbed the subtleties of Finnish identity.

Finns played down the origin of their exports. Most Americans barely registered an awareness of Finland, presuming nothing of great importance came from there (with the exception of the music of classical composer Sibelius, certain Marimekko floral prints popularized by Jackie Kennedy in the 1960s, and wonderfully-made chairs). Inside the Nordic nation, Nokia and Linus Torvalds—the creator of the open-source software Linux—were synonymous with technological prowess. Nora appreciated the contrast between the humble impression Finland conjured of itself to the world and America's bombastic superiority. The Finns also panicked about Y2K disruptions, believing firmly in the "precautionary principle" and assuming the worst-case scenario.

Jussi represented his nation. Accomplished, yet modest. Restrained, yet flamboyant. Polite, thoroughly elusive and somewhat unavailable. By the end of lunch, Nora could have released Jussi's hair, twisted and held in place beneath a leather barrette pierced by a wooden stick, to flow into her hands. He had to be at least ten years younger than she was. But staring at the rings on his fingers and his snake-skin belt, she refused to get caught up in a number. Please find me exotic, she prayed. More desirable than Bobby Zimmerman.

Her quest to know Jussi represented a yearning for the local: her desire to act on a scintillating attraction would blot out memories of Nate. In a foreign culture, it helps to have guides. Lonnie's old high school acquaintance, Bethany Mayles, served that purpose. She had married Mikko Pentimenen, giving up her country to live with him.

A few days after Nora had lunch with Jussi, she met Bethany. A large woman with green eyes and straight, dark hair, Bethany dressed in a flowing garment and a jaunty hat. As an American expatriate residing in Finland for fifteen years, she qualified as an expert on the culture; working with immigrants and refugees familiarized her with the trials of assimilation. Nora might have appeared to Bethany as a curious, opportunistic visitor, clinging like plankton to her host.

Bethany sat at a table in the pub, reading the *Helsingin Sanomat* newspaper. A Donald Duck comic book, *Aku Ankka,* lay on the table next to her pint of beer. Kids and adults read the thick, paperback tomes

Off the Yoga Mat

devoted to Donald, his uncle and cousins.

"The artist who draws Donald Duck created *The Quest for the Kalevala*, a comic book epic set in Finland," said Bethany.

"We're reading sections of the *Kalevala* in my culture class," Nora said. "Why do ducks excite the Finns?" She was amazed at the contradictions of these Northern people.

"We'll never know. They also love the epic's witches, singing warriors and its determined mad women. The quest for the Sampo is their version of The Holy Grail."

Bethany said she recalled Lonnie from their high school days in Minnesota. "She was always trying to explain my behavior to others. She was diplomatic when I was crass."

Nora was grateful Lonnie had led her to Bethany. They sipped their beers.

"How do you like living in the *Tammela* neighborhood near the market square? There's a café next to the gas station where old men spend their mornings."

"Yes. I love that place," said Nora. "It reminds me of my dad's R.O.M.E.O. group—retired old men eating out. But here they play slot machines."

"Finns gamble in kiosk markets, at train stations. They're not shy when they're in groups. Then there are the saunas," said Bethany.

"There's one in the basement of my building. I call it the 'dungeon,'" Nora said.

"It's pitch dark, next door to the room with a washing machine I have to sign up to use. The lights are set on timers that go off as you grope for the next switch, located somewhere on the wall. Fine place to commit a murder. My sauna slot is 6:30 on Thursday evenings. I'm scared to go down there."

"Let me take you to a fancy sauna. That'll initiate you to our cold weather diversions. I'll have my *lapset* with me…unless you know anyone who wants to buy a couple of kids."

"Actually," Nora said, "I might. I'm 39. I want a baby. I was dating someone who used his unfinished thesis as an excuse…to avoid procreation."

"The fairy dust has come off my kids. I had them young. If it was up to the hubby, he'd have made me pregnant a few more times. We can barely afford the two we have. I'm round enough without a loaf in the oven. Let's find a horny Finnish boy to give you a baby."

"I may have found one."

"Already? Do tell."

"Jussi's a doctoral student who talks softly and parties hard. Probably has a girlfriend. I'm much older."

"He'd sleep with you. Finnish women take initiative. Hell, if I didn't reel in my Mikko he would have stalled endlessly."

"There's more," Nora said, assuming Bethany, like Lonnie, would weigh in on her every option. "I work with this Welsh guy named Winn. I enjoy his company, but I'm not attracted to him."

"One of life's great misfortunes. Welsh accents make me melt. Might you change your mind? He could be good daddy material, whereas your young Finnish partier is probably trouble."

"You sound like Lonnie! Trying to be practical when my heart and loins won't hear of it."

"Then ask Jussi over. Fire up the pea soup."

"The what?"

"Pea soup. It's a Finnish tradition to eat pea soup on a Thursday. My Mikko likes to make whoopee after."

Nora laughed.

Bethany continued: "I'll get you a recipe, convert the measurements. I know what it's like to be an American who can't function with liters. Take it from me. Even the heavy metal dudes of Tampere eat pea soup. With ham, not much else. It's all about the peas."

When Bethany spoke, you listened. They settled on a date for a spa and sauna afternoon—with the kids but no husband. Nora called her parents when she got back to her apartment. She wanted to hear her dad's voice. As she spoke to her father, she thought about cooking pea soup for Jussi, pictured his long hair and silver rings beneath her stiff white sheets.

On a Friday afternoon, Winn asked Nora if she'd like to take a train the next day to see the Museum of Contemporary Art Kiasma in Helsinki. "We'll get inspired by the designs," he said, after noticing when Nora made a sculpture from spare parts of phone handsets. She and Winn divided up surveys they were asked to conduct on cell phone usage. Winn would run some focus groups in Tampere, while Nora agreed to research Nokia's competition, in addition to conducting surveys in the Helsinki area. Nora thought about what Bethany said about him being more appropriate for her than Jussi.

On a snowy Saturday in early March, Nora and Winn boarded the fast train to visit the museum. Inside, they stood in front of a painting of an animated yellow pig, highly stylized in a coat of arms. In the center of a room stood a sculpture of four pigs, shiny and glazed, gathered round a table with a food grinder in the center. Nora scrutinized the porcine figures. Then she checked out images of blue-and-white Finnish flags on the walls. In assorted canvases, it was burned, crucified, and sliced in half while flying at half-mast. She laughed while surveying the room again, enjoying the satire.

The artist Harro Koskinen was known for his socially critical works of pop art in the 1960s and 1970s. His influences came from counter-culture art, poetry and journalism, including members of New York's underground scene: Andy Warhol, Jasper Johns, the Beat writers. Thinking of New York, Nora felt a twinge of homesickness.

"He blends camp with satire like a political cartoonist," said Winn.

"Haughty pigs," Nora said.

Whenever she and Nate had gone to the Museum of Modern Art or the Whitney, they argued over what constituted brilliance or meaninglessness in a painting. Nate's taste in art was parochial, whereas Nora felt at home with experimentation—the saturation of colors and lines, smidgens, blurs and confusion.

After the museum, she and Winn took a self-guided tour of Helsinki's Art Nouveau buildings, appreciating the gold-leaf carvings and the terra cotta owls and eagles. They barely noticed the spires and cupola of the Russian Orthodox Church down the street because of the snow blinding them.

"Let's take refuge in the Marimekko shop," said Nora, and they made their way down *Esplanadi,* the shopping street. Shaking wet snow from their coats, they warmed up immediately after they entered.

Winn sorted through the textiles and pillowcases with swirls and bold prints; Nora cataloged Winn's dark eyes and neat beard, noting their shape and size. He's handsome in his own way, she acknowledged.

Winn held up a floral purse and spoke with sincerity. "I see a symbolic dimension—decorative yet responsible. Make a profit, but not merely so."

Winn pontificated like Nate, but without bitterness. Plus, his accent—how glorious! Bethany was right. Nora originally found Nate's self-underestimation sexy. His lack of awareness that he was above average appeared refreshing…until it grew tiresome. Winn made the most of his attributes: well-groomed, au courant. He didn't complain.

"Look at the colors and patterns in those dresses," Nora said, gesturing towards a rack. "Bold pinks and blacks, red and blue flowers, stripes galore. We're being pelted with snow. Inside its spring."

Nora shifted from exteriors—mere window dressing—to interiors, where most of life unfolded. As the snow cascaded outside in heady splendor, Nora, thinking in Darwinian terms, willed her nature to mutate. Winn could make a good daddy. Her father would like him, and even her mother should find him acceptable.

Usually, she gravitated towards whatever struck her fancy. She didn't care to roll any dice or wait and see; when she admired the merchandise, she grabbed it. A saleswoman asked if she could be of assistance. "No thanks," Nora said. "I'm still deciding."

Would Winn be willing to move to the States, or might she relocate to Wales? Did he even want children? Was it possible she'd become more attracted as she came to know him? Her mind raced as she clutched a set of hand towels. She stood at the crux of uncertainty, but time couldn't care less.

She fell asleep on the train ride back to Tampere, her head falling to Winn's shoulder.

***

The next afternoon, Sunday, she went to the spa with Bethany and her children, Lilly and Antti.

The nudity in the dark, dry sauna unnerved her. Mothers and children, old women and young, puffy and shapely sat next to each other on wooden benches. They placed small paper towels under their behinds to prevent burning. Bethany's belly fat hung over her lap, and Nora found her cheerfully unselfconscious as her kids splashed her with water from a bucket. On the other hand, Nora itched to cover her long-ish bellybutton, the ridged cellulite on her thighs and buttocks and her dark nipples, disproportionately large. She ran out of methods to cloak those parts with her hands or by crossing her legs. A thin elderly woman grabbed the ladle.

"She's about to make it HOT. Brace yourself," Bethany translated. "That's a *kiulu.*" Bethany pointed to the bucket, "and the ladle is a *kippo.* She'll throw water on the rocks in the sauna's stove."

It sizzled like meat on a grill—the blast of *löyly.* Smoke rose; the room grew sultry with the scent of brine.

Nora broiled. "Too much. I'm leaving."

Lilly and Antti stared.

"That's understandable," Bethany said. "Go shower in cool water. Come right back for another round. That's how it's done. Cleansing and relaxing. Then we will drink something."

Detritus rinsed from her system—Nate's doobie roach sucked down the drain. Jeremy's toxic odor scrubbed away with dead skin. She scurried naked through the locker room to the shower, a bare stall with no curtain. After the blast of cool water, she slipped back inside the sauna cabin. Vapors hissed as the old lady poured water. Some women talked. Others washed or meditated. When they left their faces glowed. I can get used to this, thought Nora. Secure and womanly. Like we're back in the womb.

Cheryl J. Fish

After a few rounds, they left the sauna to drop into a small, cold pool. "Mommy, let's go into the big one," Lilly insisted.

Next, they swam in a large heated pool where giant shower heads pelted bullets of water onto their backs, a rough massage. Hot and cold perfectly coordinated. Bethany lifted Lilly into the spray. "Nora, would you be so kind as to hold up my big boy?"

"Sure," Nora said, grabbing for Antti, ducking under her legs. She tried to catch him by one foot—he swam off splashing her with scissor kicks.

"Just out of arm's reach," said Bethany.

"Typical guy," Nora responded.

Nora swam after Antti. She caught him and held him under the powerful spray. He finally relaxed; she liked his boyish energy. What would it be like to parent a boy? After all, she might not give birth to a daughter.

"I'm going next," Nora said as she gave him a shove, forcing him to share the space beneath the pounding spigot.

Later over snacks and drinks, Bethany told Nora that Tampere had three public saunas, including a very old smoke sauna—the original form with no chimney—located in the *Pispala* neighborhood. The other two were down at the lake. Nora decided to make it her mission to visit them all. This heat opened sweltering cracks, releasing toxins. Nudity and alternating hot and cold temperatures, stripping away guardedness. A lulling, satisfying transformation.

Chapter Ten
Happiness?

(Nate)

Nate ended up on the trail of young Mariel Day, an anarchist dancer who presided over free swaps and dumpster dives with Anita Willis, a former vice president at Secanor. Nate decided to hang around with the freegans. He skipped a few yoga classes. Soon he felt guilty, which led to his missing more classes.

Mariel and Nate stood in the courtyard of St. Mark's Church on Second Avenue amid old headstones. Famous for its cultural programming, the church's iron gates held posters for theater and dance events. Musicians picked on their guitars and poets smoked outside the sanctuary door, setting up for a reading that would take place at the Poetry Project, inside the church. At the free swap, folks poured over books, clothing, shoes, purses and vinyl records to take away and they discarded videos, an old turntable, *New Yorker* magazines and a set of Rangers shot glasses. Mariel asked question after question about Nate's dissertation and his yoga practice. He noticed her slick boots and designer jeans.

"Nice Ferragamo's," said Nate. Dating Nora had upped his fashion consciousness.

Embarrassed at being bankrolled by her parents, Mariel admitted she didn't live on air.

"I survive off credit cards," she whispered, knowing it was a dirty secret among the freegan anti-shopping inner circle.

"You don't have to prove yourself," Nate said, not mentioning his own reliance on his parents. "The Finnish philosopher Pentti Linkola said 'unemployment is better than doing harmful work.'"

"Aren't they socialists in Finland?"

"They have social welfare...not the same thing. But they take care of their people."

"My parents think I'm a parasite living off of others' taxes. The freegans challenge greed and waste in capitalism...somehow that message is not getting through. All anyone mentions is how we eat from dumpsters."

"You are not what you buy." It was Anita Willis.

Nate had believed Nora shopped as a reflex against disappointment. Anita once worked at the same firm as Nora. "How did you get from Secanor to freeganism?" he asked. She didn't bother to ask him how he knew about her job history.

"I was an ideal consumer, a corporate spokesperson. Obsessed with real estate and investments. I voted Republican," she said, coughing into her sleeve. "Then they found a hole in my heart, and I almost died. After surgery, I realized I was lucky be alive. I had savings; the corporate grind wore me out." She smiled, revealing teeth that could have used a cleaning. "I want to give back. I'm happier now."

Nate took a deep breath. What did it take to be happy? Nate had rarely thought about it. He avoided the dissertation he needed to complete or abandon. He antagonized Nora without reflection and hadn't been willing to compromise to make her happy. He held out hope for a career in higher education but was blocked by the unfinished thesis. Happiness: a human construct, perhaps non-existent in the animal brain. But what about pleasure? That was something else.

Whose advice should he take? Monica's or Offendorf's? Get more personal or emphasize the philosophical? Why bother to dwell on happiness? William James, his favorite pragmatist, wrote "to give up pretensions is as blessed a relief as to get them gratified." Maybe so. Or as Ms. Lulu Betancourt said in class, "we must not forget to practice yoga *off the mat*. Are we serving our community?" Nate imagined working with students as confused and thwarted as he. He'd love to lecture at that specialized conference he stopped attending, fearful of questions like, "Why haven't you published anything?" He longed to teach, but without a Ph.D. in hand, his job possibilities appeared grim.

The previous evening, his mother had said, "I want you to be happy."

"Don't you worry," he replied during their weekly phone call. "I hope I'm not a constant disappointment."

"Of course not. But nothing comes easy for you. I wish it would." She discussed cousin Daniel's promotion to junior partner in his law firm and mentioned some woman Daniel was dating. "Perhaps I shouldn't speak of him."

"I can handle it, mother. Don't coddle me."

Nate had nearly blabbed about his break up with Nora. And his involvement with Mariel and the freegans. On second thought, he didn't care to explain his or their agenda to his mother.

He watched the crowd recycle possessions. He ate food "pulled from the garbage and cooked with love," as Mariel put it. Vegetable and herb stew over noodles didn't taste bad. After he and Mariel cleaned up the dinner service, Mariel turned around and planted a hard, wet kiss on his mouth. She jumped into his arms. Then she invited him to her apartment, which was shared with two other young women in a luxury doorman building on lower Fifth Avenue. He didn't say a word about the fancy building.

No spouting post-structuralism or endorsing corporations…refreshing. Kneeling on her mattress on the floor, Mariel said "Come and get me Natey." So, he did. The sex was mechanical yet rigorous. She was around 25, with lean, unblemished skin. Nate tasted a speck of happiness, a crumb on his lips.

Nate spent the days that followed in empty buildings filled with squatters on the Lower East Side and in Brooklyn with hardcore anarchists. Mariel gathered supplies to cook for them as they debated how to stop real estate developers in Mayor Giuliani's circle from putting up luxury towers, shutting down their community garden and ignoring the homeless and the working class. Mariel and Anita sought advice from housing advocates on the best way to legally gain access to vacant buildings by virtue of occupation.

As the freegans tended to the compost in the garden on East Houston, thinking about what vegetable and flowers they'd plant in April, Mariel and Nate encountered others who spoke about developing permaculture—a system for conserving water by designing a pond. Nate admired their idealist hands-on approach. Was activism a better fit for him than theorizing in a swivel chair? Might he choose it over inertia and the struggle to please Offendorf? Couldn't he find paid work in community or non-profit organizing?

One evening Nate joined a dumpster dive, and he was amazed at all the perfectly fine bakery rolls, cut up veggies still in plastic wrap and packaged pies they found unopened as they went through the pile of discarded food. He listened as a cohort within the group planned a protest to save community gardens from the bulldozer. Word went around that a couple of die-hards intended to commit sabotage. He thought of Edward Abbey's classic novel, *The Monkey Wrench Gang,* that had inspired the founding of the real-life environmental activist group, Earth First! In that fictional story, the gang committed sabotage in response to overdevelopment, the building of dams, when mines destroyed forests and Navajo lands. Did these freegans understand the risks? They could be arrested and charged as domestic terrorists if they tampered with construction equipment or pulled up stakes. If he objected, they'd find him square. He didn't want to scold them by suggesting that non-violent direct action was a better alternative. But in his conscience, he felt he should challenge them.

While hanging out near the garden on Houston Street, Mariel approached Nate: "How would you like to teach a mini class on political theory at our free and open university? I bragged about your credentials."

"It'll be my first-time teaching since I was a TA in grad school."

He remembered an insecure sophomore asking him to read multiple drafts of his paper, begging Nate to convince Offendorf to raise his grade. He did so without hesitation. Another time, he had offered to intervene in a skirmish at a young woman's sorority house. It didn't matter that her problem was personal; he felt invested in those kids. He was asked to mediate, and it made a difference. He'd have coffee with them in the student union and listen to their anxieties and distractions. As he agreed to give teaching a try, he was already gathering material for his mini course in his head. He couldn't wait to tell Mariel about Antonio Gramsci's concept of cultural hegemony: the way that the state is maintained through the status quo in a capitalist society. That's what they were experiencing.

"Bring it on," Mariel said.

His years of education and reading theory books might mean more than a grasp of obscure language and in-group understanding. Nate carefully planned his talk. He got out old notebooks and sat at the computer: cutting, pasting and creating a narrative thread. Would they respect what he had to offer?

In one of the freegan squats they had visited, Mariel grabbed his hand. She pulled him inside a dilapidated room with broken beams, mice scat, dust bunnies and loose wires. Nora would have run from such a place, whereas Mariel wanted to make out here. He found himself surprised he could withstand the squalor. It turned out to be a fine day of grime, theory and sensuality.

After several weeks of this life, in which Nate digressed from his stalled dissertation with some satisfaction, he stood across the street from Lulu's studio on Second Avenue. He gazed up at her window—thought he saw a shadow of her bent arm through a curtain opening. Then it hit him. He'd become cut off from what mattered: the manuscript, job applications, Lulu's corny metaphors and the feeling of relaxed accomplishment in her studio. She mentioned nightmares. Why hadn't he offered solace to Lulu—she who made his dull life better? He bailed out after introducing Gil to the practice. Now Gil struggled with planks instead of Nate. With time away, the cricks in Nate's spine shot flares again. Peering up, he saw light seeping inside 2 Squared's window, highlighting the red in Lulu's bangs like silk petals. Has she noticed I've gone AWOL? In his heart of hearts, she kept one eye on the lookout for his sorry ass.

That evening, Gil phoned Nate with an update.

"When I'm not practicing with Fox Hole or at the office, I've been hanging around Ms. Betancourt. Did you know she left N'awlins for Maryland as a young girl? Lulu married some Jamaican boxer a long time ago, but it didn't take. She studied in an ashram with the same guru as Allen Ginsberg. Cool, huh?"

"I've been busy." He held the phone far from his ear as Gil talked trash.

"I am right about her diabolic aspects. In the most pleasing way. I will get to know her froggy down to its Louisiana pores."

Reveling in salacious commentary, Gil neglected to ask Nate for any of his news.

"Lulu will attend one of my gigs," Gil said.

He told Nate he was going to dedicate a song to her, a sure-fire path to seduction with 99% of women. Gil let out a self-satisfied laugh.

Repulsive, thought Nate.

"You can't handle it," Gil said.

Lulu ought to know better than to consort with him. Thinking of the two of them together, Nate's face grew heated and his nostrils flared. He hung up without another word.

Chapter Eleven
Bystander

(Lulu)

"We'll tell Nate we've slept together," Gil said, attempting to kiss Lulu in the stairwell of her studio after class. He stroked her hair as she exited the building. "Nate hung up on me when I said you were coming to a gig. He can't stand it."

"I am not going to your gig," she said. As the lasso of Gil's lust tightened, Lulu hoped that Gil would disappear and Nate would come back. He had practiced mindfulness amid distress and worked through his physical pain. When she watched him struggle to hold a pose, she reached for something too. Gil trailed her and she felt a chill in the air. Lulu noted artists and entertainers in the street and she felt as if they silently berated her. She pretended she danced on a cloud.

"I have the perfect plan," Gil said. "Come to my place for a few minutes. We'll figure it out. You will appreciate how I practice feng shui—a harmonious balance of the elements in my apartment."

"Five minutes. Then will you promise to leave me alone?" She wanted it to stop. "I'm not joking."

"Sure I will," he said.

Upstairs in his illegal sublet apartment on Washington Place (which was owned by the giant university in the process of evicting her), Gil showed Lulu a mini fountain with pebbles and a tiny spray of water. A pleasant gurgling sound came from the center of his room. As she stared at the fountain, Gil bent over her, pushing aside the collar of her shirt and licking the frog's fly-catching tongue. Lulu went blank.

"What's our plan?" she said as he kissed her neck. Then she understood there was none. As a little girl, all she could do was cry and push with her small fury. Lulu slid from Gil's grasp. He walked over to his desk to pick up a lighter, took a hit from a bong. "Want some?"

She shook her head, no.

"The only plan that matters…is satisfying you."

He walked up behind her and stroked her shoulders. Then he pushed down her leggings, scooped her up in his arms and placed her on the sofa. Hands, lips, tongue on her skin, her mouth, her tummy and her breasts. Fingers pressing inside of her. "Stop," she said, but he didn't stop. If only she could distance herself from her body, from her feelings. She could have escaped. Instead, she relinquished control. Watched it unfold as if on the outside.

He attempted many different angles and moves with his hands and lips to get her to climax, but she felt no arousal—no pleasure. "I said, I don't want this," she spoke into his ear. She recalled how the ugly bald man grabbed her beloved doll. He asked her to touch his stubby penis to get Chatty Cathy back. Could one violation displace the other? That man called her a little whore. Same as your mother, he said.

As Gil started to unbuckle his belt and pull down his pants, Lulu heard the steam pipes hiss amid the pungent stench of weed. She felt like a bystander in the presence of a monster.

She stood up, catching Gil off guard. She pressed her knee into his groin, grabbed her leggings and fled.

Off the Yoga Mat

Chapter Twelve
Idiot

(Nora)

In culture class, her teacher, Mrs. Marakola, distributed free passes to the Tampere Short Film Festival, which was set to invade the town over the weekend. They were asked to choose a film by a Finnish director and to write a paper about it. Winn requested an extra pass.

Outside, as she and Winn walked the few blocks to their Nokia office, Nora asked "Why the extra pass? Are you bringing a date?"

"I suppose. My wife Doris will be visiting," he said.

Nora nearly choked. That bloody Welshman! Her inner Lonnie kicked in. You *assumed* Winn was single, she could imagine Lonnie saying. Of course—he wore no ring, had failed to mention a wife—unusual for a man who was happily wed. He had been attentive, even doting. Living away from home must have given him license to imagine being unattached.

Nora picked up the pace. Winn scrambled to keep up.

"Slow down, love," he said.

"Don't call me that."

"All right then. Shall we stop for a pint?"

"No."

"What's the matter? You hadn't any clue I had a wife?"

"How would I?" Nora asked, biting her lip. They had often discussed their lives back home. She had short-listed Winn as a potential partner, father of a yet-to-be-conceived child. She had told him she wanted a baby. "I love the little ones," he said. "I would fancy two or three."

"I didn't think it mattered, one way or the other," said Winn.

"It doesn't," Nora said, thinking what a bloody idiot she'd been.

At the office, she slammed her door and put her feet on the desk. If only she hadn't arrived at this juncture, where she felt the necessity to consider every man as potential mate. Her mother long ago predicted if she couldn't snag a fellow in college, or soon after, she'd end up an "old maid"—a modern version of that gray-haired, elderly woman on the deck of cards. When the son of one of her mom's childhood friends moved to Manhattan soon after Nora, they played around in the downtown theatre and arts scene. Nora fell for him, thinking they'd please everyone at home if they got hitched. But he became besotted by a Mohawk-bearing poet who shook a tambourine while reading at The Nuyorican Poets Cafe; then the new couple moved to Bolinas, California. One of many doomed attempts at partnership.

She could not waste energy on Winn. The film festival would keep her occupied. Bethany promised the pea soup recipe. She'd invite Jussi over. He dared not be married, or gay.

Opening night of the film festival in mid-March: winter loosening its grip. Darkness fading bit by bit. Light encroaching. Nora entered a red-brick industrial building previously a factory transformed into a posh movie house. Attendees exchanged handshakes and hugs, showcased credentials in the form of large badges and made plans to dine. Nora didn't know these luminaries, but she found it exhilarating to hear conversations in French, Finnish, Swedish, Italian and German—overlapping Eurospeak. At the concessions, she got herself popcorn and sprinkled cheese powder on top. A few of her classmates nodded to her.

Nora was tired of opening an imaginary drawer and finding fragments of her past. She had come across a photo in one of the books she brought from New York. From a time when she and Nate threw a party for a friend's 40th birthday; in the shot, she gazed upon him, but his attention was focused elsewhere. Despite his shortcomings, she couldn't help but feel he would have been a perfect companion at this festival. Although she had come to dread his insistent, know-it-all critiques, she could almost hear him: "View that film on Sami reindeer herding. You know nothing about indigenous tradition."

Scanning the program, she read the description of the films by and about the Sami people. Traditional reindeer herders who lived in Finland, Sweden, Norway and the Kola Peninsula of Russia, the Sami spoke a number of languages related to the Finno-Ugric family—the same as Finnish. She hadn't realized an indigenous population lived in Scandinavia. For a long time, Nora had avoided thinking about global politics, war, famine, natural disasters or poverty. In New York, she couldn't help but be aware of class distinctions and racism. It was in your face.

Living in the north of Europe, she resolved to pay attention to the struggles and aspirations not only in the United States, but on a global scale; Mrs. Marakola's lectures awakened her to the limits of her geographical and historical sensitivity. She hadn't heard of the wars in which Finland lost land; she didn't know they had been colonized by Sweden and then Russia. Until she had met Bethany, she knew nothing about refugees from Africa and the Middle East that needed asylum and applied to live in the Nordic countries. She started to read the *International Herald Tribune* and watch the BBC World News. When she heard what they had to say about the U.S., it often sounded distorted.

Nora became transfixed by a short film on international logging interests that encroached on forests in the north of Finland where reindeer fed on lichen in the winter. Some Sami were involved in protests against logging and mining; she was glad for the English subtitles that enabled her to grasp this struggle. Another film highlighted tensions between assimilation into modern life and how the Sami preserved their languages and unique form of ritual song, the yoik. In a video, a Sami musician, Pekka D., performed hip-hop in the Northern Sami tongue. He rapped in baggy pants and wore a backwards Yankees cap; behind him stood small mossy hills, known as fells. In another short film, Nora discovered a Sami tradition: giving birth in a smoke sauna. Often the first dwelling built in old communities, saunas were a gathering place and a spiritual portal.

As Nora vacated the screening room, she caught sight of Winn and his wife Doris, a brunette with a heart-shaped face—in flats she had two inches on him. Nora decided to attend the reception for Sami artists at a nearby restaurant. She pushed open a side door and escaped into the night.

When she entered the reception, her teacher, Mrs. Marakola, gestured for Nora to come over.

"I'd like to introduce you to Heidi Somby. Her movie will be screened later."

The woman wore a traditional dress of red and blue cloth with ribbon and fringe, known as a *gakti*. It was patterned specifically for her home village. Her shoes were narrow, sewn of reindeer skin and fur, with the toe pointing upwards in the direction of her face.

"Will you tell me about your film?" Nora asked.

"A little bit. It is my first full-length documentary. I am Sami on my mother's side, Swedish on my father's. My mother was denied the language and traditions. She was called 'Sami bastard' as a girl. I went to Sami festivals to discover the culture. They didn't embrace me. It has been painful."

Nora was struck by Heidi's openness; the filmmaker had explored an unacknowledged part of herself.

"It's courageous. To film your discovery and disappointment."

"I had to."

Regret and discovery co-existed. "I love your shawl," said Nora. "Can I touch it?"

"Go ahead."

Nora took the fabric between her thumb and forefinger. Fringed, light blue and soft—it kissed the filmmaker's shoulders. Her boxy hat repeated the dress's pattern. "Would I be able to buy one of these?"

"It's traditional style. Some of us accessorize with the latest fashion," she said, displaying the leather belt that cuffed her waist and a black onyx necklace. "We do not like it when women in Helsinki and Stockholm who are not Sami wear our clothes."

"I'm sorry." Nora tensed up, understanding why it wouldn't be appropriate for her to wear fringed Sami shawls or colorful *gaktis*. Even if they might have caught on in New York. Out of the corner of her eye, Nora spotted Winn and Doris. "I have to go, Heidi. Maybe we can talk again later."

Nora went to sit at the far end of the room. She envisioned a shield to keep out Winn and his wife. Then another Sami woman in a shiny red dress with an oversized bonnet rose from the center of the room.

"This is Kaisa-Maia from Inari," announced Mrs. Marakola. "She'll perform a yoik."

Kaisa's throaty, low-pitched chant signified what had been taken or lost. Yoiking connected the Sami to their ancestors or spirit guides. Somewhere between a wail and a growl, her song softened Nora's dour disappointment. I am alone, she acknowledged. It's going to be fine. The moon is full. Vibrating notes connected her to longer periods of light, greening the world. Her time in Finland was limited; she must sing her own song.

***

Later that night, she met Bethany in the small karaoke bar nestled beneath the railroad bridge. She and Nora jointly belted out "Crazy on You," by the Seattle band Heart. Nora watched as couples danced drunkenly. The overhead monitor displayed lyrics and panoramas of the Finnish countryside. There were white birch and fir trees, red cottages, reindeer, magpie, and a white swan, the national bird.

They drank *Lonkero*, bottled gin and soda—known as the 'long drink.' It didn't taste strong, but its effect accumulated. Although Bethany's husband wanted her to come home, she lingered.

It wasn't Winn and Doris haunting her again, but after an hour in the bar, Jussi entered with a tall woman in a white coat. It had been that kind of day, ripe with untimely entrances and exits. Nora tried to ward off her sense of disturbance, but she could not.

"What's going on?" Bethany asked as Nora's eyes narrowed.

"It's Jussi. The one you said I should invite for soup. The lord of the rings. With a stunning young woman."

"Oh no." Bethany cocked her head to get a look as Jussi as he

Cheryl J. Fish

carried drinks to his table.

"Shall we leave or say hello?"

"Take the high road," said Bethany.

"It might help if I was high. Is she his girlfriend?"

"Who knows."

"He sees us."

Nora pulled Bethany to his table.

"Jussi. *Moi. Paiva. Terve. Mitä Kulu.*" She sprouted off a string of Finnish greetings. "This is Bethany."

He shook Bethany's hand, smiled and introduced Ulla—another student in his department. She could have been a fashion model with her high cheekbones, sleek brown hair, and white go-go boots.

"Can we join you?" Bethany asked, and sat down at the same table as Jussi and Ulla. The four of them sipped the *Lonkeros*. Nora thought she was going to faint, sitting next to him with that stunning girl.

They were all putting on an act, laughing at the karaoke Elvis and the Abba girls singing "Take a Chance on Me." Nora's favorite performer came up to sing; for a minute she stopped feeling inadequate and obsessing over her attraction to Jussi. It was that earnest, older woman Nora had seen before, whose pancake makeup and mascara melted under the lights…whose heart had been pierced by disappointment. As she crooned a Finnish torch song everyone recognized, a couple slow-danced the Finnish tango. Even while drunk, the woman expunged bittersweet memories. Tears of hope and futility welled up in Nora.

"You should go up there," Nora said to Jussi, touching his arm.

"Unfortunately, I can't sing. How's your evening been?"

With moist eyes, she told him about the Sami films, the yoiking and the experience of singing a duet with Bethany. "It's been a night of song. But after the Sami chant, our cover was a travesty."

"I bet you sounded at least as good as the others," said Jussi.

"At least."

If only she could become the object of his affection. Or lust.

"Is Ulla…your girlfriend?" Nora perched on the edge of losing all inhibition. After finding out about Winn, could she accept another bitter pill?

His hair cascaded over his face. "We are classmates. More than friends...but not exclusive. I'm all for freedom. How about you?"

"More than friends" meant they were sleeping together. "Freedom is overrated," said Nora.

He nodded, stood up and went to buy another round.

Bethany was speaking to Ulla about her kids. She asked if she wanted to procure one of them. The young woman didn't understand.

"I trained my husband to let me roam the bars once or twice a week," Bethany said. "As long as dinner is made, and the kids don't kill each other. He works odd hours. Poor, poor Mikko."

In a land of introverts, Bethany's volume suggested a rant. But after drinking, the Finns upped their intensity. A man on the stage yelled in halting Finnish, gesturing with middle fingers to the crowd.

"A spoken word poet in between karaoke," Jussi said. "You're not missing anything."

Nora sought Jussi's mischievous gaze, and she found it. Loud melodies blasted, familiar and unfamiliar. Then Dylan indicted her.

"You're a Big Girl," a favorite song from *Blood on the Tracks*.

In the tune, the singer claims that love is simple, and the woman in the ballad knows it, while he has yet to learn. Bittersweet guitar chords pushed Nora to the brink. They moved towards the year 2000: a black hole with dimensions, too large or too small. The character in Dylan's song made it through. She could too.

Nora played more songs in her mind. She found the idiot wind, roaring. When it came to sexy men, she was an idiot—a big girl with a child-like need.

Back at her apartment, melancholy and tipsy, she tripped over a baby carriage in the hallway. Impulsively, she dialed Nate's number, intending to blab about the Sami films. She considered trying to yoik at Nate but knew she'd merely howl. As soon as his machine picked up, she cut off the call.

Chapter Thirteen
Humiliation

(Lulu)

On a dark and gusty evening, a week after she'd been assaulted by Gil, she felt a presence in the stairwell to her studio. Her first impulse: run. Then, she discerned a familiar shape. Caught a whiff of marijuana.

"I didn't mean to creep up on you," Nate said.

"Are you stoned?" she asked. "Why are you here?"

"I'm not stoned," he said, gripping the banister. "I wanted to ask you something."

He had played hooky from yoga for about six weeks. She fished around her bag for the keys to lock her door. "Bear with me," she said.

The pungent odor seeped through the narrow passage, reminding her of the dense smoke from Gil's bong. She couldn't locate the keys. Thoughts about fighting with Gil ran through her mind—kicking and punching and biting him before he touched her. She scratched around in the bag, pulling at tissues and fingering her wallet. Perhaps in absent-minded exhaustion she had left them inside.

Nate stood in silence until she felt the keys, and took them from her bag. She turned one in the lock. They exited the stairwell and the outer door of the building.

"Let us walk," she said, longing for the sanctity of repetitive motion. Why should she trust him?

Along First Avenue, she decided he might have found out about her and Gil. All of a sudden, she imagined a hot hand pressing her throat.

She felt a wave of nausea.

Jealousy might blind Nate and distort his reality. She could not handle any outburst, any violent gesture. After what she had witnessed in her family's drama—her mother and father's accusations and suspicions, their flare ups, battle cries, rough blows. Her father hadn't hesitated to pummel Rosa if he could get a hold of her; Rosa always remained defensive, ready to run, or poised to strike back. She feared for the child who witnessed warning signs: the younger version of herself who knew both more and less than she should have known.

Lulu's hands grew clammy. Should she go home? Tell him to go away?

Heat tunneled up her coat, replacing the gusts of late March. She led them to a public place.

In a cozy café on Fifth Street, Nate pounded his thigh. "I've been away a long time. I make no excuses. I hope you're doing well. There's something I need to ask."

He uttered a stream of anxious expressions that had the effect of time-lapsed photography slowly getting to the point. What finally registered in her mind were the words "two readers." This was not about her. Not about sex. She settled into her chair.

"One wants a confessional narrative. The other asked me to cut the heart of my research. One demands academic focus, while the other encourages a turn towards a general readership. Something to get me on Oprah Winfrey. I thought you might give me sound advice, Lulu." Nate gazed at her. "I want to know your thoughts."

"I'm not sure I understand," she said.

"If you and I talk about the options, I might gain insight. Like Ralph Waldo Emerson and Margaret Fuller, those Transcendentalist authors. They'd go back and forth in conversation."

Her breath slowed. What was he saying about Emerson? Who was Margaret Fuller? Conversation?

She stared at her bitten down fingernails. Kept on her coat. He finally stopped talking and sat there like a small boy awaiting approval, rubbing the stubble on his face. He was clueless as to how much she yearned to be comforted, to be heard.

After a few minutes of silence, the server brought their tea.

"I don't have much to say, Nate. Write the book you want—that's in you. Advisors advise, just as yogis unlock our potential for higher love. I won't quote philosophy, but my mother and I lived with a rough drunk. My father tried to dictate, but that wasn't our truth. Aren't you pursuing your degree to discover something?"

"Yes. But it's been so long. Full of nasty rites of initiation," Nate said.

"Didn't I play a part in the research?"

"What do you mean?"

She hesitated, but only for a few seconds. "Gil said you needed to experience…sexual jealousy…to improve your work. It sounded crazy."

He frowned. Squeezed his eyes shut.

"He said we'd…make you envious. If we slept together. Jealous. In a productive way." She gazed at him, realizing how pathetic it sounded.

"What? That sly dog," Nate cried. "My own private Iago." He reached for and pressed her hand. "I'm sorry. I hope you didn't believe him."

She felt like a wave had knocked her down. "He didn't force me," she said bluntly, although she was thinking, there had been no consent. Cold perspiration soaked through her garments.

He stared at her, unnerved. "Lulu, when you said you have nightmares, I was concerned. I wanted to help. Instead, I ran away. Soon after, I met this woman. That's why I haven't been around."

Lulu felt a burning in her chest. Betancourt women refused humiliation at the hands of drunk or lying men. We are women to be reckoned with. Nate Dart was not even close to jealous. He was making time with some new lover, worried about his thesis. She felt like a doormat.

"I'm going home," she said. She stood, tilting her chair.

"Don't go. I'd like to get you something to eat. You don't look well."

"Leave me in peace."

"I'm sorry," he shouted into the overheated café.

That Gil, she thought as the cold air hit her face. A lying asshole, an abusive attacker. She should have never gone to his place. Those guys could go to hell. She'd care for herself. Go home to her sanctuary, light candles. Burn incense on her altar. Take comfort in meditation and *viloma* breathing. Consult the yoga sutras, which would remind her that this rage and past traumas would dissipate someday. She would seek divine light.

Chapter Fourteen
Primal

(Nate)

Nate remained seated in the café for a long time, listening to Whitney Houston sing about dancing and feeling the heat with somebody. Time teeter-tottered with the nighttime crowd. If he ducked outside to take another hit on his joint, it would ease the clatter and eventually let him sleep. He knew he was a lunkhead. A dick.

It should have occurred to him that Lulu had been used. He didn't need details to imagine the worst. He might have offered to confront the rival who harmed her. To listen to her instead of blabbing about his thesis. Hadn't he internalized his Darwin? Grasped his Freud? Considered the primal behavior of men and beasts? No, he remained dense and clueless.

While dating Nora, he made emotional progress after years of insecurity and isolation. But clearly, he had a long way to go. What could he do about Lulu now that he knew what he knew?

Lulu appeared jealous of his involvement with Mariel. But in Nate's mind, Mariel was not a serious girlfriend, just a lovely young woman he had the blind luck to attract when he needed attention. Lulu's reaction proved him guilty, an asshole. Recalling her defiant hazel eyes, strong sensual limbs and intelligent grace, Nate realized how morally-deficient Gil had to be in order to harm Lulu. I'm as big a jerk as Gil for thinking with my penis. He grasped the depth of her emotional vulnerability, let himself envision inhaling her jasmine-scented skin and rocking her all night. Why would she lower herself to fulfill Gil's childish jealousy scheme? Lulu harbored her share of damage. He considered the evidence: a drunken father, nightmares, casual sex, nail biting, mood swings in class. Frailer than when he had met her, emotionally untethered. Gil had taken advantage.

Nate wanted to kill him. And to meet Lulu in her sanctum of pathos. Her obvious concern and tenderness for him left an invisible tattoo.

He hadn't listened. He didn't deserve her.

Chapter Fifteen
I'm Your Venus

(Nora)

Following Bethany's advice, Nora invited Jussi for lunch and decided to make pea soup, *hernekeitto,* the traditional Finnish way. As Nora converted 240 milliliters to one cup of peas the previous night, she considered Mrs. Marakola's lecture. At the time, Finland was a part of Sweden. Taxes were levied for the King, money was scarce and peas were served as a form of payment. Considered pig food, the legumes could gain status if soldiers received a weekly portion for soup. Thursday became the day to serve it.

Nora poured water into a large pot. After twenty minutes, the peas softened and combined with the chunks of ham and carrots. As she stirred the mixture, American and British hits from the 60s, 70s and 80s—courtesy of a retro radio station—provided an upbeat soundtrack for Nora's restless musings. The recipe called for "salt to taste." Did she suit his taste? Jussi said he had sixty minutes, including the walk to and from his office. He was bringing her a book written in English about Sami culture. She told him she needed to interview him about the impact of Nokia products, part of Aino's assignment to research cell-phone usage in the typical Finnish household.

Jussi knocked and she let him in. The peas emitted their earthy aroma.

"Nokia made rubber boots and tires initially. When did your

family begin to use their telecommunications products?" She'd get the business part of lunch out of the way.

"My mother bought her first mobile phone recently...to keep track of us and also for work. I don't have one."

She jotted down his answer. Soup beckoned.

"Can I offer you some pea soup? I cooked it in the traditional style."

He smirked. "I ate it in school. The women in the cafeteria made sure we didn't waste a morsel. You didn't have to go to so much trouble."

"I like to cook," she said, although she rarely did.

Nora ladled it out and carried the bowls to her small table. Jussi appeared tired. His hair was bound in a leather clip married to a wooden stick. Oh, to be that piece of wood.

He wore a tan vest over his shirt and a silver chain connected to the vest. Ornate rings with curves and rhinestones shined from most of his fingers.

They silently spooned soup into their mouths. She served him coffee in a Moomin mug.

"You appreciate our heroes, the Moomins," he said.

"I got a hold of one of the books. The one about the family getting caught in a storm, building a shelter and then eating marmalade. The grumpy one, Little Mi, is my favorite. And her sister Mymble. She falls for the wrong fellow."

"I would have thought you'd favor Snork Maiden, with her sense of fashion."

"I like her too. You're the stylish one, Jussi. A heavy-metal Bob Dylan."

"It's a bit of a game." He ran his spoon along the edges of his bowl.

For a graduate student, he didn't seem anxious. Nora learned that the government would fund his research for at least three more years.

She hardly touched her soup.

He glanced at his watch. Her radio played upbeat wails about desire: "*I'm your Venus, I'm your fire.*"

It's now or never. Bethany said it was up to the woman, so Nora cheered herself on. You can make a move! The Finns stand up for equality. The thought of waiting, unbearable.

They got up from the table. He went to get the book about Sami culture and history. Just as he was about to hand it to her, Nora spoke: "Jussi. I'm...drawn to you."

He paused. "Thanks. I find you attractive."

She reached for him. He stepped sideways. The book thudded to the floor.

Undeterred, she put her hands against his chest, over his vest and pressed close.

"I'd like to be one of your women," she whispered. "To boogie and drink with you on an all-night adventure. Do whatever it is you do."

"We'll see," he said, but he looked away.

Kiss me, Nora screamed internally. *Please.* He didn't make a move.

She bent forward. Brushed his lips with hers. His mouth stayed small, so she inserted her tongue. When she did that, they made out briefly. Polite compliance? Not what she had in mind.

"I have to go," he said, stepping away. "But thank you for the soup and coffee." He picked up his coat and book bag.

"Wait," she shouted.

He marched out the door. Left it ajar. She watched him walking away.

She closed the door and slammed off the radio. Stood in the silent cloud of cold soup.

Is there anything more humiliating than being deserted after an ill-timed amorous advance? Nora didn't believe there was. Why had he run from her? The kiss was lovely. He said she was attractive. So, what was the problem? She sat crumpled on the floor, and tears burst out like rain. It was snowing sharp crystals outside. Almost time for her weekly sauna session. The dry, dry heat and the sizzling vapor on the rocks would purge everything. In that dungeon sauna, she would sweat. Then, in the cool shower, she would experience sweet relief, repeating the process until she purified her dashed spirit, her unravished body.

Chapter Sixteen
The Job Interview

(Nate)

Nate's cordless phone rang at 7:30 a.m. Mariel requested his company to forage for wild edibles in city parks. Then, they'd blend what they found with what the others gathered, making a comforting stew with beans and rice to feed the squatters. The leftover herbs would go to the homeless shelter on the Bowery. She sounded breathlessly enthusiastic. Instead of getting caught up in the activities of the freegans, he hesitated. He hadn't slept.

His back and neck ached. It was too soon to return to yoga; he needed to figure out how to approach Lulu. He wanted to support her, and the time had come to change his relationship with Gil who crossed a line. They had known each other since high school, when Gil's flirtations and conquest stories created a scandalous legend; Nate had lived vicariously through others back then. Those old identities seemed ridiculous, even dangerous. The connection with Lulu hung by a fragile thread.

She sought a path towards transcendence; she guided him out of his darkest gloom. Now, Nate's head filled with static and white noise. Along with Gil's ruthlessness, his own stupidity scared him. He couldn't show up.

He would rendezvous with Offendorf and confront him. If only he could rise from under the covers. He told Mariel he couldn't accompany her. There was a long silence on her end. Then he apologized. Somehow, he fell back to sleep, dreaming of a forest where he lay covered by a pile of leaves and dirt. A winged maiden stopped to dance. She held onto her skirt and kicked up her heels. He barely felt the imprint of her toes or the indentation of her soles; her weight barely registered. Sticks and soil covered him even as she hovered and shined in the sun. She didn't notice there was a person underneath the pile; she took her winged glory elsewhere.

Jolted awake by the phone, Nate picked up. It was Offendorf, sounding incredibly sober.

"I've been waiting to hear from you, Nate. What's going on? I arranged a job interview. A one-year teaching position at a small college in upstate New York. You need to prepare."

Nate bolted up straight.

Offendorf knew the chair of the English department there—he had told her Nate would fit the bill. He could cover many of the liberal arts courses: English composition, Introduction to Philosophy, Literary Theory. He could even teach a course in psychology and literature.

"Bowl them over," Offendorf said, clearing his throat. "They may be located in bumfuck, but won't act like it. They'll try to appear hipper than thou."

Nate rubbed sleep from his eyes. Did Offendorf consider him hip? He got out of bed.

"I only taught two semesters as a teaching assistant," said Nate, pacing, staring at his shelf of vintage radios. "Won't that be a liability?"

"Not necessarily. Read up on pedagogy. First and foremost, everyone seeks a brilliant scholar."

No chance Offendorf considered him brilliant. He hadn't been encouraged in ages. During his first few years working as Offendorf's assistant, they had been like Falstaff and young Prince Hal. Nate absorbed the older man's advice and humor. It had been easy to gain his mentor's approval then. If he had faith in me now, Nate thought, he'd sign off on the dissertation. Release me from purgatory.

"Shall I discuss my research?"

"Of course. Boil it down, don't go on too long. I sent them a copy of your proposal."

That outdated document. Nate couldn't remember what he'd written.

When he hung up, a million questions popped into his head. What were the students like? How many courses and preparations would he have? How much would they pay? Could the job last beyond one year? It seemed foolish to move away for that. On the other hand, it's what academics did to jump-start their careers. They often careened from short-term position to short-term position—didn't always land on the tenure track. Or sometimes they opted out completely. His mother had quit graduate school to make a stable home with his dad. Nate had to take it seriously. An actual job!

He didn't mention the interview when he spoke to his mother.

"I hear that quality in your voice, Natey, a twinge of fear with possibility. You're up to something. Is this about your writing, or is there a woman?"

Boy, she was good!

Nate didn't say a word about the job to Mariel or to Gil. Not even to Monica Portman, who could have provided valuable advice. He wondered what Lulu would have thought about him moving away. He had only a week to prepare. He felt terribly deficient. It had been years since his department offered mock job interviews to help students rehearse the exchanges they would encounter on the job market. He was not a good play actor, so the interview would be trial by fire.

A week later, he found himself on a bus passing through Albany, then Schenectady, and finally east of there, before entering a small town where the college was the center of its universe. Bare trees and piles of snow created a stark impression. He shivered in a suit jacket on the poorly heated bus, wondering what to do about Mariel since acknowledging his concern and desire for Lulu. Students crossed the quad in boots wearing heavy coats. There had been no snow down in the city. About 2,000 students were enrolled, and the school had a solid, if not an elite, reputation.

He had gone to a hair salon. For the first time in a long while, he paid to have his mane trimmed and styled; no one but Nora had been allowed to place sharp objects near his neck. He'd purchased a second-hand suit, as moths had eaten into his other one (he must call an exterminator). Being on a campus reminded him that graduate school had been a refuge and a place to sequester. But, as he had no other prospects, he was grateful for this chance.

The ivy retreated on the old brick buildings. He had been informed there'd be a committee of three. He considered how to talk about his dissertation and pedagogical theory. They were taking him to lunch. He'd be deferential.

After climbing the stairs to the third floor, Nate found the department office. On the wall, they had posted the names of the job candidates, along with scheduled interview dates. He found that odd. His competition included a person named Mekaila and another named Arno. She had already visited; Arno was next week. When the search chair, Janice Dominick, came out to greet him, she didn't crack a smile. The other committee members entertained each other as Nate shook their hands in the corridor.

"We'll go to eat first, if you don't mind, since its noon," said Dale Bryson. They took Nate to the parking lot, drove to a restaurant a few blocks from campus.

"You'd have to wear an overcoat," Dale said. "Winters are hellish."

At the table, Nate couldn't believe it when Bryson and Agatha Wheeler ordered whiskey, neat.

"It's on the dean's dime," Wheeler said. "I don't teach until 4."

When Nate had participated in a mock interview many years before, they insisted job candidates never should tie one on. But interviewers? Were they exempt? Nate ordered a Diet Coke with lemon.

Janice Dominick refrained from drinking alcohol. "So, Mr. Dart," she began grilling before food arrived, "wouldn't you miss city life if you took this job? Would you be able to live in a small town?"

"I can live anywhere," he said. "I'll be working hard. There won't be time for much else." Was that answer acceptable? He couldn't tell by looking at Janice. He should have said he adored college towns, that he'd grown up in the suburbs.

She continued her quest for personal information. Had he a partner and a family? How many years since he had begun graduate school? Nate wasn't sure if those topics were legal. How woefully unprepared he was for this interrogation. Offendorf should have warned him that lunch could be a subterfuge.

That was only the tip of the iceberg. When Janice excused herself to use the restroom, Dale and Agatha sang harmonies to an old Pat Benatar song that came on in the background. "Join us," said Agatha, moving her hand to the beat. "Heartbreaker," they bellowed. Nate couldn't carry a tune, but he opened his mouth so as to fake it.

"What's the matter, Mr. Dart? Are you a musical elitist?" asked Dale.

They laughed about someone named Jonathan, whom Nate took to be an adjunct.

"You know what Jon said this morning," Dale said to Agatha. "He went to the wrong room to give the exam. In one column of the handout, it listed 'test room' and in the other column, 'regular classroom'. So, they had to change rooms after everyone sat down. The test started late."

"Never should have listed two rooms," responded Agatha, chugging her second Scotch.

"We can't always read a form," confirmed Dale.

"Hey, Nate," said Agatha with speech slightly slurred, "do you know Raul Zazŭk— he's now at Maryland State, I hear? He has some sort of bionic leg, or maybe it's his arm."

Nate bit his lip. "No, I don't know him. After my time."

When Janice returned, they clammed up. After they had cleared their plates, it was Nate who headed to the men's room. When he returned, he didn't see a soul. Where had they gone? Glancing out the window, Nate noticed the others getting into the car in the lot. He considered boarding the next bus home.

He stepped outside and scurried over.

"There you are," Agatha said. "What took you so long?"

Cheryl J. Fish   *91*

Back on campus, they began the formal part of the interview in a conference room. As Nate described his research, they slouched in their chairs with drowsy expressions. After a while, Dale Bryson lifted his index finger.

"I see you focus on jealousy as a theme in literature. What's Darwin got to do with Shakespeare?" Dale asked.

"Why look at Shakespeare *and* also refer to Julia Kristeva? It seems like apples and oranges," complained Agatha Wheeler.

"How does your teaching fit into our core?" It was the practical voice of Janice Dominick. "We emphasize great books, but are being challenged by a multicultural requirement. How would you handle that?"

Nate looked at them one at a time. They didn't consider it impolite to talk over each other. He'd handle the questions simultaneously.

"Darwin's ideas about adaptation and natural selection reveal that jealousy could serve a biological purpose. Shakespeare plumbed human nature and the cycles of life. He considered the scientific values of his time. Someone like Kristeva or John Dewey adds psychological and philosophical resonance, making for a complex approach that can serve the core."

"What you just said would confuse the average undergraduate," said Janice. "How do you teach Shakespeare? Or Nathaniel Hawthorne, Nathaniel?"

The others laughed at her double-entendre.

He had never taught either author.

"I would ask them to compare the conflicts in those works to their own lives. Think about what *they* would do." He was delving into Monica Portman territory. "We'd discuss the student responses—then they'd write."

"And I hope you'd include women and people of color, and never omit social class," Agatha said. "Our previous interviewee specialized in those areas."

Dale shot Agatha a dirty look.

Agatha continued: "Our students demand diversity. In fact, they want to meet the candidates to ask about a gay and lesbian club advisor."

It felt as if gasoline was being siphoned from Nate's tank. How dare she bring up the competition?

"Some of our students have been exposed to Shakespeare. Others have not. Would you show any films? How do you cope with plagiarism?" Janice asked.

"I would show films," he said. "There have been some very good adaptations of Shakespeare. And I could design an assignment where they apply concepts from Kristeva or Foucault. We did that in graduate school, but the theory can be simplified. Undergraduates recognize that *The Lion King* is a rehashing of *Hamlet*."

"But Mr. Dart," said Dale. "Undergraduates are addicted to TV and video games. Shakespeare should not be dumbed down. I, for one, have them read the scenes out loud, emphasizing proper diction. In nothing less than well-articulated Renaissance-period English. I have won teaching awards."

Nothing Nate said could please this self-validating posse.

At last, they asked if he had any questions. He had prepared for this.

"I want to know if the job would possibly last beyond one year. And will there be support for my research?" The last part was risky. They might assume he intended to skirt service responsibilities.

The committee members turned to each other, as if they were trying to figure out who would run with that one.

"Well," said Janice. "Right now, it's a one-year replacement for someone on sabbatical. We are uncertain if a line will open beyond that. Our budget has not been flush."

"But I started out in a replacement position," said Dale. "Today, I am a tenured associate professor. There's always a chance."

"We would expect you to show us you are eager to stay. To serve on committees, be collegial. The load is four-three. In the spring, you'd get off one course. *That* is considered research support." Agatha cleared her throat. "We expect...that you will defend your dissertation by the time you'd start in September. Is that likely?"

He wondered if Offendorf had mentioned his stalled progress.

"I plan to defend before then. But it depends on my committee," Nate said.

"I smell trouble," said Dale.

"Nothing extraordinary," he said, realizing his *faux pas*.

"If you haven't defended, you'll be paid less. It's painful to finish a dissertation while teaching a full load," said Janice. "We have one more candidate to interview. We shall make a decision within three weeks, if not sooner. Now we'd like you to meet with two student representatives. One is from the English department, and the other is from the lesbian, gay, and bisexual alliance."

Nate sat on a bench in the hallway, fuming. They hadn't listened. Showed scant interest in his research and teaching. What happened to sophisticated conversation? They were going through the motions and preferred the other candidate; perhaps she was a shoo-in. If they represented the professoriate, he wanted out.

"Hey," said the voice of a student, whose hand was held up for a high five. Nate stood and hit the hand with his.

"Armand Davis, English major. What do you think of our campus? I hear you're from the city. Same here. I received a scholarship to transfer from a community college."

"How are your classes?"

"So-so. Some profs are dull, others fine. But it's freezing cold. There's a ton of rich kids partying. I'm here to ask what you would prefer to teach if they hire you. And I want to know," Armand said.

"My work is interdisciplinary. My dissertation looks at jealousy, evolutionary biology, literature and psychology," Nate said.

"Deep. I read about jealousy between the two brothers in James Baldwin's story, 'Sonny's Blues.'"

"That's a great piece about sibling rivalry, generational divides and the American Dream," Nate said. "Harlem is a character too, with rhythms that echo in Sonny's music."

"Makes me homesick. I'm from Brooklyn. Bed-Stuy."

"I should tell you about the freegans I met in the city—you might find them interesting, or maybe absurd. But I feel shaky."

"What went down, Mr. Dart? That's your name, right?"

"Call me Nate. The committee didn't show much interest. Two of them were drinking."

"No shit. I mean no way," Armand started laughing. "Who?"

"I can't say. What do you miss most about the city?"

"Everything."

They were interrupted by a tall, thin woman with an eyebrow ring and white blond hair.

"Armand and Mr. Dart. I'm Carrie Joan. From the lesbian, gay and bisexual alliance," she said. "I'm not an English major. I want to know if you'd consider advising our club if you got the job. We are just getting started. This college is way behind."

"I can't promise anything," said Nate. "I don't know what sort of service they'd require from me. By the way, I'm a hetero guy who supports gay rights."

"How?" Carrie Joan asked. "Are you inclusive in your course offerings? Do you assign only dead white males? Are you aware of date rape on campus and the rampant homophobia here?"

Nate was taken off guard. "I would not tolerate it," he said, realizing nothing in his research on jealousy had focused on same-sex relationships, or for that matter, on persons of color.

"Now that you mention it, what is called 'queer' theory would be required reading in my courses. I plan to consider the gay and lesbian angle in my research."

"So, this is new for you," said Carrie Joan.

"Not really. I live in New York City. I support diversity, I read feminist theory." He realized he hadn't done the relevant work.

"If you insist," said Carrie Joan "But I am suspicious of men who claim to be feminists."

Armand chimed in: "Those guys want to get laid. Or they're hecklers in disguise."

"That was true in my intro to women's studies class," said Carrie Joan. "Except for the gay guys, who were serious. Maybe one straight guy was authentic."

"Well, I hope more hetero men get it," Nate said. "Anyways, I don't think they'll be hiring me."

"Why not?" asked Carrie Joan.

"He didn't feel the love," said Armand.

"They will be asking us about *you*," said Carrie Joan. "I would prefer if they hired an out gay, lesbian or transgender person. But I think I could live with you."

"We wouldn't have to share a room," Nate said.

They all laughed. The exchange with the two of them was the highlight of his day. Perhaps he did belong in the profession. After all, it was largely about teaching and cultivating relationships with students.

They accompanied him back to the English department so he could formally wrap up the interview. Janice had retreated behind her large wooden desk; as Nate entered, she grounded out a cigarette on the windowsill. Then she got to her feet.

"Defend that dissertation, Mr. Dart.. Defend away! There is nothing as disheartening as a colleague running around ABD. As I like to say, it stands for 'Aborting Basic Duties."

Who thought committee chairs had no sense of humor? Nate made a face, and should have walked away. Something inside him snapped.

"About to Bloody Disappear," he blurted. "Absently Bleeding Dissent," he continued. Janice stared.

"Absolute Bitter Disappointment," he cried. Now she looked cross.

"Assure Better Developments." There! Take that.

"Abruptly Betrayed Drunken."

"All But Done?" she asked.

"It appears so," he answered. Then he waved.

He kept it going, his volume rising as he slinked down the hall. What if I cross my name off the posted list of candidates, he thought, taking the stairs. His voice ricocheted off the walls.

"Assholes Buttfucks Dickheads."

"Asinine Bastards of Dimwittedness."

Off the Yoga Mat

"Atone Blowhards, Dastardly."

"Assume Backwards, Duds."

"All But a Disaster."

He exited the building—cold air clobbered him. Gliding towards the bus stop, he spied Armand with a couple of friends.

"Hey Mr. Dart," shouted Armand. Nate raised his arm. He didn't want to reflect on how badly the day had gone. He had been unable to cut his losses.

"Allegedly Blowing Dust," he murmured to himself. "Alarmingly Bedeviled. Devastated." Nate walked over and patted him on the back. "Listen, Armand. You and your friends, want to go smoke a joint?"

Arrested Between Drags. That couldn't happen. He'd be Absolutely, Blatantly Discreet.

Chapter Seventeen
Evil Eye

(Lulu)

Lulu found Ginny, the woman she had met at the soup kitchen, dozing outside her studio. As Ginny's chest rose and fell, she reminded Lulu of all the others in need of support—Rosa, Uncle Monroe, her father Maximilian. Lately, both sleep and daytime hours featured glimpses of the bald stout man. She remembered he'd said, "Let's read a book together," grabbing her hand, removing it from her doll. At some point, he exposed himself. He had been spending time with Rosa—too much time—before they lost their house. There was talk of a terrible storm and discussions about how best to prepare. Board up the house, leave town? Should they believe the forecast? "They like to put the fear in us," Rosa uttered.

Lulu watched Ginny snoring. Shaking her awake, Lulu brought over a cup of tea and some biscuits. She set her up in a chair.

"You can observe class in session."

"You should eat a biscuit or two," said Ginny. "You look malnourished."

Lulu went back into the studio where students remained on their hands and knees, tilting their pelvises and buttocks.

"Move your *gluteus maximus*, as if you're cleaning out a peanut butter jar," Lulu instructed, using a silly old simile.

Ginny had burst into the room and let out a cackle. Lulu excused herself, escorting Ginny away.

"Stay outside or sit quietly on a mat."

"What were you saying about peanut butter?" Ginny asked.

"Don't worry. I have to get back," Lulu said. They must be peeved with her for walking in and out.

Ginny opened her hand. "Spare some cash, dear? A twenty, like last time."

Lulu went into the closet and grabbed her purse. She held out the twenty. "Please don't interrupt us."

"They're only shaking their bums."

"It looks silly. But what a marvelous way to release the hip joints."

That crisis subsided and Ginny left. A few minutes later, Gil Nudleman appeared in the back of the room with an air of insouciance.

She carried on with her routine although her breath quickened. She considered halting the class, but that would gratify him. Luckily, he didn't join. Students lifted their torsos in preparation for shoulder stand. How did he summon the nerve to show up?

"Can we lower ourselves?" Bina asked. It had been a long, hard shoulder stand.

"Sorry about that. Yes. Come down one vertebrate at a time." She stared at Gil through Bina's legs.

"Now move into fish pose. Lie on your back and tilt your head, keep your elbows on the mat. Expand your chest. You are a fish temporarily captured. You'll flip back into the sweetness of the sea."

Gil didn't flinch.

She made believe he was a shadow. Silently she shrank.

After class, a few students stayed to chat. A young hipster attempted to flirt with her. She brushed him off coarsely. If only she could fly away.

Gil approached.

"What do you want?" Lulu asked, voice trembling.

"To see you. To be with you."

"You've got to be joking. I want nothing to do with you."

"You're angry. I'm sorry. I should have listened to you."

She looked down at the floor. "And I saw Nate. He's not jealous.

He's seeing someone."

Gil's eyebrows arched.

How unsatisfied she felt, sick of her terrible choices. But Lulu had done some research. Nate paid her a compliment when he compared her to Margaret Fuller, a woman of singular abilities and erudition. A renegade and mystically inclined, Fuller was a Transcendentalist thinker and early American feminist who found happiness with a younger Italian man. She became involved in the revolution in Italy during the 1840s. Romantic and tragic, they died with their baby in a shipwreck off of Fire Island.

"Nate gets a medal," Gil said. "As a perpetual student, he knows it's not proper to hit on his teacher. My buddy found a new squeeze? Who is she?"

"I have no idea. Just steer clear of here."

"I'm sorry that I used him as an excuse. I'll keep him out of it." Gil tried to gather her in his arms. "Is it wrong that I want to be with you?"

"I'm not interested. Don't keep sniffing around here."

"Nate can't be a yoga dude. He's the smart, angry loser. You know what? You've got it bad for that decrepit brainiac. Lulu Betancourt falls for a *schlub*."

She shoved him. "How dare you! Mess with me again and I'll get a restraining order."

"I don't doubt it. But you'll change your mind," Gil said.

"Don't come back. And you're no friend to Nate," Lulu said.

She locked the door. Spat into her hands, rubbed them together and rested them on her forehead, like Rosa had taught her. She made circles there, chanting to ward off the evil eye, as if such a gesture had any power to protect her. She inhaled and sucked down breath…holding then releasing it. Anger gave way to a sensation of calm. Lulu had to admit that Gil was right about one thing: she should know better than to care about Nate and the woman he spent time with instead of taking yoga. So why did she wish that woman would disappear?

April, 1999

Chapter Eighteen
Sisu

(Nora)

In southwest Finland, sunrise in April begins early and twilight descends late. Light ignites a frenetic energy; people sit outside well into the night. They take to the lakes in row boats, fill the streets and flea markets, shop and eat ice cream (even if the temperature hovers at freezing).

Nora's father slowly recovered from prostate surgery. Hearing his voice across an ocean comforted her. She tended to her surveys on cell phone usage, aware that she was more than half way through her time away. Some middle managers invited her to a dinner at a restaurant where they ordered steak and bottles of wine. (No liter measurements were taken.) They discussed the switch from the Finnish markka to a common European currency, the euro, while also preparing for Y2K. Nora listened. She volunteered to research how other nations were coping with restructuring their keeping of time and the threat of crashing computers. There was talk of delivering her to Espoo, to the illustrious headquarters, to meet with the top brass. But pressing for more details would have seemed out of order, so she kept quiet. Meanwhile, official letters and emails arrived from Jeremy Frankl and Rebecca Magum-Chin back in New York. Jeremy was staying on in their department.

"You are to report back to Secanor on July 1." They did her the favor of allowing an extra week for the transition. Perhaps they feared she'd abandon ship. Nora fantasized about coming home pregnant. She'd immediately take maternity leave, and avoid Jeremy and her old job. Another thought: remain in Finland. See what happens in the year 2000, watch technology fail or prevail. The changing seasons and her upcoming fortieth birthday reminded her of the constancy of inconstancy. She imagined herself riding a bus with her baby in tow, boarding in the middle with a stroller and paying no fare—one of many benefits for Finnish parents.

She reflected on the Finnish concept of *sisu,* brought up by Mrs. Marakola in class and mentioned by practically everyone. A mix of bravado and tenacity, it referred to the ability to keep fighting long after others would have quit. Determination that was *not necessarily* rewarded. During the Winter War—which was only the first of three battles the Finns fought between the late 1930s and 1940s—they entered Russian territory on one front while on another they withstood attacks. Although they were inferior in number and in weaponry, Finland temporarily gained the upper hand. However, they ultimately lost. The Finns had a taste of revenge in the late 1980s: During the fall of the iron curtain, Nokia flooded Eastern markets and former Soviet republics with cheap cell phones, profiting greatly from this market infiltration.

Nora wore a red coat of *sisu*, unearthed from her favorite flea market on Laukontori Quay. The ice had cracked and the river flowed once more, signaling the pleasure-boat season. Many young women revealed their mid-drifts, wearing minis over tights despite the minus Celsius temperatures. Cold weather and disappointment would have nothing on Nora. She outlined her eyes with a dark pencil and accessed her glamorous side.

One of the boutiques she passed walking home from work had the slogan in its window *"If you're going through hell, keep going."* She bought magnets and stationery proclaiming those words, originally said by Winston Churchill. She plastered them throughout her apartment. She wrote her friend Lonnie a long letter, finally, as they had been out of touch. But just as she intended to buy stamps and send it, she received an email written in all capital letters, as if it were spam: "GUESS WHAT, GIRLFRIEND? I AM MARRYING DANIEL MOSS!!! HE PROPOSED!! GLAD YOU'LL BE BACK IN TIME FOR OUR JULY WEDDING."

"I don't believe it!" Nora shouted to the walls. Lonnie's marriage would change everything. They wouldn't be single together, wouldn't be each other's priority. They had cared intently for one another. Always aware of each other's whims, making time any time. Nora faced that void as if the walls were hollowed-out dry board. Now everything would revolve around Daniel, the guy Lonnie began dating shortly before Nora left the country. Before the reality of cutting things off with Nate had set in. Three months and they're engaged already? As Nora let out a gasp of anguish, she understood what had factored into the decision. By the time people reached their late 30s, they panic about aging, being alone, finding someone to love who would love them back. It was ridiculous and inappropriate, but they were raised to writhe in the grips of that panic, even at the close of the twentieth century. Nora grew up hearing she had better learn to please a man so she could attract the right guy, but, in the next breath, her mother claimed a particular fellow wasn't worthy of her time. Her mom felt she had compromised by marrying Stephan Lester, an engineer from a working-class family. Zelda never let them forget she came from people saturated in the best kind of money: old and invested in gold. As a teenager, Zelda groomed and showed horses, even won ribbons. But she hadn't attended college, although her parents could have sent her anywhere. Married and settled into upper-middle-class Bethesda, she was the mistress of a suburban colonial home with a two-car garage. And as of recently, she was also the owner of a timeshare in Aruba. Nora felt like the victim of Zelda's unacknowledged aspirations. I will never hold my failures or personal choices over my daughter's head, Nora swore.

After a while, Nora stopped fuming. She focused on things that brought her gratification: living close to two giant lakes and working for a high-tech firm that valued her input. She was immersed in a culture of *sisu.* Despite Winn's deception, Nora relied on his company. She'd be smart to make the best of what he offered as a friend. Nate? Yesterday's child. And her oddly frustrating connection with Jussi, like some undiagnosed condition. Nora decided to recreate herself.

Bethany had invited her to the band's concert that night. Nora planned to make a grand entrance, inspired by Finnish textures. The women would don a tank top or bustier with a short sweater tied high or some slinky shawl or sweater. Leggings with a tiny skirt. Keds sneakers with striped socks, hair dyed one or two shades, a nose piercing. Kerchief or bandanna on the head, a woolen hat, like the ones baby girls wore with their snowsuits.

Long skirts or slacks were for work. That evening, showtime. Spring arrived freezing, but no matter; cleavage and arms must be bared. Even big girls showed skin. Bethany posed for an artsy photo as an angel with beating wings. Her butt crack and naked limbs unabashedly displayed as she mugged for a campy tableau; she handed out cards with the erotic display. In the U.S., it wouldn't have played as well.

"She inspires me," Nora wrote in her revised letter to Lonnie. "And I am psyched about your wedding. Tell me all about Daniel." It was easier to absorb the news and appear supportive with the wide sea between them.

In Tampere, nothing more than a stroll, bus ride or taxi separated you from the next party. Nora left her apartment and walked downtown to the main drag, *Hämeenkatu*, where there were scores of others in weekend mode. Some young guys clutching cardboard cases of Koff beer were roaming the street, exhaling smoke.

When Nora entered the Sahara Desert Pub, there sat Winn. "You look amazing," he said. She wore black leggings, a short purple skirt and a sleeveless top with a gauzy blouse over it. Finished it off with low boots. Plenty of blush, eye shadow and mascara. Her small breasts and shapely thighs nearly thrust from their restraints. She decided to talk to Winn like she would have spoken to Lonnie.

"As I dripped in the sauna, I realized women strut their reserved butts around town," Nora said. "I'm turning forty, facing a new millennium. Forty is the new thirty."

"Maybe in the States," Winn replied. "In Cardiff, forty is the old forty-eight. You go to the pub with your mates, get pissed, and aspire to cheat on your wife. Then out of guilt, you take her to Mallorca."

She giggled. That's probably why Winn had kept Doris under wraps. He wanted to live the risqué life.

"I am going to dance," she announced.

"I'll watch."

She danced on a slightly elevated stage alongside a group of twenty-something girls wearing shower caps, towels and underwear. In Finland, they called it a hen party. In the States, it was called a night out for the bachelorette and her pals. The point was to humiliate the bride-to-be. She'd spend a drunken evening partying, laughing, the victim of pranks; her fiancé would be exposed to even more debauchery, similar to the antics of a fraternity hazing. Nora imagined throwing such a fete for Lonnie. She'd parade her down 72nd Street, past the Gray's Papaya and the Dakota building. They'd raise hell in the grass, dive naked into the Bethesda Fountain. Give head to hot dogs. For starters.

Nora shimmied with the shower-cap girls to where she noticed a few men—some alone, some with partners. With one wiry guy, she dallied for three or four songs, scrunching her shoulders up and down. She lost track of him, winding her way among the strangers with light refracted off their silhouettes. At home, she didn't know of any places where folks over age thirty-five could dance as comfortably. This evening felt like a blessed relief. She fit like a daisy among other pretty weeds.

When she sat down, Winn offered to buy her a drink. She accepted and knocked back half of it. The guy with whom she had twisted on the stage breezed past. He was tall and thin, with brown hair and piercing eyes. He probably assumed Winn was her date. Nora wouldn't clarify anything. She needed a hiatus.

Nora spotted Bethany at the bar. She walked over and listened as her pal spoke animated Finnish to the bartender. Nora envisioned Bethany as a social worker, helping Somali and Iraqi immigrants adapt to life in *Suomi* after they'd abandoned their war-torn homelands. Bethany provided a comforting respite. She had told Nora about the difficulty of securing jobs for some of the qualified candidates because of racism or xenophobia, and about the children sometimes orphaned while others came to Finland with a parent left behind. Bethany advocated for them with mixed results.

As her crew set up on the stage by the plate-glass window, Bethany greeted friends packing the room.

"Nora, this is Tomi Vaisto. Here are Markku and Mari Tolvonen. This is my pal and colleague Giovanni Degli." Bethany reeled off the names of those she knew, and then there were some others.

One of the guys in the crowd surrounding Bethany was the one Nora danced with. Thin, with a piercing gaze. His name was Ville, pronounced Vill-eh.

Before long, Bethany and her band took the stage, blessing them with a version of "Little Wing" that was more akin to Hendrix's than Clapton's: sultry, lovingly pitched, the electric guitar providing a sweet background. Everyone clapped wildly. Then, Bethany and the guitar player sang a corny duet about "lovin' that hot sausage pie," a blues collaboration they had concocted during rehearsals. Nora wondered how Bethany found time with her job and kids to rehearse, write songs and flirt. The crowd whistled. When Bethany walked off stage for a break, two guys trailed her; one carried a fresh pint of beer, placing it into her hands, while the other fanned her with a magazine.

"Bethany's groupies," Nora said to Winn.

It was hard to find a place to stand or to sit. Winn called it a night and left.

Nora downed a shot of whiskey and fought her way towards the bathrooms; from all her years of living in New York City, she could penetrate a crowd like a running back desperate for a first down. Lowering her head, she stiff-armed her way out, but she accidentally smacked into Ville.

"Oops...sorry," she said, slurring her speech. "Didn't mean to. Didn't see you." She felt like a clod. "Do you know Bethany?"

"No," he muttered. "Someone mentioned she'd be here. To wake us up."

"When Bethy's in the room, it's never boring," said Nora.

She introduced herself. They shook hands. "I'm a visiting American," she mumbled, striking a pose against the bathroom door marked *naiset*. When someone exited, the swinging door hit her.

"Ouch. That's not funny!" she shouted.

"I apologize," Ville said with a straight face.

"For what?"

"The lack of snow this winter."

A non-sequitur. Not the first time Nora had heard it.

"Don't worry. Plenty of snow for my purposes. But why don't they clear away the ice on the sidewalks? I'm glad it's melting. I thought I'd die in my boots."

"A winter without much snow is a subtle punishment," Ville said.

"Maybe."

Ville gestured for Nora to step outside the small club to get some air. In the darkness, she noticed two women shoving and grabbing each other's hair. Then a man rode up on a motorcycle. He got off, attempting to break up the fight. One of the women kicked him. Ville pulled Nora aside.

"Stand next to me."

She took a few steps closer. Her red coat flew open; the night air frisked her.

"I'm frozen." She put her beer mug on the ground.

Ville pulled her close. "Beautiful Nora…balm for my misery."

She welcomed his firm arm around her.

He looked her in the eye. "My wife left me for someone we know. Life is such shit. I couldn't leave my apartment. Until tonight. Now I meet you, an American. So open. I've been drowning in my drink. I'm sorry."

"Don't apologize. Hand me my beer."

Nora felt tempted, but refrained from offering to serve him pea soup.

"You aren't the only one drinking like a fish," she said. Since moving here, she had consumed more alcohol than at any time in her life (except for college). It was beginning to feel normal.

"I don't know you," she said. "But you'll get over it. You've got to." She did a little bump and grind into his thigh.

"Like that?"

"Very much. I fear I'm headed to the underworld."

"You believe in heaven and hell?"

"Only the latter," said Ville. "My mother gave her soul to a minister preaching intolerance."

"Sounds American."

"So I hear."

"Promise me," Nora said. "No more gloom!" She gestured with her empty glass. "Look at me."

He obeyed.

"Kiss me."

He leaned over. Planted one full on her lips.

"Finally," she said.

"Finally," he echoed.

"Again."

He called a few days later, and Nora learned more about Ville. Separated, he lived in a nearby suburb with part-time custody of an 11-year-old boy. The wife had been carrying on with one of their closest friends. He worked for his father's firm in contracting, engineering and design. How about that? Ville, the Finnish equivalent of William. Darkly intelligent, an above-average kisser, grateful to know her. In *sisu* she trusted.

Chapter Nineteen
Insect Over Nectar

(Nate)

Back home after his flubbed job interview, Nate sat in his swivel chair wracked with back pain. As he moved, each chair squeak incited a dull throb. He needed to stretch. Mariel insisted on becoming his pillow, his comfort. But her insistence made him want to pull away. Finally, he let her drag him to Times Square to behold Reverend Billy's Church of Stop Shopping, located outside the shrines of capitalism, the chain stores and the flashy billboard displays of 42nd Street. Dressed like a Southern evangelist in a white suit, Billy had teased poufy hair and preached against mass consumption.

"Let's exorcise cash registers. Throw away credit cards," he shouted into a microphone.

"Amen," responded Mariel, and many of the others. A small choir joined Billy to perform songs and skits. Nate stood silently.

Mariel couldn't fathom his dread over the failed job interview. How had Nate ended up at her cuddle party? Nora might have rolled her eyes at his fatalism, but she made room for it.

"Get your mind off the interview," Mariel said, pressing her petite frame into Nate's bulk as they stood watching Billy. "I bet you did better than you realize."

"No. I blew it. They wasted my time," he said. He had skipped his regular call to his mother; she would have guessed he'd screwed it up.

Since Nate started to hang around with her, Mariel hadn't attended any dance classes. They were both avidly avoiding something. If he had to perform a dance, he'd pirouette—spin *en pointe*, round and round with a hardcover book on top of his head. Then, in his mind, he became a swinging skeleton, like in The Grateful Dead and Day of the Dead iconography.

He needed to get back to Lulu's studio. That was where he became the graceful version of his dancer—the one who could *plié* and take a bow. Even if some of the *asanas* stung and the chasm between his knees and toes loomed large, he missed that dusty room with its slanted light, bodies flowing to their own rhythm. The regimen provided meaningful structure to his stilted life. He had begun to understand that failure did not diminish him. Any possibility of spending time with Lulu flooded him with relief. Yes, tension lingered between them. At the very least, she would understand his need to resume yoga. And he must write his way out of the trench—it mattered more than anything to move on. Hadn't Nora nailed it by taking that next step? It was his turn.

He imagined Lulu checking his alignment and applauding his progress. Would it be legal if he kissed her while she adjusted his pose? What could they name that *asana*? Insect over nectar. Yes. But he would never have the nerve.

Offendorf urged him to come to Maryland. "I have been expecting you," he said. Nate might feel centered enough to go there after a dose of yoga.

He told Mariel he had to take care of something. She tried to keep him close, but to no avail. He showed up at Lulu's, ducking into the darkened room as class began. He inhaled Lulu's jasmine cologne or body wash. Sweet and spicy.

"Take a breath of this new day." Her familiar voice: calm, low pitched. "Breathe through your nose. Let it flow all the way down, fill up your throat, your chest, bring it into your stomach. Until you cannot hold it any more. You are a blowfish. No, you are a whale. Gone under. Finally, you surface. Exhale REALLY BIG. Ahhhhhh."

Everyone let out their pent-up breaths. Blowfish and whales. Back to the routine. Best medicine. He took stock of Lulu. She'd lost weight. Wore a tight orange and pink tank, black spandex shorts. Basking in morning light. A deep red swath glinted in her nest of hair.

Was she eying him from a gap in her bangs? She blew them off her forehead with an upward whoosh. Her voice stayed level, but then she smiled. Glee floated towards his mat. Was she pleased he returned? Or was he the one beside himself? Had she forgiven his lame reaction to what transpired between her and Gil? She once said, "I like to keep my regulars regular." He wished he had never left.

During the salute to the sun, his bending, lunging and stretching fell off rhythm. He forgot everything. He needed to push his legs out with his hands when it came time for the big step forward. As he raised his arms on the way up, his oblique muscles cramped. His tree pose lacked tensile strength—a sapling about to snap. Triangle became rectangle. Lulu made no adjustments. She stayed in the front. He'd have to ease into the postures on his own.

A few months away and this is what happens. You lose fluency, become estranged from the supple sense of yourself. He felt stiff and stuck together like a newly opened cardboard puzzle. Imagine, he thought, if I wrote like a streamlined round of sun salutes. What would that entail? Whose theory would that enable?

Nate sank into the floor during *savasana,* just as Lulu instructed. He tensed and released and released and tensed. He put up no resistance, experiencing nothingness.

As Lulu narrated a visualization of tightening and loosening, an image emerged: Nate embracing Lulu like circling the sun. The hallucination aroused him. Maybe it was her orange and pink top or her high, rounded breasts. Waking him, prodding his every center. Her oddball instructions spoken with a slight Southern accent. Why hadn't he noticed her accent before? Returning to this space after being away, he felt at home, and he realized the truth in his heart. Her attention was magical and genuine. She was a complex woman—passionate—with an underlying fragility. He had been wrong to avoid her. He should run to her. He gave himself the green light, despite the possibility of rejection. *She's your life. Perhaps you can be part of hers.*

Nate couldn't say how it unfolded. Maybe his doppelgänger stood in for him, ripe and possessed. After the class ended, Lulu welcomed him back.

"I know you're struggling, Nate. Give it time. We all struggle. The important thing is you're here."

"What took me so long?"

"I don't know. You needed a break."

"Maybe. But that's not what I need now. And what do you need? I...want to help."

She let out a quick breath. "I appreciate that."

After everyone cleared out, Nate accepted her friendly hug. Lulu's head rested on his chest, childlike. He held her. Then he took a chance, running his hands along her hair and over her arms. His eyes locked onto hers.

How soft and firm she felt: the complete package. She seemed surprised, searching his face for answers. A swath of hair fell across her forehead. There was a sweet obviousness, like a sense of returning to where they had begun. Being that she was Lulu, she understood a shift had occurred. She blessed the universe. She stood on her toes and lifted her face to his. His heart leapt.

"Nate," she said, "what's happening?"

He didn't know what compelled him to act. He softly kissed her lips.

She kissed him back.

Emboldened, he kissed her deeply. She opened her mouth; their tongues tangled. He gathered her to him like a bouquet. Then he lifted her to nibble her clavicle, her shoulder blade. His lips lingered on the crescent swells of her breasts. She stroked his hair, kissed his facial stubble and threw back her head.

"Nathaniel Dart. Slow down."

"Sure," he said, out of breath, "I wanted to let you know the experiment was double blind. It needed time."

He could feel her heart thumping.

"We must take this elsewhere," she said.

"I'm portable," Nate said.

He recalled that time a few months ago when he first set foot here as an anxious interloper.

"You live close by, don't you?" he asked.

"Yes, but…I'm sorry to say I can't invite you. I have to protect my privacy," she said. "I don't encourage visitors."

He touched her cheek. "Please make an exception." He felt like an actor living some fantasy Hollywood life. She threw her arms around his neck.

He ran his fingers over the curve of her spine. "I believe I am enrolling in the advanced class," he whispered.

"Not so fast," she answered.

Chapter Twenty
The Boudoir

(Lulu)

Lulu hesitated to invite Nate to her white-walled apartment, her sanctuary and retreat. However, recent circumstances dictated she break her unwritten rule never to consort with lovers there—to keep it free of intruders who might cross a line. Nate was not one of those risky bad boys or taut yoga dudes that she accepted for a quick thrill, but he was friends with Gil. A throb in her side accompanied anticipation. She would not be toyed with. The locked outer gate leading to the courtyard of her pre-war building swung open. *I am making an exception for him,* she thought, but with conditions. They entered the path together.

Inside her apartment, she took his hand and led him past an altar containing scented candles of various sizes and a collection of deities. There was a small replica of the Hindu god Shiva, a symbol of yoga and purification, a pottery head of Aphrodite, the Greek goddess of desire (and jealousy), a voluptuous carving of Aku'aba Asante, Ghanaian fertility symbol, and a small bust of Sappho, the poet of Lesbos. She stopped to chant a few words of Sanskrit. Nate's voice echoed after her, without hesitation.

"Who are the women in these photos?" Nate said, pointing to two framed snapshots resting on the altar.

"My grandmothers. Dee is Rosa and Monroe's mother. She grew up under Jim Crow, was a dressmaker. They say she knew her share of amore and might have been a voodoo priestess. She died young. My mother thinks I've inherited some of her tendencies. Francois, French Creole, is Maximilian's mother. A discreet drinker, fabulous baker, tough on her kids. She loved the limelight. They say her recipes live on in the desserts of the French quarter, and beyond."

"What fantastic characters," Nate said.

"No shortage of those," she said.

They entered her boudoir. Her bed was queen-sized and high off the floor, covered in a pink chenille spread, with many pillows on top. A magenta canopy hung atop the poster bed like a veil. Mardi Gras-beaded curtains of red, blue, green, orange and pink separated the bedroom from a hallway and a bathroom. A pile of books about yoga, including the Sutras and a volume titled *Dissociative Identity Disorder*, sat atop her dresser. There was a framed series of risqué pin-up covers from old pulp novels on the wall. Some showcased half-undressed women, smoking. Others were lounging in garters or sexy nighties.

"My version of the graces and hours," Lulu said. Nate perused the images of her unique variation on Zeus' daughters and the seasons in Greek mythology. He gaped.

"I'll worship at your temple. Girly-girl meets carnal bohemia, with you reclining on your mile-high throne." He reached for her.

"It's not that simple," she said, stepping back. "Don't imagine you understand."

He nodded. "I'm sorry if I jumped to conclusions."

She had gone and done it: revealed her eroticism, spiritual allegiances, struggles and contradictions. She hoped their being together would move each of them to a better place. Still shaken by the encounter with Gil, Lulu's nightmares remained. She and Nate could never return to where they had been. She gulped her breath. They should take their time.

"I have a request," she said.

"What is it?" He placed his hand on her back.

"I don't want you to bring around Gil, and I don't want to hear about him. I am even questioning why you want to be his friend."

"I am asking myself the same thing," said Nate. "I won't mention him, and I'll do my best to keep him out of your hair."

"It's important. Can we lie down? I'd like to be held."

He took his time embracing her firm shoulders and muscular arms. He kissed her neck.

They fell asleep.

Lulu dreamed of flowers. The lotus blossom with its openness, representing purity of the body, speech and the mind. Rooted in mud, lotus flowers blossomed on long stalks as if they could float above the waters of attachment and desire. They also symbolize detachment because drops of water easily slide from their petals. She didn't know how long she had slept, but when she opened her eyes, she saw Nate, snoozing next to her.

She placed her hand on his belly. After he woke up, she moved his hand to her hand. She alternated between watching and closing her eyes as he slowly undressed her. She felt cherished as he moved, his touch firm and inquisitive.

As the clothing came away, he embraced her on top of the covers. They stayed that way for a long time: eyes closed, arms encircling each other.

When Lulu felt ready, she pulled off her undergarments one at a time and straddled him. They kissed deeply and he slid off his pants; she helped him remove his clothes. He tasted her erect nipples; she bent down to cover his face in kisses, frenching him. Slow, long and tender. "Can I touch inside of you," he asked, and she nodded yes. Placing his fingers inside her wetness and licking her navel, he kept it going with a rhythm until her orgasm rocked her backwards. She rolled a condom onto him and rode him. Barely speaking or coming up for air, they rested in an embrace before shifting positions. He raised her legs and she cried out as he came towards her, moving deep within. Nate bellowed as he came. They held each other, eyes open and smiling before closing them again. Time lapsed, languid. Sunlight, cutting through the slightly drawn curtains and reflecting in the colored beads, was casting blue and purple

Off the Yoga Mat

shadows.

Lulu realized that she had to run over to her studio. "My next class begins in fifteen minutes," she said.

They got up, dressed haphazardly, and parted in a blissful haste.

Chapter Twenty-One
Hiding

(Nora)

Since Bethany seldom stepped out on the town with her husband in tow, Nora decided to offer babysitting services to her friend. Nora needed a break from running around. She had plans to see Ville soon. She'd been assigned to conduct interviews with consumers in Helsinki and Espoo about their mobile phone use—the information was going to be used by Nokia to develop strategic plans and for statistical analysis. When she checked out the list of interviewees, one surname, Nurmio, rang a bell. Nora wasn't sure why.

She looked forward to an evening alone with Antti and Lilly. Despite her yearning for a child, Nora hadn't spent much time with little ones since her days as a teenage babysitter. She'd had multiple charges then—from babies to eight- and nine-year-olds. She'd observed the children of Tampere: yellow vests over snowsuits, holding hands in packs led by teachers, making their way to the ski trail or playground. Did she have the patience and mettle—the heart and the head—to be a good parent? She believed so, but this evening she put herself on trial.

Nora carried the frilly dress and Dr. Seuss books she had brought from New York. She boarded a bus from the *Keskustori* town square, and after spending nearly an hour weaving through Tampere's outskirts, she finally arrived. She followed Bethany's directions; soon, she was approaching a yellow wooden house in a glade she'd describe as "rustic suburbia."

The ten-year-old boy and eight-year-old girl shouted Finnish phrases from the yard. A cat and dog scurried onto the dirt path.

"The cat believes she's a dog," Bethany said, stepping into the yard. "She follows us to the bus stop." Bethany scooped up the large white feline, opening the front door.

"Welcome to our messy, overcrowded lodge. The kids have eaten dinner. They can have one snack and watch TV. Honestly, Nora, I'd like you to read with them from English books. To keep up their skills," Bethany said. "They speak just fine, but they're behind in reading."

"Look what I have for you." Nora held up English versions of *The Cat in the Hat* and *Fried Green Eggs and Ham*.

"Those books are for babies," said Lilly, grabbing at Nora's bag and finding the purple frock.

"That's a dress I picked out. In New York City," Nora said.

"I will wear it." Lilly yanked off the tags and walked away with it.

"Say thank you," Bethany shouted after her.

"Good luck tonight," Mikko said, emerging from the bathroom in a neat blue shirt, scent of fresh aftershave. "You're brave—they're used to me or my mother. But it's time I accompanied my wife to whatever entertainment she has in mind."

Bethany winked at Nora.

"I am going to hide," Antti announced, taking off.

"Stay in the house," his mother reminded him. She turned to Nora. "That one likes to hide in the yard or down the street, even in the woods. Don't let him drink too much pop or you'll never get him to sleep. I expect we'll be quite late. Your bed is the sofa—I left some sheets. I'll cook you a hot breakfast."

"Sounds great," Nora nodded.

"We have to scram," Bethany said, grabbing her coat and releasing the cat, "or we'll never get out. The bus arrives in six minutes." The dog and cat attempted to follow.

Bethany blocked them. "Stay inside, blessed creatures. Goodnight, Lilly. Please behave." Bethany blew her a kiss. Lilly had thrown the frilly dress over her clothes. It was about one size too small and strained across her chest and hips.

"Doesn't that pinch?" Nora asked.

"No," Lilly said. "It's perfect."

Lilly stroked the cat. She lunged as the dog charged past. She turned her wide blue eyes upon Nora. "Antti is so disgusting," she said. "Can I show you something in my room?" She presented a collection of Barbie and other dolls along the floor. "Let's play."

"Sure," Nora said. It brought back memories of fighting with her brother Ben after attempting to include him in multiple doll scenarios with little success. Lilly's dolls sported puncture wounds: some were missing limbs. A few were covered in magic marker and had straw-like hair. Nora's Barbie dolls had been finely combed, heartily worshiped, stoically behaved. She had hidden her darlings from Ben and his cronies—one of whom had bitten Nora on the forearm.

"Antti ruined this one," Lilly said, holding up a Barbie with a lame leg. "But she's still my favorite."

"Of course," Nora said.

Where was Antti? Should she search for him? Nothing must happen to him on her watch. Why had his parents let him bolt? I would not permit such rude behavior in my child. Then again, Nora believed she'd give birth to a fairly docile daughter.

"I should go find your brother." Nora stood up.

"No! He always hides." Her tone of voice resembled her mother's. "He wants attention."

"Okay. We'll wait a little while."

They dressed the dolls in various outfits, fixed their hair and improvised with shoes and purses to prepare for their trip on a boat; a tissue box stood in for a cruise ship. "Have you ever been on a ship?" Nora asked.

"Yes. The big ferry to Stockholm. It has one thousand rooms."

"Did you have a good time?"

"We played games. Ate licorice and *Dumle* candy. Antti hid in someone's room. There was an amusement park in Sweden with a big roller coaster…I was afraid. I fell into the water."

"What water?"

"By the shore. In my clothes."

Nora could only imagine.

The dog bounded in.

"What's his name?"

"Boho."

Nora petted him, recoiling. "Boho has bad breath."

Lilly giggled.

"I should look for your brother."

"I know where he is," she said. "He's outside."

Lilly held Nora's hand. They entered the backyard, where an outdoor clothing drier held sheets and towels hanging from clothes pins. In the tight party dress, Lilly pranced as best she could, grabbing the sheets and wrenching some down. Nora picked them up and hung them again.

Lilly led Nora to hedges with toys strewn about. Then over to a deep hole where they found a small gaming device, a bottle of soda and a batch of scattered Legos.

"Sometimes he stays here," Lilly said, and she herded Nora to a spot in the hedges where the fence was low. "Let's climb over," Lilly said, pulling the dress over her head and discarding it.

It would have been easier to walk around to the front gate.

Lilly crossed the fence in a breeze. Nora almost swung both legs free and clear, but her stocking snagged. "Oh shit," Nora mumbled. Lilly laughed and placed her small finger on the spot where the nylon caught, freeing it. Nora thrust that leg over. A jagged run erupted down one side of her tights.

"They're ruined," Lilly said. "I see Antti." She took off across the road without checking for cars.

"Lilly," Nora called. "Look both ways." Had Lilly and Antti planned this clueless chase? They couldn't have.

Nora trailed Lilly, breathing heavily as she entered a wooded area. "Wait up!" she bellowed, squinting. Finally, she reached the girl.

"Did you *really* see your brother?" Nora inquired.

"I thought I did. He comes here sometimes with a friend." She pointed to a bunch of branches that were tied and stacked, almost forming a lean-to shelter.

"Antti, come out of hiding!" Nora cried out, not knowing what else to do.

"Antti go home," Lilly screamed.

"Let's get out of here." Nora took the child's grimy hand.

When they entered the house, they heard a TV playing in the living room. Antti sat on the floor drinking soda with a straw from a tall glass. He gripped a doughnut. "*Hei,*" he said.

Nora wanted to laugh. And cry.

"You took the last one. Give me half," Lilly tried to grab the doughnut from her brother's hand.

"*Ei...*no," he called out and shoved the pastry into his mouth while Lilly jumped onto his back.

"Antti that isn't nice!" Nora scolded. "Let's see what else there is to eat." Nora followed Lilly into the kitchen.

"I want this." Lilly grabbed a large unopened bag of potato chips from a basket.

"Fine," Nora said. She had no idea whether or not there were restrictions. Her parents hadn't allowed her and Ben to eat salty snacks after dinner. What kind of rules would she enforce for her child? It seemed like something she'd never plan. She hadn't given much thought to becoming a disciplinarian and what persistence it required. Parenthood had been an abstraction. She watched as Lilly tore open the bag of chips. The salty treats scattered across the floor. The pooch scurried in. "No, Boho," Nora said, brushing away the chips, attempting to pick them up as the dog devoured them, growling at her.

"Help me, Lilly," she called. The girl reached for a few chips, placing them into her mouth and crunching with delight. Then she scuttled off with the bag to the living room. So much for cooperation. Nora seriously doubted her ability to persuade these kids to read any books.

She found a broom and while sweeping up the mess, spotted a

Moomin mug on the counter. A stack of newspapers, gossip tabloids. She sat down for a minute to catch her breath. She couldn't allow them to have the upper hand. She wanted a drink. Might she check the fridge for beer and the freezer for vodka? Better check on the kids.

When she entered the living room, Lilly had her arm inside the chip bag. Pets guarded the ottoman.

"Antti's hiding again," Lilly announced. "I think he stayed inside."

Nora took a swig from the large soda bottle; some dark fluid dribbled down her shirt, leaving a stain. "Oh great," she said, sitting down. The night was young. She paused and thought for a minute. When would she interview the Nurmio family and the others around Helsinki? She ought to go this coming week. Nora heard a loud crash, like a box flying off a high shelf.

"What was that?"

"Antti," said Lilly.

"You know what? We are going to play a game that I choose," Nora said, her voice terse. "Let's make a movie. I'm the director; you and your brother are the actors. I'll be back with props. You'll listen to me."

"Can I be the star?" Lilly asked.

Nora opened the front door to the house. She leaned into it. A car whizzed past. It was still light. Evening insects unleashed a rapture like a chorus. A few birds made clicking sounds from trees. Magpies screeched like crows. When she went back inside, she'd direct a thriller. Someone would get whacked, immediately.

Chapter Twenty-Two
Gravitational Pull

(Nate)

When Nate returned to his dowdy apartment, an ecstatic aura, better than any drug, surrounded him. He fell into his bed, converting the ceiling into a screen upon which he replayed the astounding events of the day. He reviewed his strange cockiness and Lulu's response. Initially reserved and hesitant. Then sizzling. Once she had accepted him, he responded like a teenager with blind dumb luck—happy as a clam, and just as lost. He called upon sexual reserves he never knew he possessed. Touching her, the weight of her body over his. She appeared relaxed and happy. In response to him!

Reality hit as he played back messages from Mariel. He had behaved less than stellar towards the young freegan. He couldn't focus on an appropriate response.

When would he be with Lulu again? He didn't recognize this version of himself: horny, romantic, inclined to experiment, anxious to please. Thankful. Blending lust and middle-aged introspection. He'd distance himself from Gil—it was time for that, and time to pursue a demon in the form of a German-born Englishman. He had to see Offendorf. If he had any chance of winning Lulu in the long run, he'd better get cracking.

In evolutionary terms, Nate figured he must secure his place in the academic hierarchy. It might appear as nonsense, but, on some level, he felt his status should approach that of a duke. He was a non-alpha male consorting with a queen. His fervor intensified because of previous denials, stubbornness and disappointments. Throw sexual ecstasy into the mix: Lulu's jasmine-scented pores, kisses he could still feel. He would do anything for her. What's the opposite of jealousy? And what would Freud say? Undress of the repressed? He sounded delirious.

Nate shut off his mind. Marveled at the white ceiling. No matter what came next, their union ignited a forecast of sunshine and daffodils. Nora had been his most serious girlfriend up to that point, but they hadn't quite fit. Their timing was out of kilter. She'd left him suddenly. How awfully he'd behaved...jealous of her career success, terrified of her plans for their future. Now he could acknowledge that destructiveness. Nora hadn't deserved it. Before her, his liaisons had been brief ones, in between long periods spent alone. He thought of stroking Lulu's two-tone hair, inhaling floral pheromones. He couldn't wait to be with her again.

Nate crawled under his comforter, attempting to sleep. Impossible. Why not clean the apartment? He wanted Lulu to spend time at his place, get to know him. He could show her his books and his music: unveil his collection of vintage radios. He hoped moths wouldn't emerge.

When the phone rang off the hook, Nate didn't pick up. He was mopping the kitchen floor. He heard his professor rant into the answering machine.

"Nate, I heard that you carried on after the job interview, insulted Janice. Threw away an opportunity. Why the childish antics? Now there's bad blood. Call me back."

Offendorf tunneled into Nate's afterglow. The professor heard only half the story; he couldn't grasp the sham. He's like my father berating me. A William James quote came to mind: "Acceptance of what happened is the first step to overcoming the consequences of any misfortune." Acceptance, humility. He accepted that Offendorf *might* change his opinion when he heard the whole story. Humility? A struggle for both of them.

But he thought of Lulu's ability to accept him, despite what she'd been through. Humbling. After he cleaned up the mess, he gathered his things for a trip to Maryland State University. He called his mother and father to inform them he was off for a few days to meet Offendorf. They wanted to know if he had made progress.

"Yes," he said to Audrey. "It's going better than ever." He sounded upbeat, breathless.

"I'm thrilled," she said. "You're exhilarated. Who is she?"

He knew if he wasn't careful, he might blurt out details. Express his bliss. He opted for silence.

Albert picked up the other extension. "Nate. Straighten it out with your professor. Have a drink. Don't argue. The dissertation isn't your life's work."

Nate was too dopamine-drenched to get angry.

"Nate," his mom's voice returned, "let us know how it goes, won't you dear? And when you meet with your professor, respect him. He'll be impressed. Don't let him ignore you. He should have your back."

"I love you," Nate said. "I'll call from Maryland."

Should he invite Lulu to accompany him? Her schedule was full. He felt like her besotted fan.

The following evening, Nate gravitated towards the yoga studio as if an iron shaving pulled by a super magnet. He didn't pay attention to which streets he wandered. Eventually, he came upon the freegan outpost. Mariel lit upon him like a hungry mosquito.

"Why haven't you called me back?" she said, her slender arms reaching towards his broad chest. He looked away.

"Sorry, Mariel. It's been crazy. I am about to meet with my advisor in Maryland. I can't talk." He knew he sounded like a bad rock-and-roll cliché, a cross between the dickhead in "Freebird" and the pompous ass in "Babe, I'm Gonna Leave You."

"Why do you keep running off?" she said. "I don't need this."

"Nobody needs this," said Nate. "I promise to explain. Really soon."

"I'm cooking tonight. We're starting to compost in the community garden. You should see," Mariel said with enthusiasm.

Her earnestness made him feel rotten.

"Let me help," he said. It was the least he could do. Rooting around in garbage would delay his hound dog hunt for Lulu.

"Go through these," Mariel gestured to a pile of large black garbage bags. "Gently open them, see what's wrapped or packaged in good condition. Bring it to me. I will cook by the fire we're setting up. And anything for the compost, place in this bucket."

He dug through the bags, wearing thin plastic gloves. Carrots, bagels, squished onions, some dried fruit, an orange with a rotten spot. It would be combined into a spicy stew to feed squatters, freegans, bicycle activists, housing rights folks, veterans, anarchists, persons with AIDS, Maoists. They would share it in the fading light, deep in conversation—some would play guitars and sing tunes by Pete Seeger, Richie Havens, Joni Mitchell, Phil Ochs and Bob Marley, while others would promote direct-action protest. Anita, drawing on her public relations background from Secanor, would urge them to do their homework. Anticipate the opposition and come across as reasonable. A joint or a bottle of hooch would make the rounds. An urban campfire: a gathering of activists. If Nate wasn't so distracted, he'd appreciate their fellowship and plans for shaking up a destructive system. But he wanted Lulu naked in his arms. He handed Mariel a bunch of salvageable items. Half an hour later he sat among them, forking food into his mouth, though he wasn't tasting anything. A gloomy cloud passed over the sunshine where Mariel basked.

"I'm sorry," he said to her.

"For what?" she asked.

"For everything. I'll explain when I get back from Maryland."

Nate put the last bite in his mouth and crumbled up the paper plate. He never meant to hurt her. But he didn't love her.

"I have to go," he uttered, dashing off.

Nate had to check if Lulu was locking up 2 Squared. It would be around that time. The few blocks he traveled to her studio felt like acres. He passed drunken revelers, working stiffs carrying briefcases and laconic couples who took their amours for granted. He couldn't.

Chapter Twenty-Three
Poetry and Radios

(Lulu)

Lulu awakened the morning she left Nate with a spring in her step. She knelt before her altar and offered a "thank you" to the universe. Their coupling had been gorgeous; she hadn't had any nightmares last night and wanted to believe she never would. Still the changed situation made her uneasy. How would they resume? She had no precedent for becoming close with a yoga student she had slept with—she'd never wanted to. The few times it had happened those folks had stopped attending her class. Nate must resume his yoga practice. A line had been crossed.

He seemed mesmerized. Lulu's confidence soared. She had sought honest self-reformation, restraint, patience and good judgment. With passion infused into a vein, her appetite returned. She decided to cook scrambled eggs with melted cheese.

Later that evening after class—puttering around with her green tea, dusting shelves, stacking mats—she tricked herself into acting nonchalant. He hadn't turned up. That was that. No big deal.

Standing on the steps heading out of the studio, in the dim light of the passageway, she heard him climb. He scooped her up, practically falling over before kissing her on the side of her mouth—klutzy gallant.

"Let's go to my place," he said.

"But I'm starving," she said. So, they went to Veselka, the packed Ukrainian diner on Second Avenue where she sometimes ate a bowl of cabbage or pea soup at the counter with homemade challah.

"She was looking for you," Lulu said when they were seated at a table. "Mariel turned up this morning in tears. Said she hadn't seen or heard from you. I told her you attended class once this week." Technically true.

"I *just* ran into her. Made excuses. The timing couldn't be worse."

Lulu spooned purple borscht into her mouth. She ordered potato pirogues too.

"I make a blessed connection with you," Nate said, "I should have broken it off cleanly with Mariel. But then Offendorf called to reiterate how badly I fucked up that job interview. I'm going to see him to settle it and talk about my dissertation," he said.

She swirled a dollop of sour cream into her soup, watched it lighten a shade.

"Nate, get your house in order." She needed to get hers right, too. She buttered her bread and bit into it, noticing Nate gazing at the strap of her shirt. She bet he could appreciate a peeper who vocalized, and a female frog treading rough stones and gullies to mate. Lulu put down her spoon, which shined under incandescent light. She recognized her vanity, her need, her edgy sense of self. Mariel had been beside herself with grief. Lulu understood she contributed to such heartbreak.

Maybe it was a blessing that Nate had to straighten things out. She felt a stinging pain in her side. She was kidding herself if she thought the darkness was gone—only on hiatus. Their union was like dough in the oven, a fullness that could burst. Something was up. A challenge on the way, a genuine crisis, an opening to illuminate dark recollections. She'd jump out of her skin.

When she was done eating, they strode to his walk-up apartment on Avenue B. He apologized for the piles of paper and books cluttering the small space, for the torn curtains and the sofa with burn holes.

"I had a friend who smoked," Nate said.

She suspected what created those holes: ash from his reefers.

"I mopped, dusted, disinfected. It's cluttered but clean," he said, beaming. "You're the first woman I've invited here since Nora. Except for my mom."

She smiled. "It has potential. I like your swivel chair." She thought he should hire a cleaning service. Throw out half of everything. It was stuffy, dark and stank of mold like some gothic library. She could barely find any clear space on the floor.

He observed her hesitation. "I'll move stuff out of the way so you can walk barefoot if you want." He picked up piles, removed some boxes. She noticed the indentations on the rug where he had vacuumed. All for me, she thought. She couldn't help but feel touched. He gestured for her to sit next to him on the sofa.

"I found the right poem," he said, and cleared his throat. He held up a book by a woman she had never heard of. There was a page folded down. His face softened. "Here goes."

"My pain/ my happiness radiates/in the curve of your mouth/in the bend of your mind/ a breaking point/ To you, I migrate."

His deep voice conveyed passages of loss and happiness. Fitting words. For the first time, she found what he had hidden beneath his unpolished exterior, in his chin dimple—a spiritual sensation. After he read a few more poems, he caressed her slowly and unhooked the tiny catch on the back of her shirt. With care, he removed each swath of fabric from her body. He undid the band on her watch. He left her ankle bracelet alone. He carried her the short distance to his bed, his sheets orderly with hospital corners.

"You're cold," he said, and he wrapped a throw blanket around her.

"Now you can undress me," he said. As she undid the buttons on his shirt, she looked up and noticed a shelf above his bed with transistors and old-fashioned radios.

"Do they work?" she asked.

"Mostly, yes. I like 'em even if they don't. Radio is where families gathered to listen to news and music before TV and computers, which leave me cold. I prefer to write in longhand and listen to commercial-free stations like WBGO or WFMU. I grew up on Cousin Bruce Morrow, the DJ on 77 WABC. My head has always been in radios."

"I like that. In New Orleans, they play music in the streets."

"I'd love to visit sometime," he said. "It's your hometown?"

"Originally. I grew up mostly in the suburbs of Washington, D.C."

"I'm from Long Island. I know the suburbs."

"Near the ocean?"

"It wasn't far, but I didn't take advantage." He kissed the hollow of her neck. She traced a line over his eyelids, nose and mouth. She arched her back, pressing into him. Stimulated and wet, she kissed the stubble on his face, the dimple in his chin, rapidly assisting him with shedding his shirt, pants and boxers. She lightly gripped his erection; he put on a condom.

"Speaking of oceans, there's something I can show you. The tidal wave."

"Teach me," he said.

She wrapped her legs around his lap, lowered herself onto him, then leaned back. She extended her body over his outstretched legs, bending. It was difficult, but it rocked every nerve in her body.

"Is this hot, sexy yoga, or yogic sex?" he asked, gasping for air.

"Both," she said. "Hold my lower back, Nate. Breathe in. Don't let go." She couldn't help but return to instructor mode. Then pleasure left her speechless. She squeezed her folded legs against his sides. Lulu swooned as she came, tensing abruptly against him. Nate let out a shout as he lost control.

Later, back on the sofa, he lifted her onto his lap. She massaged the length of his arms, legs and chest, then kissed his face and chest, admiring the yoga toning and belly pouch. She was thinking how much she'd miss him, even as she contemplated the right time to leave his side. Lulu almost always had the urge to escape her partner after sex. They shouldn't possess her or assume anything. With some of them she'd intuited an undercurrent of roughness and risk. As she admired Nate's sated face, she knew she'd stay all night.

"Read to me some more," she said, grabbing a book by June Jordan. She caught a glimpse of small gray-white moths fluttering from his closet. "What else lives in there?"

"Sorry about the wildlife." They laughed, holed up with all the creatures of the tenement.

Chapter Twenty-Four
A Proposition

(Nora)

Nora defined Ville as existentially depressed. In her company, he felt at ease. "Nora, you don't judge. I admire your American openness."

Was she really so open? Nate had found her controlling. Together, Ville and Nora reveled in temporary lightness. He took her to play mini golf, an amusing sport that the Finns took seriously.

Tampere's mini-golf course featured three courses built into one: hard, impossible and brutal. The ball had to travel through tiny, narrow ramps. In some cases, the golfer could not stand on the green. Instead, they were forced to tilt against its side and swing from there. If you failed to hit the ball up the ramps or through the mini archways, your access to the green could be denied. No windmills, clown faces or tunnels of love. Access to the green included hazards on all sides. Nora realized the contradiction of designing a mini-golf course for grown-ups and for kids. Clearly not a concern here because Finnish children were as rugged as soldiers. She'd been in awe of little ones trudging with ski gear on their way to the cross-country tracks in the woods, part of their normal school day. No wonder they skied like Olympians by the time they were six. She'd also heard that mothers wrapped their babies in layers before placing them in their strollers out in the cold for long naps in fresh air—a toughening up. Nora imagined swaddling her baby in her arms. Nate was about to take over parenting duties. Why did she still imagine him in the picture? Thinking of Nate, she recalled her association with the name Nurmio on the list of those to be interviewed for Nokia. Wasn't Nate's mother's maiden name on her Finnish side Nurmio?

"It's your turn." Ville nudged her.

"Sorry," she said, paying attention. "How am I supposed to hit the ball through such a narrow canal?"

"Try."

"Who designed the course? A tech guy spending too much time in his cottage?" She crouched down to study the set-up.

She hit the ball, attempting to roll it up the narrow ramp. It went off the course. Nora picked it up and put it back on the green outside the ramp, near where it had flown free.

"You're a cheat," Ville said. When the ball was hit out of bounds, he insisted on starting over, placing it back on the original starting spot.

"Cut me some slack," countered Nora. "You're anal."

He let out a belly laugh. "You don't talk that way at Nokia, do you?"

"No. At Nokia we discuss handsets. Which features matter most? A tactile keypad? Buttons leading to an artery of functions?" Nora said, swinging her club in the air. "The year 2000 bug would cut into profits."

"What do you think?" he asked.

"They're right. We can't begin to imagine the chaos when technology fails us. We may have to start over. If we don't plan ahead, we could face some real trouble."

"Don't hit me with that club," Ville said, as Nora practiced her swing wildly.

She hesitated. Then the "pro" mini golfers pulled up—two overweight guys who took from carrying cases their own clubs, multi-colored balls and a gripping tool that picked up the balls so they needn't bend down. One of them pocketed a can of *Karhu* beer. Those two blazed a trail through all the courses with alarming speed and accuracy, barely needing an extra stroke, never speaking.

Ville stared. "That's how it's done."

"Who are they?"

"The mini-golf mob."

She smiled. Studied Ville's physique as he putted with concentration. Wiry, in good shape; so far, they had smooched and cuddled. She wanted to sleep with him. She and Ville had dined a few nights before at the Telakka restaurant, which was also a music and arts venue. Jussi had walked in with one of his babes. Over the sound check of the Led Zeppelin cover band, Hammer of the Dogs, Nora called out a greeting. She had made enough emotional progress to bypass her mortification over Jussi's womanizing and his rejection of her advance. Ville fidgeted. Nora and Jussi exchanged furtive glances that signified nothing.

Nora took a breath. Ville was separated from his wife. *I am his rebound fling. He is mine.* Might this become something more? She hoped it could.

Lonnie would have said "just enjoy yourself!" She was getting hitched—maybe she'd have a baby. Perhaps she'd move away. Bethany seemed to sanction unprotected sex that could lead to pregnancy, but Bethany didn't romanticize parenting. She struggled to maintain her identity as a singer and social worker, while also guiding Lilly and Antti. Nora had no clue how to reconcile her most pressing goals while still existing in the present moment. She accidentally bit her tongue as she remembered to putt—it bled onto her finger when she touched it. "I'm going to run to the toilet," she told Ville.

"It's your turn."

When she returned, she whacked the ball with abandon. It zigzagged unpredictably, landing in the hole on the first try. "Did you see that?" she yelled, hugging Ville. "A hole in one."

"Without cheating," he said. "Let me treat you to some sausage."

They sliced into hot portions of *mustamakkara*, a thick black sausage of intestine skin filled with barley and sold at an outdoor grill. Nora mentioned her assignment on Sami film.

"My mother is part Sami," Ville replied. "She was forbidden from speaking the Inari-Sami language in school."

"Sounds like what they did to Native Americans in my country. Were your mother's folk reindeer herders?"

"I don't know. She never mentions it. She's become an evangelical Christian. My father is the opposite. He doesn't believe in God—he's a fanatic social democrat. My parents barely co-exist. On Saturday nights, they meet in the sauna."

"What if they have other plans?"

"They skipped a big party because of their blessed appointment. The week begins with purification. If it wasn't for sauna, they'd be finished."

Nora imagined such a ritual might help her parents reinvigorate their union. With her dad's slow recovery, they needed to emotionally recharge. He was fighting off an infection, back in the hospital for observation, which worried her. Her parents weren't religious. Their habitual renewal: watching TV, playing cards, bickering. Her mom played bridge and attended Weight Watchers meetings. Her dad preferred to stay at home doing crossword puzzles or tinkering in the garage. Nora and Ben didn't visit them often. What if her family embraced a sauna ritual? What might they discover about each other if they relaxed in a hot, dark cabin?

Finnish families spent a good deal of time in each other's presence. Grandparents helped with childcare. They'd visit their ancestral towns and, in summer, take to the woods at lakeside cottages. Since her folks resided in Maryland, Nora couldn't count on them to help with a baby in Manhattan. When her dad was doing better, Nora would suggest that her parents seek out a sauna or steam room, or maybe a meditation center.

What about Ville's son? She hoped to observe her new guy as a parent. Soon, she'd uncover more details of Ville's world, including where he lived (a nondescript condominium complex) what kind of music he liked (Beatles, classical) his favorite TV shows (*The Simpsons*, Eurovision singing competitions, programs on the state-sponsored channel, *Yle*). Glimpses inside the wreckage of separation—lessons for how to move on. She'd classify Ville as the most "normal" man she had dated.

"I will take you to an outdoor sauna," Ville promised. She liked the thought of sweating next to him nearly naked. She wanted to plunge into the hole in the ice, meet the extreme sublime.

"I'll guide you into the lake," he said.

But first, Nora received a modest proposition.

***

Winn entered Nora's office without knocking.

"You startled me," she said, looking up. "What's going on?"

"I keep thinking of how to say this, but there is no delicate way. We are in the final throes of our time here."

"Out with it then," said Nora.

Winn delivered rapid fire. "You want to have a baby. My wife doesn't fancy having children. How do I put it? I would be happy to contribute to your cause."

He turned crimson. Nora's eyes bulged.

"I don't mean to suggest we'd have to have sex. There are scientific methods."

It was the kind of thing they'd joke about if it didn't concern them.

"You're offering me your sperm? Your jism. Your love juice?"

He looked terrified. Then he nodded, chuckling. "Yes, it's all yours, for free. My parting shot."

"A little bit of you to take away," said Nora.

Now that they'd had a good snicker, she considered it a generous offer. Not her first choice. But in the back of Nora's mind, donor insemination had always been an option.

"I don't know, Winn. You caught me off guard."

Would she go through with being a single parent? He lived far away. What about Doris? Might she object? Anonymous sperm donors give up their parental rights. There's also adoption. Really, so many ways to become a parent. It crossed Nora's mind that she wouldn't want her kid to inherit Winn's bald or short genes. Was she a monster for thinking like that? What if Winn's wife sued for custody of the biological progeny of her husband? There were so many factors to consider, on top of the shame.

"I've made you uneasy," Winn said. "Don't sweat. Think on it. If you want, call me. I'm around for the next month and a half...then I go back into my box."

She imagined that when her hormones raged—while she was ovulating—she'd summon Winn to try to impregnate her. Maybe he wanted to have a last-minute fling. Here he could appear as a Good Samaritan. Quite ingenious. Why couldn't she produce a baby the old-fashioned way? Nora sensed she wasn't destined for tradition. She had been anointed a time traveler in the age of high-tech reproduction. Her options were multiplying even as they spoke. Technology-inclined Nora could embrace them.

"I'll let you know if I require your services. Let me return to my editing...as if I can focus."

That night when she fell asleep, she dreamed of floating on a sea of ice. Winn sashayed across the cracks, calling "I have a bucket." Jussi appeared submerged, his head the only visible body part above the water, shouting "Help me!" Nate powered along the shoreline in a dune buggy with Lilly and Antti sitting in the back seat. Lilly held a can of Coke. Antti waved a Barbie doll. Nate yelled "I'm calling the cops." Absent from the dream, Ville would be the one actually walking into the heat and ice with Nora. The others could become bobble-head figures she'd fling with her fingers.

Chapter Twenty-Five
Not Good with Darts

(Nate)

Nate's bus ride to Maryland provided him with four hours in which he could plan his encounter with mighty Offendorf. He'd flatly refuse to purge Darwin or take feminism from his thesis. He'd provide his side of the interview fiasco. Hopefully, they'd set a defense date. Nate would kill to meet that deadline—get the doctorate out of the way and then land a professorship. Cease being bankrolled by his parents and pay off those loans. Get tangled up in Lulu. On I-95, he dozed for ten-minute stints, and, whenever he woke up, he couldn't remember where he was.

Lulu had hit the road, too, heading to New Jersey. She received a call that her mother was being hospitalized for pneumonia. Before she took off, she embraced him.

"Good luck with Offendorf. His name, you must have realized. Do not offend Orf."

"That's right," Nate chuckled. "If you or your frog has any power to influence the gods, persuade them to be on my side with the callow professor."

"Of course. In Morocco, young women pray to frogs for a good marriage—they burn incense at the edge of ponds. Light candles. Ask for guidance."

"I don't think I'll burn incense. But I'll imagine I'm kissing your collar bone," Nate said.

"You speak so sweet. Fill me in on what happens."

"I will."

She planned to drive her mother to New Orleans as soon as possible. She gave him the phone number for her Uncle Monroe's place.

"Don't be gone too long," Nate said. "It'll all be in my convoluted head."

"I don't know how much time it'll take to get her settled and recovered. Would you check on my studio, please? I asked this other yoga teacher to take over some classes. And keep up your practice, dear Nate."

When she called him dear, it hit him like a trumpet blast—a flourish of sensual guitar.

"Of course. I'll check on your studio," he said, kissing her long and slow. "Don't forget about me."

"As if I could."

The bus hit traffic after Delaware. He hadn't called ahead. Offendorf often holed up in his dormer office on the top floor of Massey Hall, a clapboard house filled with sagging bookshelves, old sofas and few faculty members. Offendorf burrowed into his cluttered office with its perfect view of the main quad.

Nate had spent many an hour there as research assistant—opening mail, sorting through requests for his boss to review manuscripts. He remembered the time Offendorf served as an outside referee on a tenure case for a woman at Oregon State University. His professor dismissed her scholarship as lacking in rigor. She was denied tenure; just like that, her career was derailed. Another time, Offendorf wrote on behalf of a former undergraduate who had applied to a prestigious Ph.D. program. Based on Offendorf's endorsement, the guy had received a fat scholarship. Yup, Nate had been naïve, but, as he opened the mail, sat in on meetings, absorbed the "yeas" and "nays" of the tribe he planned to join, he grasped their biases. The power of certain individuals to make or break others. Did he still want in? He supposed so…but he'd push for reform.

If given a chance, he'd play fair. First, he'd refine his teaching skills. Figure out how to motivate students, especially the doubtful or the confused. He enjoyed the patter with Armand and Carrie Joan during the doomed interview; they also made him realize he hadn't thought enough

Off the Yoga Mat

about bias against women, people of color, and those who might identify as gay, lesbian or trans. When he met with the few freegans who attended his teach-in, they argued that social class re-structuring under capitalist institutions—including universities—was just a ruse. If the gatekeepers let him enter the kingdom, Nate would try to dismantle it from within.

He also believed in the value of research for creating possibilities. When he initially realized his focus on jealousy and envy, those psychosexual behaviors that appear in Shakespeare's plays, he wrote furiously in his spiral notebooks. How thrilling to exchange drafts with his study group and swap perspectives with Offendorf.

"I have not shrunk…I have not dwindled," Offendorf responded that time, drawing on Shakespeare's phrases, when Nate role-played as Prince Hal, thrusting at Offendorf: "All else falters but your love of sack, my liege." Sir John in *Henry IV* favored sack sherry. Offerndorf was a beer and whiskey drunk. Back then, Offendorf could take a joke.

In the early days, they would talk for hours, drawing on references and insights, poetry and theory. Then Nate's unconscious mind would process those dialogues; by morning, *voila,* new patterns had emerged. At some point, Nate's inquiries became less about discovery, more politically motivated and self-conscious, as his status depended on winning approval and hoop-jumping. He'd stare at his computer screen, grow dazed by the dense theoretical writing that had come to seem normal. "The hegemonic discourse of learned men in the determinist nation-state preserves a boundary for the subject." Must *he* write like that?

Offendorf had asked Nate to compose his correspondence, fact-check, file and order lunch. All of this cut into Nate's research and writing time, but he depended on the fellowship money so he couldn't complain. More his father's son than he liked to acknowledge, Nate believed in keeping Ralph Waldo Emerson's idea of the transparent eyeball on the elusive prize. Teachers must respect students; contempt and power-mongering undermined noble objectives. Nate had little faith Offendorf would treat him with dignity.

As the bus pulled into the depot, Nate pledged to be optimistic. He thought of Emily Dickinson's line, *Hope is the thing with feathers.*

It was late afternoon when he arrived. He checked into a cheap motel before heading to campus. The door to Massey Hall, propped open. Although April daffodils pushed through the grass, winter lingered on in a few patches of snow on the ground. He climbed the creaky steps, passing a student dozing on a couch while another student spread out her notes, a Big Gulp soft drink by her side. On the top floor, across from Offendorf's office, Nate found a chair. He composed himself, did some yogic breathing.

Voices. Muffled laughter filtered from the half-open door.

"He didn't try to hide anything." Nate recognized Offendorf's stuffy British accent.

"Yup," a female responded. "He doesn't deserve a B+. Maybe a B. Watch him during his presentation."

"He mustn't mimic."

"But you like it when your ideas come back at you, Mickey," she said. "You reward students who recycle."

They tittered.

Mickey? Nate had never heard anyone call Offendorf Mickey. Hardly anyone even called him Michael. Who was this person, discussing some graduate student's fate?

The conversation continued. Nate picked up bits and pieces. More giggling. He fanned cigarette smoke as it seeped out the door. He stood up and edged closer. The conversation covered lousy arguments, faulty logic, underdeveloped examples and misread theories in some graduate student's essay. If she was his assistant and a current Ph.D. candidate, that was inappropriate; it wasn't the same as being the professor's TA. Their job was to grade undergraduate essays under supervision. They might as well have been deriding *his* chapters.

He started to slink away. Then, a woman in a navy suit with streaked blonde hair emerged. She looked about thirty and had blotched mascara under her eyes. She wore no shoes.

"Are you waiting for Professor Offendorf?" she asked.

"No. Um, yeah, but I'll come back," he stammered.

"Go right in."

Nate composed himself. He entered, facing the advisor he hadn't seen in years.

"Good afternoon, Professor Offendorf."

Offendorf lifted his bag-laden eyes from a paper. It took a few seconds for any recognition to register.

"Nathaniel Dart! You made it." He came out from behind his desk. He looked shaggy, smaller in stature than Nate recalled. He had a tuft of a beard, tangled gray-white hair and one part of his shirt was statically clinging to his trousers.

Nate shook the extended hand.

"Sorry I didn't call. I have to be in D.C. anyway. Stopped by to discuss my dissertation. Also, I want to tell you what happened at that job interview. But if you're busy, I can come back."

Offendorf fingered his beard. He looked dazed, his eyelids fluttering. "I am finishing up with a graduate student who holds your old job. Heddy McKendry, of Scottish-American extraction. Quite dazzling. We will head to the pub in about an hour. Meet us there."

"All right, but I was hoping I could have you all to myself," Nate said. "It's been a while. Some of this is sensitive."

He remembered how Offendorf took late dinners in the pub. The Mrs. had left him years ago (although there had been no formal divorce). She was a Catholic—didn't believe in it. Nate used to relay her messages.

"I can vouch for Heddy. She's sharp. Don't worry. She might even resolve your writing quandaries," the professor said.

Just then she burst in.

"Heddy, this is my former research assistant, Nate Dart—an ABD toiling endlessly. He's come to find his way out of Plato's cave. I believe I mentioned him. Writing on jealousy, with Shakespeare and Darwin."

"Oh yes. Pleased to meet you. It's awful what you're going through. My heart goes out."

Was she being sincere or mocking him? How dare Offendorf divulge his problems? "I'll see you at the pub," Nate snarled. He left the building, head down, his back aching.

With an hour to kill, he gravitated towards a favorite tea house where students eyed each other as much as they studied. Two boys flirted behind a propped up hardcover edition of Raul Zazŭk's book, *The Post-Nomad Uncanny.* Nate sat down and thought for a moment. He distrusted Heddy. As for Offendorf's behavior, he'd label it deranged. A realization returned that had dawned on Nate before he left the school. Offendorf lived off long-faded glory; what kind of power did he *actually* wield? Even back then, people were saying he wrote the one book as a junior professor: on sin and salvation in Shakespeare and Melville. He hadn't produced much since. In the academic pecking order, you're only as hot as your latest work. Maybe the professor had written one substantial essay in the past few years. So how did he operate? How low had he descended? What did that mean for Nate? He thought of his own chapter on King Lear. "Nothing will come of nothing," Lear lectures Cordelia when she hesitates to flatter him like her sisters, and so she loses her share of the estate. Offendorf had already punished Nate for having ideas that diverged from his own. Nate no longer had time for mind games.

When he entered the bar, Heddy and Offendorf clutched half-drained pints, the next ones waiting nearby.

"Ah Nate, you want to plead your case," said Offendorf. "But first, let's order fish and chips. Hear the latest from New York."

"I love the city," Heddy said. "I got my B.A. from Barnard."

"And then she came here instead of staying in the Ivies," said Offendorf. "Their loss."

"I was offered a full ride here...I don't come from money."

"She's made the best of her time, Nate. The lass wrote an essay for *PMLA*. She has an anthology under contract." (*PMLA* was a prestigious journal in literary and linguistic studies.)

Impressive, Nate admitted, peeved the conversation focused on *her*. "Congratulations," he said. "How did you find the time to do all that?"

"I suppose I'm a workaholic," she said. "I don't sleep."

Offendorf beamed. "You know my piece—came out three years

ago, Nate, on sin, as reflected in American secular identity and biblical original sin? She sat in my seminar, absorbed my concepts. Ran with them, pushed the work so that it took immigration and popular culture into account, like Clinton's ordeal with Monica Lewinsky. Heddy knows her way around French theory. But she's not interested in feminism. Quite refreshing."

Nate felt woozy. The two of them had set up a little enterprise—building up some, shooting others down—based on their combined aesthetic. A twisted power grab that could spell his doom.

The next hour proved to be a series of pints, greasy food, dart throwing. Nate tried, but he could never score as high as they did.

"It seems Mr. Dart is not good with darts," declared Heddy. "You suck."

"Yes," said Mickey. "Whereas I am a prick who finds my target." He fingered one of the missiles. Tensed his arm all the way back, taking aim. His shot dug into the cork just below the bull's eye.

Nate wished he could launch one at the prof's bloated chest, shoot another to pierce Heddy's head. His last shot hit the wall, thudding to the floor.

"Now, now. Someone needs another drink," said Heddy.

When they sat down, Nate surmised nothing would be accomplished. It was all drunken revelry, smug innuendo.

"Nate Dart. Do what you have to do," Heddy uttered, banging her shot glass on the table. Offendorf's head drooped on her shoulder. "As my mother says, 'aye...my darling, your life's worth more than a fixin' o' haggis.'" Heddy giggled. "Do as you're told. Then put back everything you removed. Who's going to know?"

"Yes, who?" Offendorf echoed. "After it's approved, then it's a whole 'nother ball of wax. Then you haveta listen to the readers' reports." His speech amusingly butchered, he shuffled off to the men's room.

Alone with Heddy, Nate's vertebrae throbbed. On her side, youth and sex appeal. He could have jabbed a poisoned dagger into Mickey's gut. Sobriety slipping away, Nate blotted sweat from his forehead.

"Isn't Offendorf too old for you?" he said. "Have you heard of a conflict of interest?" He wanted to ask, "Are you like an ingénue on the director's couch?" but he refrained.

"Give credit where credit is due," Heddy replied. "Don't get defensive. Your ideas are decent. Someone else'll beat you to the punch and publish them if you don't get off your ass. Offendorf will retire soon. Then what?" She laughed.

Nate yearned to retaliate with sharper, wittier words. He grasped her point. The threats she spoke of were viable. He inhaled his rage.

"You're grading your peers' essays," he said.

"Someone with talent has to slog through the slush."

"Any chance you've heard of what we call ethics?"

"Save the philosophy. Goes with the jealousy thesis."

Offendorf slid back into the booth. "How are you two getting on?" The barkeep rang a bell to signal for last call.

"Let's call a cab," Offendorf said. As soon as they stepped outside, he lit up.

"I like an older Brit with a pipe." Heddy looped her arm through the professor's, glaring at Nate. "You're not so bad. Wipe that desperation off your face."

As they piled into the back seat of the taxi, she leaned forward, catching Nate off guard. She planted a kiss on his lips. It happened too quickly for him to recoil into the cushion. Heddy and Offendorf let out a howl. Nate wiped beer-flavored spit from his mouth. "Let me out," he told the driver.

The cab stopped short. Nate cracked open the door.

Offendorf shouted after him. "If you want to see me tomorrow, drop by around three. But I might forget."

"I'll call you," Nate said as he scurried off, almost tripping over his own feet.

***

When morning came around, Nate winced. His head felt fully loaded, his stomach lurched. They had wiped the floor with him, even as he caught on to their scandal. He needed to strike back, yet he depended on Offendorf's approval. He yearned for Lulu's sympathy, her touch. He'd negotiate his escape from that man and his demon accomplice, like a kidnap victim slinking out unseen before ransom has been paid. He dialed her number. A man who must have been Lulu's uncle picked up.

"Who is this? What you want? Lulu's not here," he mumbled. "She's with her mother in Jersey. I don't know when they're coming."

Where was she? Nate stared at the gray walls. He hadn't any dope, scant cash. He managed to do a few planks on the thin, stained rug, holding himself taut, arms beneath his shoulders. He could laugh at the ludicrous events of the previous evening, but he needed to talk to someone. Monica?

She answered on the first ring but couldn't talk. It was almost time to go to teach. They were riding her hard, she said, and she'd have to prove herself as the most junior of the junior faculty. He explained his discovery.

Monica grew incensed. "Tell Offendorf he's an unethical slut. You'll file a grievance with the chair."

Oops. They realized the chair wouldn't care. He was going on leave and his time was taken up with mentoring and handing out scholarships to those he favored. And the Dean? She had a reputation for being on the side of students, swooning over precocious success stories. Someone like Heddy would bring tears of joy to her eyes. Permanent ABDs (All but Dissertation) like Nate, paying only the matriculation fee until they completed their degrees, represented a nasty statistic in graduation: lower job-placement rates, inferior ranking. In other words, a parasite.

"Don't worry, Nate," Monica assured him. "I'll find something to take down Heddy. You deal with Offendorf...don't let that bastard get in your way."

"All right. And one more thing Monica." He couldn't help but say it. "I've met...this amazing woman."

"What? Oh my God," she said. "You sound like a teenager. Who is she?"

"She's a yoga teacher. Big heart, complicated past."

"Is she anything like Nora?"

"Not really. Nora left town. Lulu's mixed-race, from Louisiana, totally out of my league. I thank the god of hormones for our chemistry." He said more than he had intended. "Jealousy played a role."

"What'd I say, Nate? It's best to listen to me. Are you making your thesis personal?"

"I'm trying," he said. "First I have to slay the dragon of the pipe and the pint."

"You shall," Monica said. "And make sure you tell me all about it."

He'd wear his suit of armor, dig out his lance.

Chapter Twenty-Six
Crescent City

(Lulu)

Lulu sat by Rosa's bed in a New Jersey hospital. Her mother had been rushed there with a chronic case of pneumonia. Jolted off her sensual cloud, Lulu responded by hustling to Rosa's side. It happened not long after she had staggered home, sore and exhausted from time with Nate, after teaching some lackadaisical yoga classes. She asked Bina to lead a short sequence of postures so she could doze in a chair.

Nate had taken off to see his advisor; he would have liked her to accompany him. If only I could have gone, she thought, instead of facing my family. On the other hand, the sooner she did, she might be freed of the mystery surrounding her abuse. She'd be back in the town where it happened, surrounded by mother and uncle, memories stirred from the bottom up. Plus, in some unexplainable way, she missed New Orleans and wanted to experience it after all these years. She'd make sure Monroe and Rosa could live together.

Lulu put her life in New York City on hold. Quickly, she requested two months' extension on her lease, citing the hardship of her mother's health. She hadn't formally agreed to the eviction. She left before that goon from the management office had a chance to visit again.

She laid out a path before she arrived: after they green-lighted Rosa's discharge, Lulu would drive her mother to Monroe's in New Orleans. Set her up there. Rosa's resistance would be weakened; Lulu would put on a brave face, sniff out evidence, attempt to uncover the source of her nightmares. Maybe Monroe knew something about the stocky, bald man.

Her mother had been struggling to breathe while Lulu and Nate were quaking with pleasure. That didn't make Lulu a bad daughter, but she felt out of synch. She wouldn't behave as she had when her father went downhill from cirrhosis of the liver. She couldn't have saved him, but she might have been there and tried to help. At that time, rage and fear had engulfed her, and she hunkered down with her boxing man, Wendell. She had never mourned the loss of her father; everything about him twisted inside her. Other harrowing incidents of her youth remained tucked away.

Lulu felt all pins and needles sitting on a hard chair next to Rosa's bed. Her mother appeared flattened—her mole turned darker. They hooked Rosa to a respirator; a nurse said she'd need a few more days under observation, then would have to pass a breathing test. In the yoga sutra, that prime document of yogic philosophy, it is best to reduce the *antaraya*, or obstacles, that deter your path through inner consciousness. Lulu sought a place for circumspection—and to serve.

She stood up, then bent forward, lightly brushing her fingers against the floor. Extended one of her legs to the side, raised her hands in prayer position.

"Don't do that," Rosa whispered. "They're bringing my lunch."

They undid the respirator for a brief spell. Lulu tried to feed Rosa. Her mother pushed it away.

"Try some Jell-O, mama. You need energy."

Her mother swallowed an orange lump.

Lulu had time to reflect on her parting conversation with Nate. As they murmured hasty goodbyes, she said she had left word for another teacher to take over some of her classes. Nate agreed to check the studio. She didn't mention the eviction. Nate was worried she'd forget him. As they kissed, she asked why he assumed that.

"I don't know. Habit?"

Rejections had accumulated for Nate; he held on tight to all of them. She decided she'd reveal her terrors to him over time.

Rosa opened her eyes, finished with her snooze. "I ain't going to Monroe's," she said. "Can't go back."

"It's temporary. Two or three months, then you can return to Ocean Grove. If you get healthy," Lulu said. "You'll keep a garden out back, near that Magnolia tree." She recalled how Rosa would kneel outside their Maryland apartment to cultivate her plot. She had grown basil, thyme, hot peppers and tomatoes. Cared for perennials, bushes and bulbs. Sprinkled herbs, diced vegetables into sauces and gumbo, filled vases with cut flowers.

"If his backyard isn't covered in weeds and junk," Rosa replied. "He's not right in the head."

"You took up painting in New Orleans, remember? Spent time by the lake," Lulu reminisced. "We'll see about Monroe. You'll help each other. Save your strength, Mama."

"You ignore me."

"I rushed here," Lulu said, stroking Rosa's hair.

She needed her uncle and mother to coexist without grenades exploding. Later, pacing in the hallway outside Rosa's room, Lulu thought about swimming as a child in the acrid waters of Lake Pontchartrain. Her father had thrown her high in the air, calling her "Little Bear." She needed positive memories. Mostly, Rosa's anger surged whenever Maximilian had gone on a rampage. Lulu ran outside at the first sign.

Thinking about those rough times, Lulu missed her students, her yoga regimen. Most of all, dear Nate. She freeze-framed the memory of his five o'clock shadow, chin dimple, attentive caresses. Their hardscrabble lust.

Rosa flat out refused to dine on hospital food. Lulu went in search of edibles in the neighborhood around the hospital. She brought her a meatball *parmigiana* hero, one of her mother's favorites.

"It's got too much pork," Rosa said, taking one bite, poking the meat with her finger. "The sauce is chunky."

Lulu rolled her eyes. "You're lucky I found it. Don't complain."

"It's expected of old ladies. I've earned it. I didn't choose to cough up phlegm or struggle to breathe. Don't plan on dying yet...got to get back to Mary's. Her sister Charlotte turned up… I might lose my place if you take me away."

"You can't behave like you used to, mama. Warm weather will heal your sinuses."

"Who elected you queen of the coven?" Rosa said as she closed her eyes.

After a few contentious days on the road, they arrived not far from where the Mississippi River lollygags into a crescent shape. Uncle Monroe's pink house was located in the old Irish Channel section of New Orleans. On the bottom of the Garden District, his modest home had been purchased with money from the Beauregards, his ex-wife's parents. He had been a reluctantly proud veteran back then, coming home with no flesh wounds from Nam. But he was messed up.

"The war was all smoke and mirrors," he often said. "I hid from myself. Where was Jesus? Didn't find him in the rice paddies. They sent us on a doomed mission." Monroe shunned a hero's welcome; he felt he didn't deserve it. Lulu barely recalled seeing the man in uniform, but she remembered marveling at the live oaks draped in Spanish moss, imagined them as charming necklaces. Monroe's house was located fairly close to the famous French Quarter and river walk; Lulu's home had been uptown, near the lake.

As they approached the streets between the river and shops on Magazine, she noticed vacant lots, empty storefronts, small churches (Catholic and Baptist), and streets filled with mostly Black and brown people. It was a warm April afternoon when they pulled in, a resigned homecoming.

Mrs. Lady stood inside the door next to Uncle Monroe.

"Welcome home," she said with a wide smile. "Have a slice of sweet potato pie. Shuck some oysters," she commanded, gesturing towards the table.

Gotta love the grub…if not the situation, Lulu thought.

"How did you know we're famished?" Lulu asked, giving them both a big hug. Rosa walked past them into the house.

Off the Yoga Mat

Mrs. Lady was not her real name. That's how Monroe knew her. She prepared some of his meals and looked after him. Brought him to First Good Shepherd Baptist Church even though he wasn't a Baptist.

"I feel at home with them Baptists," said Monroe, watching as they dug in. "My people was Catholics, maybe a touch of hoodoo in the mix. We lived over by North Rampart for a while before they put the down payment on this house. Betsey leveled your place. We weathered that storm."

Mrs. Lady gets him, Lulu thought. How remarkably gracious. Her kinfolk boarded with her, but she took the time to help Monroe.

"This pie is…exquisite," Lulu said taking a bite, noting that Rosa only jabbed it with her fork. "I am ready to collapse." She hadn't done so much driving in many, many moons. Lulu's hair stayed matted to her head. She longed to stare at the insides of her eyelids, take a luxurious nap. But could she succumb? Closer to the source of her terror, that stout bald man touching her. Lulu stayed awake. She prepared the small junk-filled room with a bed for Rosa, just off the kitchen. Lulu watched fountains of light emerge from windows as tall as the front door.

Mrs. Lady helped Lulu tidy the room.

"Your uncle has been taking home empty covers from musical disks," she said.

She meant CDs; evidently, he thought the empty containers were filled.

"He wants to know why we can't hear anything. Monroe picks things off the street and refuses to throw them away…old newspapers and mail. He's a good man. I'm happy to assist. He served our country."

"You're *our* savior," Lulu nodded, mentally hugging this woman living the sutra. I can assist her too. She noticed Mrs. Lady had developed a hump in her back: probably osteoporosis. Might this good neighbor salute the sun? Lulu would guide her though a few yoga *asanas* if she was willing.

"Here's Rosa," Lulu announced, as she and Mrs. Lady entered the living room.

"My half sista," Monroe proclaimed. "Married a white man—a

drunkard who beat her. Further diluted our African blood. My niece Lulu, originally Luanne, is from the Big Apple. Welcome home." Monroe often remarked on the difference in complexion between him and Rosa.

"Monroe, Jesus loves all his children," said Mrs. Lady. "Don't you go name-calling and paying mind to skin. He's glad you're here," she said to Lulu.

"I know. And I get to spend time with both of them."

Monroe appeared hyper. Rosa was subdued. Lulu knew she'd have to find something outside the house to do when she wasn't needed. Sometime after they planted a garden, when Monroe adjusted to their company, she'd wander outside the orbit of family ties. It had been many years since Lulu spent time in New Orleans—a spectacular city she knew little about. But for the time being, she focused on scrubbing, vacuuming and organizing. Making herself useful to her family was no small feat. She noticed some scrap books, a mess of photos in one corner of the living room. She felt a chill as she straightened up the albums and stacks of snapshots. She saw one of herself as a child, a dark-haired Chatty Cathy falling from her arms. The child's eyes lacked focus, her mouth downturned and stretched on one side. She hesitated to go through the stack.

Later on, when everyone shut off the TV and retreated to their beds, Lulu opened the screen door. She stood on the dilapidated porch and smelled the river mingled with magnolia blossoms, tobacco from a pipe, fresh mint. She heard hesitant voices, melodies from other porches—dogs and crickets—a serenade. Wiping her damp brow, she realized her exhaustion. She recalled some words from a poem Nate had read to her.

"Do I prefer the beauty of inflections or the beauty of innuendos the blackbird whistling, or just after…"

Lulu preferred the beauty of inflections. Everything of significance began with innuendo.

Off the Yoga Mat

Chapter Twenty-Seven
Trouble

(Nate)

Tired of playing hack-Hamlet, Nate decided to suit up. He knotted the tie from the ill-fated job interview, pressed his pants with a borrowed iron. His pen stood in as sword. On campus, he tore up the stairs to Offendorf's office. Empty. So, he went back outside, walked back to the building that housed the English Department and took the steps, rather than the elevator. He checked the schedule posted on a board near the department office, sneaking around to avoid professors who'd remember him (and ask why he hadn't graduated).

As he sharpened his rhetorical dagger, he fought an impulse to dwell on his past. He could still recall a time when he loved his classes. He wasn't clear on how he'd appeal to Offendorf but reasoned after the revelations of the previous night, he'd stand on firmer ground.

It was after 3, but his professor had left no word. The secretary said he hadn't posted office hours, and he wasn't due to teach until the following evening. Indisposed, Nate imagined. Nursing his hangover with a boilermaker.

Nate stood in the hallway trying to figure out his next move. He thought he spotted Heddy coming down the hall, so he ducked inside an empty classroom off a corridor. Sitting at a desk, he starred at the phrase "generative cognition" scrawled in marker on the dry erase board in Zazŭk's seminar room. Nate had fallen out of sorts. Only one productive activity remained. He walked over to the student union, drank a big cup of coffee, stuffed down a muffin. Proceeded to Linwood Library where he found a vacant computer. He slipped in his disk.

The densely-worded body of his dissertation had been a neglected partner. It took courage to face it again. First, he wrote on the small slips of paper left for anyone to jot down call numbers. "You can't do this, puddle brain. Quit for God's sake. You're worse than pitiful, pothead." He scribbled missives until his hand ached. Wicked ass-wad. Unqualified scum bucket. Somewhere he had heard about clearing out negativity before sitting down to write. Finally, he tore up the ambassadors of annihilation and sprinkled the scraps into the waste basket.

He opened his manuscript file on the library computer. Let it aerate. He imagined he was about to lead an Argentine tango, a dance he always found beautifully cagey. He approached his cyber partner with new moves; the dissertation stood on its toes, waiting to be paraded for a tango close. Without the crutch of his books and notes, the equivalent of a dancer's sturdy frame, he walked firmly forward, dipping it, wrapping his leg against a bare knee. He revealed fresh moves, a stark turn, rose in his teeth. Not with Monica's gait, nor Offendorf's turn. They came from that place that cannot be named, an internalized muse. He dance-wrote, pivoting, *ocho Adelante.*

.   Nate transformed his tome on jealousy. He abhorred being upstaged by Heddy, disemboweled by Mickey, disrespected by Monica, infantilized by his parents, bested by another job candidate, dumped by Nora and abandoned by Lulu. He typed as if doing a *molinete* counter clockwise, going sideways with his foot, sweeping it away and back, hooking, hooking. He'd bury his rivals, refute the naysayers.

He varied his instinct to ensure his survival—domesticated procrastination. Darwin, but with a dip.

When Nate emerged, tapped out, exhilarated from his three-hour library stint, he clutched his newly minted pages. He spotted his professor lumbering across the quad like a distracted bull. Nate chased after him.

"Professor Offendorf!" he shouted.

The prof looked up, bewildered.

"Nate. You're still here. Come on up."

Nate trailed him, agitated.

Before Offendorf even unlocked his door, a spigot opened.

"I have it right here." Nate held up his new pages, ruffling them. "You see, I've been working frantically. It's my best work. I know you'll approve. I respected your wishes. Made radical cuts."

In fact, Nate added *more* Darwin, additional feminist scholarship and queer theory. But he exchanged theoretical jargon for poetic fluidity, metaphor, alliteration, as if a practiced flamenco dancer. He spoke in phrases with Heddy and Monica hovering, keeping tabs. Offendorf should kiss the manuscript. He held his breath. Then he spoke.

"You know you had me chasing my tail. It ruined my life," Nate said. "You've written just the one book. It appears you may be…in an inappropriate relationship with a graduate student. I don't know why I've been afraid of you."

The professor stood motionless. "Are you finished?"

"Not quite," Nate said. "There's that hideous interview. Janice and her colleagues never took me seriously. I suppose you meant well by recommending me. I became snarky, yes, after they mostly dissed me. What were you thinking?"

Offendorf motioned for Nate to take the chair across from his desk. There were essays scattered about. On the floor, one of Heddy's sweaters.

"Well, well, Mr. Dart. A fine outburst. Has Heddy provoked the fear of Satan in ye?" He coughed. "I was wondering if you'd ever summon the guts to speak your mind. I'd have preferred a more diplomatic approach or parlay, like in the old days. You mustered some heat, Nathaniel, although you were named for a man of Puritan ancestry, as windy as a New England squall. Good God, Janice Dominick is insufferable, isn't she? Never did care for her when we sat on the literature and philosophy division of the MLA. It's not surprising she and her cohort pelted you with tomatoes, as one of Offendorf's twisted lot. Why'd you think they'd take you seriously? They need one body to replace another," he said, blinking. "They'll pick who suits them. You're supposed to be grateful for the chance."

Nate felt confused. So why had he sent him? Had Offendorf deliberately set him up? He realized this bloated billygoat was testing him. Like Hamlet's play-within-a-play, intended to evoke recognition. Knights of the round table. Don Quixote's chivalric errantry. In a quest for the grail, one endures contests. Nate failed.

"So, you suspected that interview would be a waste? Or was it Heddy?" Nate asked.

"Well now, don't blame her. There's only so much credit I'm willing to share. I thought it would be a worthwhile experience. You didn't have to board a jet, did you? How many other interviews and conferences have you attended lately? It's good practice," said Offendorf.

"I get it. But why didn't you give me a heads up?"

"Oh, I don't know," the professor tugged on his beard. "Just thought I'd let it play out. I have been waiting for you to gloriously defend your prize, rationalize your need for Darwin—like one of his finches attacked by a parasitic fly. Ignore Monica Portman. She's a frustrated novelist. A shrew who should step aside."

Heaven forbid: writing fiction amidst literary theorists or composition pedagogues.

"Monica has unorthodox ideas," Nate said, relaxing after the reference to the finch and the fly. "She suggested I incorporate personal jealousy into my thesis. After I received your remarks, filled with expletives, cross outs, damnations."

Offendorf smirked. "Maybe I was excessive. Why didn't you spar with me instead of burying your head in the sand? If you want to go on *Oprah*, or become a self-help guru with your nose up your own petard, don't belabor it. You're not some kid. Forget me. I'm on my way out. They took away most of my seminars, committee chairs. I don't supervise many theses. They have this hotshot, Raul Zazŭk."

Then rumors of Offendorf's retirement were reliable. Now Nate grew flustered. Would a deflated Offendorf sign off on the manuscript? His adviser clung to a febrile power. Nate handed over what he had printed. "The rest will be coming. Soon."

"And don't threaten me, Dart. You'll need a letter of recommendation. If I'm on your side, maybe your defense committee will pass you without much fuss."

"I know."

"But expect trouble," Offendorf said. "Bear down."

Chapter Twenty-Eight
Serious History

(Lulu)

As Nate wrote in a state of near *bodhisattva* in his university library, Lulu dialed his home phone. When he didn't pick up, she chatted into his machine:

"I hope you aren't struggling with your advisor. Rosa's improving slowly. We are going to plant. I mean I am, since she's frail. It's tense between her and my uncle. The weather is warm. Call me back. You've been on my mind."

Lulu upended Louisiana dirt while Rosa fingered seeds, handled samples from Mrs. Lady's garden that would propagate new species. They worked in silence under the strong sun. Then Lulu showered in Monroe's stall (the bathtub needed fixing). When she emerged clean, refreshed, she did some planks and downward-facing dog before transitioning into "wild thing." She lifted her head, extended an arm over it, sharply curved into a rapturous backbend. She'd get through plough, a headstand, eagle, pigeon, child's pose, even *dhanurasana*. Finish with alternate nostril breathing and *savasana*. It would have to do. The photos sat in a corner.

She walked over. Picked up a few loose snapshots, dreading the sad, long-forgotten images. Looking closely, she saw two of the crossed-eyed girl with the doll. Lulu stared at that face. After offering her candy, he licked his curved mustache. At some point, he wedged her doll from her arms. "Here's what I am going to do….it won't hurt." How had she responded? What had he done? Those details did not come into focus.

Lulu's knees buckled. She collapsed on the carpet. Something smelled sour. Was it coming from the kitchen? She went through a few more photos, fast, wanting to stop. Uncle Monroe and his ex-wife; Rosa and Monroe, even one of Maximilian and Rosa. No one seemed at ease even when they smiled. Still, she felt a small relief that she wasn't in most of them. Then one photo made her turn purple. "NO!" she shouted. Between Rosa and Monroe, there was a stocky balding man with arched eyebrows and a thick mustache. Was this the fellow who had invaded her slumbers, refused an exodus from her dreams? He forced her to touch his penis. Did he place it into her mouth? She heaved her lunch, ran to the toilet.

What was Rosa's connection to him? She threw the photos in the air. Screamed into dull silence. She had to get out of there.

She needed fresh air, solid pavement. Lulu went to the small family room where her uncle and mother slouched in a TV stupor, watching reruns of MASH, a bowl of peanuts between them—minds, mouths stilled, neither commenting on or acknowledging her scream if they had heard it. "I'm going out," she said. "Don't wait up."

As soon as she left, Lulu took a few deep breaths and stopped her hands from trembling. Her bitten down nails had grown back; she'd gnaw at them again. Her head felt smashed between two rocks. Objects in her path vibrated. She held on tight to a branch. She wandered a few blocks, past gardens ripe with purples and pinks, mums and gladiolas, native Louisiana irises in blue and white. Sweet sap tickled her nose, radiant hues astonished her. Beauty co-existed with horror. Rows of live oaks rustled, and a sliver moon appeared over the Baptist and Catholic churches. Wind harsh one second, then a mere prickle against her skin. She came upon Magazine Street, ambled down its uneven sidewalks. Passing antique shops and boutiques, she stopped and stared at the front of a tattoo parlor.

Recognition shifted her focus. She took out a tissue, blew her nose. It was similar to the one in Baltimore where she had acquired her frog tatt shortly after divorcing Wendell. She had needed to mark herself—reclaim her body, define her style. Her dad gone, her marriage bogus, life in disarray, no clear plan. She chose a frog. It was slippery and ugly, alluring, watery, exotic, ornery. Spoke of the bayous and woods, of her favorite pond not far from their Maryland apartment. A frog croaked at night. She stood before the shop and asked the universe to help her recover.

A few blocks later, she spotted a welcoming café with outdoor tables. Folks sipped coffee and chatted. Rue de la Course offered the tart aroma of java beans (they roasted their own). A Cajun accordion player and fiddler jammed in one corner, singing *"et trois."* Her first instinct was to compare it to Café Orlin on St. Mark's Place, where she ordered her usual espresso, and Caffé Dante, off Bleecker Street, where gelato ruled. But Lulu decided to experience the city of her birth on its own terms.

One of her ancestors had been a free woman of color, in the days before the Louisiana Purchase transformed the city from French to American. The matriarch of Rosa's family worked as a cook, a hostess, and a jewelry designer and lived as a mistress in a bungalow not far from Esplanade Street. Who was the white man that had kept her? No one knew for sure—he was a Creole, most likely a military or business man. Most certainly cruel or drunk with power. It gave Lulu perspective. I come from free and artistic women who worked hard to earn their keep. We are successful—but we've paid a price.

On a whim, Lulu caught a bus. She stepped off in the warehouse district and wandered among dilapidated factories converted into galleries. Tourists were not plentiful; she needed to escape her mind. She navigated streets her ancestors haunted for generations. Pink clouds settled low. A few art galleries remained open, so she chose one at random. When Rosa regained her strength, maybe they could check out the art scene together.

Lulu stepped up to the front desk. "Do you have any information about the paintings on the walls?"

"Just what you can read on the placards," said a man with spiked hair. "Where are you from?"

"New York City. But I was born here. My uncle still resides here. Any chance you know of a decent yoga studio? I teach hatha, but haven't worked out seriously since I arrived."

He waved his hand dismissively.

The woman next to him laughed. "You won't find him sittin' cross-legged. I can find out," she said.

"Donna teaches Phys. Ed. But she's no drill sergeant."

"I work with a population that has had the book thrown at them. I provide a healthy outlet."

"Donna here is salt of the earth."

Lulu offered her hand. "I appreciate that kind of service. Great to meet you. I'm Lulu Betancourt."

"Donna Canamalo," said the woman, standing up. Lulu took in her gait. About 5'8" and muscular; she pumped iron for sure. Her hair was short. Her large eyes brownish gold.

"I'm originally from Chicago," Donna said. "Then we lived in Houston. Finally found my way here, where I belong. As you might gather from my name, my father is an *Italiano*, my mother, African-American. South side, Chi Town. This here is Jeffrey Stanton Lee."

"Yes," he nodded. "Closeted-queer Southern WASP and straight Chinese-American. Case of opposites distracting."

Lulu cracked up. "I'm grateful to meet you two. I don't know anyone around here. Mostly I'm in the house all day with my elderly mother and her half-brother. Neither is healthy. They pick at each other. And, to be honest, there's some ugly personal history I'm dealing with." Lulu bit her lip.

"Whoa," said Donna. "Something is up...I get it."

"We know great places, especially if you're cool with the gay and lesbian scene," Jeff said.

"I am," Lulu said. "Everything depends on how things are going at the house. And on my state of mind."

"Where you staying?" Donna asked.

"Near the river, below Magazine."

"I will ask round and get back to you about the yoga," said Donna. "How about a drink, some music in the quarter? We're closing."

Lulu hadn't peered at a single work of art.

So they took a streetcar to Canal Street outside the French Quarter. Meandered to a small gay bar, just off Rampart, where patrons were squeezed elbow-to-elbow. Then it was onto Bourbon Street—Pat O'Brien's. Jeff said they had to imbibe a Hurricane.

"Frat boy's drink, I know, but it's what tourists do. You, dear Lulu," Jeff pointed out, "are a tourist."

"Yeah, you're right," Donna said, "but Jeff gawks at them frat boys, heckles the strippers. He's hoping we'll run into that old lady who keeps a duck on a leash."

"The duck died," Jeff said.

Lulu nodded. "I'm not much of a drinker."

They entered an alley that served as a path to a restaurant and small bar; a terrace towered over a flight of stairs in the rear of the courtyard, featuring pots of plants and a fountain spraying water. There were wrought-iron balconies up above. Lulu admired establishments with outdoor seating, gardens beyond their store fronts. They shared two hurricane cocktails adorned with mini umbrellas and glitter, pledging the tall souvenir glasses to Lulu as they slurped the drinks. Then they stumbled out onto the cacophony of the quarter, bands jamming, crowds refusing any hiatus, hawkers hawking with unrelenting din.

These two seemed like old friends already. They strolled to the statue of Andrew Jackson on his mount in the square that bore his name. The air was clammy.

"Yup, Andy Jackson pushed back the British in the Battle of New Orleans in 1815," Donna said.

"Bad ol' history," Jeff added.

"When I moved here, I wanted to know how it all came to pass," Donna said. "There's barely any trace of what was the most infamous slave market in the U.S.A. It peeved me then. It still does."

Lulu nodded. "I had an ancestor, a free woman of color who ran a small business. Could she have been enslaved? What about her children, how did they grow up? What kind of threats did they face? Living up north I hadn't thought much about it."

"Better that you do," Donna insisted, eying Lulu carefully. "There was always a risk that free Blacks would lose their freedom. Nothing could be taken for granted. If one of those mistresses ever rocked the boat, her white lover would kill her. Get away with it too. Happened all the time."

"Does not surprise me," said Lulu.

They continued their slow stroll to Chartres Street where they waited on the long line at Central Grocery to order one of the large, circular muffuletta sandwiches piled high with salami, ham and provolone, and topped with chopped green and black olives, anchovies, garlic. They carried it down to the river, sat on a bench and broke off slabs of meat, cheese and bread, watching the mimes posing for tourist bucks. A trumpet, trombone and drum trio struck up "Won't You Come Home, Bill Bailey," and "Hello, Dolly." The Mississippi loomed dark, rolled slow, shards of moonlight illuminating a paddle-wheel boat tooting its horn without diminishing that brass.

Lulu thought of Nate, quite the jazz fan. The distance between them had widened.

"My mother's mother was a dressmaker," Lulu continued. "Took out ads in the local paper. Found clients among the white elite. She did well for a while; then she got sick and couldn't get decent care. She died young, from a hernia that should have been fixed in routine surgery."

"Oh yeah? That's awful," said Donna. "Caring for colored folks wasn't a priority. Still isn't. You have some serious history. You ought to be proud."

"I am. But there's shit just coming to light."

"Tell me all about it. I've known my share of ye old domestic trauma," Donna said.

"I feel better saying it out loud," said Lulu.

"Must be the hurricane blowing through," said Jeff.

"I hope I can see you again real soon." Donna squeezed Lulu's hand. "Let's break bread. We got more to discuss. Am I right?"

Lulu's pulse raced. She nodded.

"Ooh, girl," said Jeff to Donna. "So bold."

Music, food, and booze. Lulu hugged Donna, then Jeff. She splurged and took a cab to the house.

At Monroe's, one lamp remained illuminated; Lulu spotted a note scrawled on a pad near the phone. *"Call Nate."*

She would. Tomorrow.

May, 1999

Chapter Twenty-Nine
Submerged

(Nora)

Nora conducted many of her surveys on cell phone usage as conversations over the phone, allowing for comments and suggestions too. But a few of the participants preferred to meet her on a Saturday afternoon in an internet café located in Espoo, a suburb outside of Helsinki. It was easy to enter their responses on the screen—they could type answers in Finnish or in English, and Nora offered the option of answering questions which she could tape on her mini recorder. When she made initial contact with the Nurmio family by email—the preferred way to connect with Finns who agreed to take the survey—she couldn't resist asking that burning question: "Are you by any chance related to a woman named Audrey Dart? She lives on Long Island, New York, but she has some relatives named Nurmio in Finland." The respondent, a Tarja Nurmio, said to call them when she was ready to set up a time.

After Nora dialed, there was a long silence on the line. The man who answered said, "I get Tarja."

"*Moi*," she said. "Tarja. That was my husband's father. Nora? We would like to invite you to our home. I can send the address and directions to your email. Yes, we have cousins in New York. Can you come Saturday at 15:30?"

"Yes of course. Thank you."

Now that she would meet them, Nora had no idea what to say.

She decided to bring them a gift of chocolate: universal pleasure.

When Nora arrived at the wooden blue house, with daffodils and tulips blooming in the front yard, she removed her outside shoes and put on the slippers they gave her. They graciously thanked her for the candy and opened the box to serve from it. She cut straight to her reason for being there. Please fill out a survey, and participate in an informal interview about your use of Nokia phones. What features would you like in the next generation of handsets? Are you concerned about Y2K? Might it affect your decision to purchase a new phone?

Mrs. Nurmio served coffee and home-made Karelian rice-pudding pies. They smelled delicious and featured a split down the middle of the dark pastry with rice poking out, plus a melted butter and egg topping.

"This is so delicious," said Nora after eating one. She would consider having seconds after the interview.

As she bit into the pie, the grandfather started to talk about bombs dropping on Helsinki during one of the wars.

"Starvation and rationing," he said. "That's what we experienced."

As Mrs. Nurmio filled out the survey, Nora asked if she could tape their conversation. When her father-in-law paused, she looked up from what she was writing.

"We gave Nokia flip-phones to our six- and eight-year-olds," she said. "We had to. They get home from school on their own."

"No one picks them up?" Nora asked.

"No. They get out around 13:00 or 14:00. We are still working," said Mrs. Nurmio. "They need to be able to reach us. They take a city bus."

Nora had learned many Finnish women have jobs outside the home. Children were left alone or with siblings. They kept in touch via mobile phones. She had been told that about thirty percent of those under 18 years old had a mobile phone and that Nokia hoped that number would rise among those under 12. Nora couldn't imagine her child walking home alone in Manhattan in the first or second grade. In suburban Maryland, where she had grown up, everyone was retrieved in a car or by a school bus; many moms were homemakers, including hers.

Nora looked at the grandfather and told him she learned about the wars with Russia in her culture class.

He took that as a sign to keep going. "During the war, I wrote to my wife from the front…they went through it, not all mail arrived. I was in the army…my wife worried sick. Rations were short. I mailed a box of food. She kept my letters."

It would be fabulous to read his letters, but she'd need a translator. Nora's tape recorder filled with alternating narratives.

"In my class, they explained the complex situation." Nora found out that during the Second World War, Finnish Lapland was occupied by the Germans, who used "scorched earth tactics" in 1944, setting fire to buildings in Rovaniemi. Finland broke off an uneasy alliance with Berlin, which they had forged to turn the tide against the Soviet Union. In Lapland, both Finns and Sami were evacuated. Nora wondered where they had gone; she never learned that part of the narrative. Of course, she knew about the Holocaust and the brave individuals that sheltered Jews; she was part Jewish on her father's side. Her grandmother had emigrated from Poland before the wars. There were displacements, refugees, partisans all across Europe. Nora hadn't considered Finland's part of the story.

They sat through a long silence. Nora had come to appreciate this quality. She conquered her chatterbox tendency with stillness. What should she say regarding Audrey and Nate? Nora got along well with Nate's mom. "My son needs to believe in himself," Audrey had said. "I know, I know," Nora responded. "While I am at work, I encourage him to settle into his daily routine." But Nate never had. What was he up to now?

Tarja broke the silent. "Our cousins in New York are related through my husband's mother, who died three years ago. Audrey and her brother Ted visited Finland when they were teenagers," she said. "I asked my husband about them. What is your connection?"

"I dated Audrey's son, Nate. I met Audrey a few times. She's lovely."

"You are not with Nate anymore?"

"It was over before I took this assignment at Nokia. I wanted to get married and have a child. He didn't."

"Maybe when you get back, he changes his mind?" she asked. "My husband, his son…" she glanced at her father-in-law, "wouldn't commit for a while."

"The young people never lived through war," said Tarja's father-in-law. "They didn't have land stolen by Soviet Union. All privileges they enjoy. Can't make up their mind. Play games on television, on the computer. Tell Nokia. Make better games on handset. Bigger screen."

"I will, I will." Nora promised. "Good ideas."

***

The Monday after that visit, early in May, Nora and Ville agreed to submerge in the still icy lake. Rain fell steady across southwest Finland. Did that mean they'd cancel their plans to visit the sauna after work? As Nora waited for Ville, she mulled over Winn's offer: Would he fly to New York to donate, or ship his sperm? She visualized swimmers swimming across the Atlantic while she stared at notes from phone-usage surveys. Some handwritten, some printed. When she played back the tape she enjoyed the layering of Finland's war-torn history with accounts of life with mobile phones. Wasn't everything cyclical, like fears about the end of the world or utopian visions for the future? Nora heard from her parents during their last call that a couple of high school students had shot their schoolmates and teachers in Colorado. It was the latest bout of craziness from her gun-loving homeland at the turn of the century: signs of approaching apocalypse, fear and madness. How terrible for the victims' families, for the other students. So many disturbances, no easy solutions. Reading more about the shooting stirred up her need to be in the same room as her family. She longed for the physical comfort of her kin.

When they last spoke, Nora told her mother about Ville. "He doesn't sound right for you," Zelda replied.

What did she know? "Put dad on the phone," Nora said.

"Daddy," said Nora when he picked up. "I've learned about Finland's role in World War II. And listen to this. Some Nokia managers want me to sit in on a product development meeting. They are designing a phone like the one used in *The Matrix*." She realized it was confidential. "Oops...forget that I said anything."

"Don't worry. I haven't seen that film. You could have been an engineer. You're technical, like your old man. Always making things."

"How are you feeling?"

"I can drive again. But I'm tired, and have trouble walking up the staircase, and...your mother is frustrated. Incontinence, you know, problems down there."

She wasn't going to ask about erectile dysfunction. "I will be home in less than two months." She'd love to embrace him—he never stigmatized her wish to become a single mom. "You'd like it here, daddy. I wish I could explain everything." He asked her to mail them a few postcards of her favorite sites.

"So we can see Finland through your eyes."

Back at her desk, she opened her notebook to a page of research for her essay on film. She had written about the Sami ritual to respect an elder who had killed a powerful animal, like a bear or a moose. No one was allowed to go near that person—his spirit must be kept at arm's length. In another Sami tradition, they honored the moon of the winter solstice by hanging a food offering on a tree. When the new moon appeared, humans were forbidden to make a sound. Nora realized most Americans didn't honor their elders, or their moons. They took out their guns.

At last, it was time to meet Ville to head to the Rauhaniemi sauna. Silly to think rain would inhibit them. She grabbed her bag, leaving the office.

Ville drove through Nora's Tammela neighborhood, winding

past walking trails, a bike path, and turning into the lot by the giant lake. Before entering the heated space, he showed her the small staircase they'd climb before descending into Näsijärvi.

Outside, the bathers placed their towels, robes, flip flops and beer on shelves. First, the locker room to change into one's bathing suit. Then, a shower before entering the hot room. When Nora emerged, she didn't spot Ville. She opened the heavy wooden door and found him on the middle bench, knees pressed together.

"The top row is very hot. For fanatics," he whispered, gesturing. "See that guy? He wears a cap so he doesn't burn his head."

Nora glimpsed Ville's pale lean form in the tight Speedo. She liked what she saw. In her one piece, she suppressed an urge to hold in her tummy, obscure her thighs. Too much beer and Karl Fazer chocolates. A one piece wasn't ideal for the sauna—it covered too much skin.

The heat blasted her bones; perspiration cascaded down her neck beneath the puckering fabric.

But the extra material proved a blessing when he took her outside. They walked on a green mat that led to the lake; it kept their bare feet from bonding to the melting ice. With her towel wrapped tightly, she let the dry heat coat her limbs. As they took the steps, then lowered themselves, she doubted she'd succeed. Already she'd lost most of the warmth.

Ville slid into the water. It was her turn, but she wouldn't take the plunge, dipping in one foot.

"Whoo!" Ville screamed. "Go under, as fast as you can, don't wait. Move around, swim." He demonstrated. "It's called *avantouinti,* ice-swimming with sauna. Come on, you know you want to."

"Absolutely." She lowered herself as he instructed, only going as far as her knees. Had icicles formed on her numb legs? Heat and ice created a sensation resembling a phantom limb post-amputation.

"I can't," she said, dejectedly.

"Are you sure? Try again in a little while. Let's sit on that bench before we go back to the heat." He climbed out of the lake.

Others relaxed outside in bathing suits or robes.

"Drink some water," Ville said, handing her a bottle.

"This is like some weird science experiment," Nora said. "It's supposed to be a rush."

Nora faced a giant, white lake covered in fog. Tree limbs dripping remnants of ice. Light rain misting, dreamlike.

It was time for another round of heat.

Not long afterwards, Nora entered Ville's apartment, sleepy and satisfied (even if she had failed to submerge her body). Her cheeks glowed—capillaries heated and cooled, blood rushing to the surface. They fell into his bed, slept for what could have been hours. Then his hard-on pressed against her.

"Nora, do you want me? It's my first time since the separation."

"Yes. It's been a while for me too." He reached around, held her. The embrace was firm; she settled into it.

Slowly they began a quiet ritual of undressing, running their hands gently over each other's nooks and crannies, all the while kissing and beholding each other. She liked his boyish firm body, the feeling of him against her on the stiff white sheet. He stroked her body in all its moist, sensitive places, saying "my Nora." Her limbs softened. The fear residing in her neck and head had dissipated.

He rolled on top of her, thrusting. She felt his weight upon her breasts, her legs, her belly—his insistent, pent-up desire as he entered her. She moaned, opened wider. After a few minutes of experiencing the rising thrill of their coupling, the intercom buzzer rang.

"*Paska,*" Ville groaned. "How did I forget? It's my son. With my ex."

Nora grabbed her clothes. At least the wife didn't have a key.

When Nora emerged from the bathroom, a boy with Ville's face glared at her.

"Nora, meet Risto. Risto, this is my friend Nora."

"*Moi,*" Nora said offering her hand.

"*Terve,*" he said, and shook it hard.

Ville motioned for Nora to come into the kitchen, where he poked his head in the fridge, removed containers of food. He and his son were speaking Finnish. "He knows some English, doesn't use it much."

Rather than sit there awkwardly, she offered to warm up the chicken and peel and boil the potatoes, hoping it would get her mind off the interruption. Risto played with an electronic gaming device. She found silverware and plates, set the table after cleaning it off. She checked out the furniture in his bachelor pad. Ikea sofa and wall unit. A computer, CD player. Unpacked boxes piled high against the walls. Game cartridges, laundry in a basket. Since it was a one bedroom, one of them must sleep on the couch. She hadn't dated men with kids. She liked it that Ville cared part-time for his child.

As they ate, Risto raised his voice, the tone threatening.

"I'll leave right after dinner," Nora said to Ville. "He wasn't expecting me, so it must be strange," she tried her best to whisper.

When Risto walked off, Ville responded.

"It's his age, 11 going on 12. He's aware of new feelings. The separation makes it worse. His mother is living with my former best friend. Risto and I are like two single guys hanging out. After dinner, I will drive you home. Then take him for a movie or a dessert. And he and I will go berry picking over the weekend."

"That sounds lovely," said Nora.

Because of Risto's presence, they didn't have a chance to kiss goodbye. But her dry spell was over.

Chapter Thirty
Momentum

(Nate)

Nate was following more superstitious talismans than he would have believed possible. Since that day in the library when he'd miraculously revised his chapters, he hadn't changed his clothes. He sat in the same chair, writing at the chosen terminal. If it was otherwise occupied, he paced and returned, eventually driving out the occupant with his body odor or creepy persistence. Nate was on a roll, writing with clarity. He referred to books in the library's collection, even though they weren't his marked-up editions. He would still have to consult notes and photocopies back home.

Anxious to share his good news, Nate couldn't believe he hadn't connected with Lulu. He didn't have anything in the city to run back to. He wondered if Lulu's mother felt better. Maybe Lulu was spending time with a Cajun fellow, a night-club charmer. Nate didn't own a cell phone, and Lulu was not on email. He left the number of his motel several times on the chance she would call when he was in his room. When he spoke to her uncle, he sensed the old man wouldn't let his messages through.

Routine saved Nate: He'd arrive at the library after breakfast, exit late in the afternoon, watch an occasional film and sit in on a lecture. He practiced a little yoga before bed.

He reflected on Lear's speech to Cordelia: "Better thou hadst not been born than not t'have pleased me better." Then he considered Darwin's concept of natural selection. For a child whose father had such a fragile ego, there was no advantage if you failed to adapt. But in certain cases, resistance trumped adaptation. Offendorf encouraged confrontation—butting heads—to maim but not kill. When Nate finally challenged Offendorf, his advisor permitted Nate to cross the bridge.

After the library, Nate jogged around the perimeter of campus, charging up a steep hill. He leaned against a tree, out of breath. When would Lulu make contact?

Instead, he received an email from Gil.

"Dude, where are you? I passed the building with Lulu's studio, 2 Squared. Some homeless ladies hanging around. Saying the door was left open. They didn't see that pretty yoga teacher...the building is just about empty! Remember those freegans? They swap stuff by St. Marks Church. I found Miles Davis and Velvet Underground albums, a copy of the book *Basketball Diaries*. Anita busted my chops—said if I take something I have to give something back. She's cute, super intense—do you remember her? Mariel and Anita are planning to protest the gathering of the World Trade Organization in Seattle. Radical. Dude, are you alive?"

Shit, thought Nate. He had to get back. The scene at the studio sounded dismal. Lulu counted on him to check on it, but he forgot! He didn't bother to reply to Gil.

When Nate and Lulu ceased playing telephone tag, they sounded breathless, slightly foreign. He held back a creeping sense of anxiety.

"It's great to hear your voice," he said. "Wish I could see you."

"Where are you calling from?" she asked.

"Maryland. I have been writing at the campus library. Offendorf approved some of my revisions. I couldn't break the spell. But I can't afford to stay. When are you coming back?"

"Fabulous news about Offendorf, Nate. I'm proud of you. How'd it happen?"

"Long story. I found him in a vulnerable position...he had to cut me slack. I stood my ground."

"You must be relieved," said Lulu.

"Yes. Soon I can remove my scarlet A(BD)."

"Nate. I would love to congratulate you in person."

"And I would congratulate with you. Multiple times. When will you get back?"

"I don't know," Lulu said. "Probably next month. My mother's still frail. Monroe is doing okay; a neighbor helps care for him."

"Don't tell me you'll be gone another month."

"All right then. I won't tell you," she said. "I made a couple of friends."

"I'll check your studio as soon as I get home." He didn't mention what Gil had written about the door being left open and what the homeless ladies said. Why worry her until he saw for himself? He kind of hoped she'd invite him to New Orleans, but he couldn't afford the ticket. Who were her new friends?

"Go and see what Evelyn is doing with my classes...make sure everything's fine. I haven't heard from her. No one picks up the phone. The machine must be broken."

"I'll go right over," he said. "Do you think we can...speak more regularly?"

"I would like that."

"Let's set a time. Because your uncle sounds pissed off when I call."

"He's a bit confused is all."

"I miss you so much," he said, "Come home soon. Please."

When he hung up, he felt ashamed for begging. He hoped her studio was exactly how she had left it.

Chapter Thirty-One
Lions

(Lulu)

A few days after they met, Donna informed Lulu of an advanced yoga class recommended by a friend of a friend, so Lulu planned to go. One evening, she greeted the gym teacher at Cafe Rue De La Course. In subdued light, an accordion player and fiddler set up. Taking a sip from a bowl of latte, Donna spoke softly.

"I escaped from Texas," she said. "I've been bringing up past experiences in a support group. I keep a journal. My mother and father divorced when I was eight. They hurt us—me and my twin brother. Shuffled us back and forth between 'em. Not sure where it was worse. This went on for years, until I managed to get sent to boarding school. My brother joined the Navy. I recently confronted my mother. She had her share of abuse as a child in foster care."

"It's terrifying. Yet, you seem strong." Lulu noted light freckling on Donna's face, changing lines on her forehead. "My daddy was a drunk. Got discharged from the military. He'd come home smelling of perfume and booze. Once, when I was on my way to school, I saw him exiting a bar as the bus stopped. He was practically passed out. This woman held him up under his arms. When I came home, I told him. 'I saw you with the clown-faced lady.' He hit me in the mouth. Kicked my shin. 'Don't think I can't wring your skinny neck,' he said. I haven't thought about that in years." Lulu's throat tightened, and her head pulsed. A few tears fell.

"What's the use of worrying? He's dead," Lulu said. "Took me to Mardi Gras when I was little. We made our costumes together."

"Coercion, threats," Donna said. "It's traumatic even if it's mixed with normal stuff. Lulu, come to the group."

"I've been having nightmares about someone else. I'm not sure… who he is, or what happened. I was six going on seven." She rubbed her eyes. "I can't be sure what's real. I'm having flashes; according to a book I read, suppressed memories can come back. Now that I'm here, I know I am close to figuring it out."

"You are brave to face it." Donna took her hand. "Abuse can turn up in your nightmares. And other times it's so insidious you won't even realize. The incidents can be repressed, then emerge with triggers. My mother had parties in the backwoods. It took me a while to recall that her friends on drugs molested me. My father didn't want me around. He left me alone or with one of his young girlfriends. I wouldn't trust anyone for a long while."

It was uncomfortable to listen to Donna. Made Lulu want to bolt from the table. Instead, Donna placed two fingers on her wrist.

"Come visit my school, watch the girls play ball," Donna said. "Working with them is better than therapy. Those girls are talented. I'll find out if you can demonstrate your yoga. They haven't been exposed to anything like that."

"I've never worked with children. But I've considered it for a long time. They'll laugh at some postures," said Lulu.

"Oh yeah?"

On impulse Lulu got down on the floor, demonstrated the lion, by arching her back, releasing a growl from around her tonsils. "It's a clearing breath, really good for you."

"Lulu, you're nuts," Donna said, and crouched down next to her. People in the café craned their heads to catch a glimpse.

Lulu thought about the other day, when Rosa and Monroe had tried the lion, their actions reflecting their competitive sides. Monroe needed help getting down on his arthritic knees. Rosa's breath was shallow, but her roar filled the room.

"I taught you that," Rosa announced.

"Yeah Mama, a long time ago."

Mrs. Lady declined to try the lion, but she rolled over sweetly into the child's pose. Lulu adjusted her sitz bone, settled her into a spinal twist. Lulu also showed her stretches to ease tension in her shoulders and back. If only I had multiple arms like the Hindu god *Ganesha* (the remover of obstacles), Lulu thought, while adjusting their seated twists, moving this one's knee, tilting that one's elbow. Since there was something for everyone in the repertoire, she considered it a success, a subterfuge from fear and arguments. Afterwards, Rosa made noise about purchasing art supplies so she could paint.

"We'll keep working on your spine, massaging your organs through breath," Lulu said. She was sure Rosa would insult her, but surprisingly she held her lip.

After Donna and Lulu's lions reared up, they brushed off some dust and settled their bill. Hugging goodnight, they headed outside, passing tables with lit wicks swimming in oil, illuminating patrons' faces. A fiddler ran her bow across a taut bridge.

"We have so much in common," Donna said. "Let's lean on each other."

"For real." Lulu had never met anyone like her. "Thanks for listening."

"I'm here."

With a quick motion, Donna lifted Lulu's chin. "Would it be okay if I kissed you on the lips?"

Lulu didn't take long to nod, affirmative. Outside the café, they kissed as if drinking water in August heat, embracing one another like that long-lost crush with whom you'd had the blessed chance to reunite. For a short spell, Lulu hadn't a worry in the world.

Off the Yoga Mat

Chapter Thirty-Two
North of Anywhere

(Nora)

Nora wouldn't be alone when she turned forty. Sweet relief! She felt old, anticipating aftershocks. A sense of regret marked her final six weeks abroad. Might she stay longer...cement the relationship with Ville, visit Lapland, Turku, St. Petersburg, Stockholm? These cities were not far away; elapsing time imposed, and they remained place names in the sky. She hustled to finish her research report for Nokia and recommended they read the British Standards Institute's (BSI) developed conformity requirements for computers and electronics for the year 2000, including century data specified by algorithms. As Nora's head filled with demarcations of time, she realized she hadn't found the gifts she wanted to bring home. As she thought about what to buy for whom, she realized, why not throw a birthday/going away party in Ville's condo complex? They could cook on the communal grill.

No. She'd rather host a final fete in her compact rooms on *Tapionkatu*. She had grown fond of using a squeegee mop to clean up after showering, and she adored her picture window—a portal into spring. With the ever-expanding evening light of May, she slept with a black mask over her eyes: brightness meant stimulation. Some nights she decided not to sleep. It wouldn't be a large party...what would she serve? At home, she would have run everything past Lonnie (since parties bequeathed surprises).

She envisioned Ville and Jussi in the same room, vying for her attention. She'd show off her shoulders, legs below the thighs, wear that lime mini she planned to purchase. Would her guys chat at all? Ville satisfied her; however, she still desired Jussi. In fact, they had crossed paths a few days ago as he headed to a Chinese lunch buffet. "Join me," he said. Every encounter with Jussi raised Nora's hackles.

"You wanted a Finnish romance. You found one," Jussi whispered. "As Dylan would say, you got your 'shot of love.'"

Never had a shot with you, she thought.

His open jacket displayed lean muscle. The ornament on his necklace resembled Prince's interlocking male/female symbol. He ate lo mein with a fork and knife.

"It's a rebound situation," Nora said. "We haven't discussed what's next." She barely touched the breaded chicken, limp vegetables.

"Do you know what you want?"

"I think so," said Nora. To stay in touch. Have him visit. Take it from there.

Jussi said he was applying for funds to attend a conference in Toronto. Nora couldn't resist inviting him to stop over in New York. She compared his situation with Nate's. Her former lover struggled, and his school support had dwindled. He received nothing from the U.S. government but debt. Jussi could count on four more years of state funds, and also receive travel grants.

"I'd like to see New York City," said Jussi.

"I'll show you around," Nora said. "In the meantime, can I put you in charge of the music for my upcoming party?" She looked to the blue sky of his eyes.

"Party?"

"My birthday. June 5."

She clung to his rejection like a vintage Marimekko purse. Why had he turned her down? She almost inquired then and there.

"I agree to serve as your DJ."

She felt certain he'd play perfectly.

Nora addressed invitations to mail two weeks before her party—give notice, but not too much. She'd also send a group email. The academic year would be over; some folks made plans to head to summer cottages. She studied her list. Aino and Winn from work, but what about Alto? If she excluded him, would he be insulted? She'd add him even if he never seemed to like her. Mrs. Marakola said she would bring her daughter, and Bethany's clan was coming "with bells on." She'd better prepare games for Lilly and Antti. Ville's son brooded the last time she had gone over there; thankfully, Risto would be with his mother on party night.

Ville offered to help Nora with the shopping. With his car, they could haul booze and sodas. For the rest, she'd procure items on her own. It would be one of her final private tours of Tampere—stopping at her favorite shops, picking out what struck her fancy. Flowers, of course. Those lovely local strawberries beginning to appear in the market square. She decided on serving a New York version of smoked salmon, with cream cheese (known as *schmear*) instead of dill and rye crackers. She doubted she could find decent bagels. She'd stop at her favorite fish stall in the Kauppahalli, Tampere's old indoor farmer's market. And what about sweets? She didn't trust herself to bake.

As for what to wear, she had mailed home two boxes of clothes. That meant she must buy that lime green skirt…maybe a blouse to go with it. As she planned the party, Nora accepted she didn't want to leave but she didn't know how to stay. She'd invite Ville to Manhattan. Recently, he had surprised her with an embrace as she sat working at the desk in her apartment. It brought her back to those times Nate slumped in his chair, reading or highlighting. She'd been desperate to mess around, wriggling on his lap or placing a hand down his pants. Nate somehow resisted her overtures while she succumbed to Ville's tapered fingers.

A week before the party, Nora prepared her final presentation to Nokia's bosses. She gathered up all the surveys and the other projects they had assigned, especially on the competition. She had spent a lot of time ordering samples, formatting statistics and trying to locate contact persons. Of course, she had been working on the biggest and best hand-made book of all time, the motherlode of corporate scrapbook art. The Finns might hate it; Nokia executives appeared technologically fixated, cool and logical (except when it came to the Y2K threat). Their paranoia about Russia influenced the gnawing feeling of impending doom and nuclear holocaust.

The morning of her presentation, she paced in circles outside her office. Colleagues filed in to discuss domestic and international markets. They carried small, frequently-filled cups of coffee, greeting each other with *"hyvää huomenta."* They had no warning as to what Nora had in store. She quietly checked it one more time, her extra-large hand-made album. Thick and laden with desire—manifested through objects, numbers and lists. More than equal to the sum of their parts. Custom-designed on the projected growth of cell phone competition in the coming fiscal year. Inside, fragments of samples shipped from manufacturers with high-contrast data displays, graphics and expanded memory functions. She crunched numbers in 3-D glitter and spray-paint. She added cropped photos with borders around items featuring the Finnish flag's white with blue cross, which stood for Nokia, and the USA's red, white and blue. China and South Korea weighing in. Talking bubbles emerging out of the mouths of her cartoon colleagues, based on photos and sketches Nora finessed over the past few months. Cut from boards with an Exacto knife, pasted into Nora's *Book of Kells*. Pithy comments added. Some pages containing Donald Duck, Formula One car racers, ice hockey (Tampere's rival teams), mini golf, ribbons, bows, velvet backgrounds on various pages. A love letter diary bricolage, Nora's finest folio.

She moved to the front of the room to nervously explain her short, traditional on-screen presentation while they passed the book around. Laughing, pointing and "oohing" and "aahing" in two languages.

Nora let herself relax.

"We're used to dull graphics, static PowerPoint slides," said Alto. "You've brought us to life with irreverent grandeur inside your almanac."

"You get extra points for making us laugh," said Aino.

"What an unexpected treat from our American guest," said one of the vice presidents. "Nora, how did you come up with this idea? Is this traditional at your firm, Secanor?"

"It's hard to explain. I love scrap books and making things out of industrial material, like plastic and metal. I went to town with a Finnish theme to acknowledge all of you and my admiration of your culture. I was asked to survey the market here, and the competitors, so I did. I have found my work for Nokia very satisfying. Scrapbooks? Definitely *not* a tradition at Secanor in the U.S."

More praise followed. Nora sat in a mental sauna, her mind aerating as the meeting carried on. Earlier that morning her mother had called, ignoring the seven-hour time difference. Her dad's scan revealed his cancer spread beyond the prostate. He needed radiation and chemo.

Nora would be flying back soon. Her mother said, "You're self-indulgent. We're glad you're having a good time, but honestly Nora. How will you settle down if you fly north of anywhere?"

"I've been trying to meet someone," Nora foolishly responded, half asleep, before recognizing the impossibility of pleasing her mother. North of anywhere placed her south of nowhere. "Let me talk to Daddy," she said.

When he came on the phone, she broke into tears. He reassured her he'd be fine. "I won't be happy unless you are, Nora."

After the department meeting, when a few people still milled around in the corridor, Winn hugged Nora, congratulated her. "They love your artistry."

"Can't artistry blend with commerce?"

"Usually not with kitsch."

Was Winn jealous? Probably, since he was leaving too. His final presentation on focus groups was dull, by-the-book.

"I expected they would hate it. My mother's angry at me."

"Why is that?"

"I am not there. My dad has cancer. And I'm still single."

Winn frowned.

What would Zelda say if Winn got her pregnant? Would she be able to show any joy amid the fear about dad's cancer? Her father would focus on the coming grandbaby.

"I am mulling over your offer," she informed Winn.

"It stands," he said.

She cut out as early as she dared, around lunch time, uncertain what errands to run first. She stood in her tracks as crowds blew past. It was a sunny day and everyone had taken to the streets. Some people wore shorts, although the temperature was only in the mid-50s Fahrenheit. Nora couldn't waste time to eat.

Walking down the main drag she took a sharp left towards her favorite thrift shop, Radiokirppis, wondering what vintage items she'd unearth. The news about her dad and her mother's bitterness flowed into angst about Ville. Did he want to continue their relationship? Was he a little bit in love with her? She could envision becoming step-mom to Risto; they could conceive another child. She wished she could discuss various paths to motherhood with her dad and accompany him for a second opinion on treatment for his cancer. He never ribbed her about her failures. Maybe for Zelda, Nora's independence reminded her how she had rushed to get married. In those days, unmarried women at twenty-five were considered spinsters. As Nora hustled through the streets of Tampere, she decided she would find out if they could store Winn's sperm at a Cardiff clinic and have it shipped to her when she was ready.

Chapter Thirty-Three
Reboot

(Nate)

As soon as Nate made it back to the city, he dug through stacks of papers and books to find the missing passages and notes he needed, searching photocopies for reference-keeping (and cursing his disorganization). Missing citations hounded him. His meager housekeeping repaid him with dust balls that induced coughs and sneezes. When he opened the closet, a posse of moths emerged as if they also paid rent. He couldn't work in that dastardly apartment. He wanted to be ready to devote his energy to Lulu when she returned. The manuscript should be complete. As for the moths, an exterminator's toxic spray hadn't eradicated those squatters, so what could he do? He hoped Lulu was as accepting of the Lepidoptera order as she was of the amphibian.

Nate planned to head over to Lulu's studio that evening to find out what happened. He sat down to open the disk where his spanking new draft lived. The screen proclaimed this terrifying script: "*disk error*." Impossible! He pushed it in repeatedly, lightly, and then with a heavy hand. In, out. Cleaned it with a rag. He let out a wail that set the moths careening. That copy was the only one he saved; except for a few printed sections, his dissertation appeared zapped. Gone. Unless some desktop magician could bring it back.

He smoked weed residue from a pipe, turned on one of his radios—a 1959 vintage Philco. AM only. Elvis Costello croaked about feeling almost human. Nate would rather have been a moth. He tried to think. Nothing. In a funk, he didn't leave the apartment.

He thought about contacting Nora; she'd know some computer nerds. But no, she'd think it was an excuse to hear her voice. He dialed an old friend from graduate school, Tom Wilder, in Brooklyn. Tom said he'd take a look and try to recover what he could.

"Write it again, Nate. While you remember. You might be surprised with what you come up with," Tom said.

"That was the new, improved version. There's not much gas left in my tank."

"Come on, man. Dig deep. Remember when everyone used typewriters? We had to start over every time."

"Maybe I can return to the era of parchment," Nate said.

"Writing was superior then. Bring it over tomorrow."

Nate determined he'd have to reboot himself.

Tom managed to recover partial sections. It looked like Nate had inherited a virus from the computer at the university library. "That's why you should have saved a copy or emailed it to yourself." The thought had not occurred to Nate. If he hadn't known any better, he'd have sworn Heddy manufactured the virus.

So, he removed himself to the Jefferson Market branch of the New York Public Library on Sixth Avenue where he played musical chairs on the three public computers until they threw him out. He emailed all the new work to himself and saved everything on multiple disks. Then he decided to take the train to Long Island to visit his parents, work in that hot-house atmosphere with free food and minor distractions. He had hash stowed away. His mom worked part-time, but she wouldn't pester him. Albert would be home in the evenings, grading papers in front of the TV. Nate would do his best to dodge intrusive questions.

His mother welcomed him with a dinner of steak, baked potato and broccoli as he updated them on his resolution with Offendorf. Better to emphasize that part of his journey.

"I wouldn't budge, so old Offendorf acquiesced." Nate condensed the entire episode into a sound bite.

"Like I said." Albert poked his potato. "You stood behind your work. A man respects another man's truth."

Nate glowered.

"We'll stop writing checks," Albert continued. "No reason you can't get a job. It's almost the end of the academic year. Some positions will open. Check Adelphi and Nassau Community College on the island. Or you can be a sub in my school, but don't bring in any of your contraband."

"One thing at a time," his mother interrupted. She topped off Nate's wine glass. "When is the defense, dear? And the graduation?"

He had no intention of attending graduation.

"The defense date needs to be set." Nate realized that since he must rewrite large chunks of the thesis, it would have to be postponed... he also needed to add someone to his defense committee. "I'd like to finish before summer." His fortieth birthday was up and coming—the degree could be his gift.

"I intend to make headway," Nate reiterated. "Avoid distractions."

"Anything we can do?" Audrey asked. "Albert, please clear the table."

While his dad carried dishes to the kitchen, his mother kissed his head.

"Stay as long as you like. Don't let your father get under your skin. By the way, I have something to show you, but it can wait until morning."

He had no idea to what she referred.

That first night in his old bedroom, he couldn't sleep. He spoke briefly with Lulu at the designated time. She asked again about her studio. Shit! He had neglected to check on it.

"I meant to, but there was a setback. Disk error as soon as I got home. I lost most of the new work I did in Maryland," he said, ashamed of such carelessness. She must want to rip his head off.

"I'm sorry to pester you. I feel nervous about everything these days. Can we chant together?"

She chanted "Hari om, hari om, hari hari hari om," over the line. Nate followed, although he hoped for phone sex. Didn't ask, as he had neglected the one thing she counted on. After they hung up, he took a few hits of hash and searched for on-line pornography. He found voluptuous yoga gals in pretzel pose with rose pedals on their breasts. A site called Derrieres of Desire. He pleasured himself, then snoozed.

Birds and lawn mowers awakened him. Albert had already departed for school. He started the day cranky. After breakfast, Audrey pulled out a sheaf of stapled onion skin paper written on a typewriter.

"This is what I wanted to show you, Natey. It's a seminar paper I wrote on tragedy and libidinal drive in *Othello,* using Freud and English morality plays. When I was going for my Master's. I don't expect it will enlighten you." She placed it into his hands.

He had never realized that his mother wrote about Shakespeare and Freud. This would have been during the early 1960s. He met her gaze.

"Why didn't you tell me about your research?" He knew she had dropped out of graduate school, not much more.

"I don't talk about it. When I quit school to marry your father, move to Long Island and give birth to you, I put that out of my mind," she said. "When you turned two, I suffered a miscarriage. Decided to get a job involving numbers. There's something satisfying about numbers. I trained to become a bank teller. But I'm proud of that piece."

"You got an A+." Nate thumbed through the pages, read out loud from the opening paragraph: "A patrician Venetian daughter, Desdemona, falls in love with Othello, a paid mercenary from North Africa, setting the stage for Iago, his ensign in the role of the devil. Iago reveals how sin lurks inside a wife's libido, and in doing so transforms romance into domestic tragedy. *Othello* is a morality tale illustrating the outcome of unchecked superegos."

His mother grew absorbed. "Pretty sophisticated for its time."

"Definitely. You're a staunch Freudian! I am going to read this over. If I use anything, I'll credit you under your maiden name."

"Wouldn't that be something," said Audrey.

"Too bad you never finished your degree. You can always go back."

"I've thought about it. I'll wait until you're done. One student in the family at a time. By the way, if I wrote that paper today, I'd draw on Foucault to show the material conditions of mercantile capitalism in Venice during the Ottoman Empire."

What was she saying? Had his mom been reading the French theorist Michel Foucault?

"You've left those theory books around. I've absorbed something. I enjoyed *Discipline and Punish*."

"You did?" He hugged her. It was one of his favorites. She never failed to impress him. "I take after you."

"Now maybe you want to tell me what else is happening in your life?" Audrey prodded. "You can't fool me. What's she like?"

He smiled. "Amazing." He would have blushed if he was the blushing type. "But she's out of town. I've got to get cracking," he said, with an off-kilter grin and a thumbs-up sign. Audrey had that look on her face—alert, hungry, wanting to be more of a confidante in her man-child's life. He left her, went to work with a lightness he couldn't have foreseen, stopping only for meals. He came away with a different, but not inferior version of the lost chapters, incorporating a few choice bits of Audrey's Freudian analysis. They decided not to mention it to Albert.

On the fourth day, Nate accompanied Audrey to Huntington, where she worked part-time in a bank branch. He dropped in on a yoga class held in a studio on Main Street. It paled in comparison to Lulu's. How he wished he could behold her. What if she succumbed to the charms of some Louisiana jazzmen? A Zydeco washboard scratcher, a rhythmic percussion beat on his metal apron. In this class, he couldn't chant; his toes curled tightly as he reached just below his knees. Saxophone blasting late night magic in the Faubourg-Marigny district...how could Lulu resist? Better run back to the city, check her studio...be her loving man.

When he exited the subway on Astor Place, picking his way

through the frantic crowds along St. Mark's, he caught a glimpse of the back of a familiar head—Gil Nudleman's. On a lark he followed, keeping his distance. His old friend was with that freegan woman who used to work at Nora's firm, Anita Willis. Were *they* together now? Nate remembered Gil mentioned Anita in his last email.

The two of them wound their way past Japanese tourists, skateboarders, the Gem Spa newsstand known for its famous egg cream on the corner of Second Avenue. Gil and Anita turned right, heading downtown. They ducked into a falafel joint near the Love Saves the Day thrift shop. He felt a wave of disgust, recalling that his old friend had harmed Lulu. What scam was Gil running now? How was Mariel? He had called her from Maryland to explain his long absence. He'd been hot and cold, his allegiances crisscrossed. She appeared in his life soon after Nora abandoned him. He told her he was sorry for rushing out without being honest and that he couldn't see her anymore. He had not confessed to falling in love with his yoga teacher. In Maryland, with time to reflect, he acknowledged his infantile behavior with Nora. One action leads to another, like swallowing a small stone—down it goes without much fanfare. But it messes up your whole system. Maybe over in Finland, with distance and time, Nora could empathize with his perspective.

He must check Lulu's studio. See what was what so he could give her some news, share how he came up with the gist of three lost chapters in four days. He'd urge her to get back to her life here. He imagined himself an admiring bog to her public frog. He couldn't resist putting a spin on Emily Dickinson's poem, "I'm Nobody."

The final night he had slept on Long Island, Nate dreamed he'd been chained in a dungeon by Heddy and Offendorf. He was having a seizure, like Othello, who in a jealous rage believes he has ocular proof his wife cheated on him with Cassio. Nate writhed on the floor while his dad laughed. His mom wrote check after check, saying "take this." The checks floated through the air as Lulu repeated "sink deep, deep down." He stopped struggling and opened his eyes. The demons disappeared. That vision loaded ammo into him; he walked with purpose.

He thought he was still dreaming when he approached Lulu's

Off the Yoga Mat

studio, spotting what looked like a crime scene. Two cop cars parked with flashing lights and a blue barrier set in front of the entrance. He could barely make out the feedback from an officer's walkie-talkie. A few folks shouted, gesturing to the cop, their voices obscured by the din of passing cars.

The officer restrained a gray-haired woman who screamed at Anita and a young man he didn't recognize. Nate crossed at the intersection.

"Those freegans ransacked the place, broke windows. Just because I'm down and out, you're accusing me? Why would I destroy a warm, safe house?" said the elderly woman.

"Calm down. We're not saying *you* did anything, Ginny," said Anita. "We just want to know what you saw. Officer, I think it might have been someone in that band, Fox Hole. They were using the studio to practice."

The man next to her shook his head. "We haven't done anything."

"Well, you have to scram, all of you," the officer said. "It's breaking and entering. Now there's structural damage. Where is the tenant? Management wants to press charges. We understand this building is under eviction proceedings."

At that point, Nate froze, realizing he needed to step forward. He appeared out of the shadows.

"Officer, can you tell me what happened?" he asked the cop.

"Who are you?" Ginny asked. "I ain't never seen him, officer."

"I recognize him," Anita said. "You are a friend of Gil's. You were dating Mariel. Came to our swaps."

"I am the boyfriend, and have been a student, of Lulu Betancourt's. She's the legal tenant of the 2 Squared Studio. How did you all get inside?"

"That's what we're piecing together," the cop said. "No one seems to want to admit to any wrongdoing. It's always the other one's fault. I am trying to contact the management company. They said damages were severe."

"I have a feeling Gil is involved," Nate said.

"He told me that the yoga teacher permitted him to practice there while she was away," Anita said.

"Not true," Nate said. "As far as I know, Lulu gave a key to a substitute teacher named Evelyn to run a few classes—that's it. I don't know Evelyn, but obviously, something went wrong."

"Go take a look upstairs," the policeman said. "It's a disaster. Get a padlock to keep these squatters away. Inform the tenant."

"I am really sorry," Anita said to Nate.

"Can you spare any change?" the woman held out her hand.

Nate went upstairs. The once homey studio smelled rank from a clogged toilet. Garbage cascaded over the floor, windows were broken, wires bared. A large hole appeared in the warped floor, over which mats had been piled, and the moulding around the windows was damaged. A few beer and liquor bottles lay in a corner. He noticed a large oval hole in the wall; it looked as if someone had walked through it. He took a deep breath as he scanned the space. Amazing how much had changed.

"I can't believe it," he said when he went downstairs.

The policeman told him Ms. Betancourt would need to file charges as soon as possible. While poking around the studio, Nate noticed several printed notifications from the university and the management office. All tenants had been ordered to vacate. Why hadn't she mentioned it? How would he convey the news of such desecration? It was his studio, too…he should have been there long ago.

Chapter Thirty-Four
Stay Hungry

(Lulu)

Lulu agreed to watch Donna's team play basketball. Entering the faux-gothic building she realized she hadn't been inside a school since her own unpleasant student days. Donna introduced her to Little Smoke, Susie Cue and Swish. They high-fived with her, in a pre-game haze, as Donna pumped them up to play St. Honore's Wolves. Of various backgrounds, disparate sizes and shapes—all in their tweens and early-teen years. Each one had a story. Immigration nightmares for the girls from Central and South America. One player came from the foster care system. Another's father had been shot by police. They came from loving families who happened to be a bit down and out, but were resilient. Lulu liked them even if they nixed yoga, but Donna sold the school's principal on her idea. He invited Lulu to come back and teach some simple postures.

Watching Donna in action reinforced Lulu's desire to spend time with at-risk youth. To have an impact on young people and revisit what had been uncomfortable or broken in her adolescence. As a painfully shy teen, Lulu never considered basketball or sports as an outlet. Ashamed to be poor in her suburban Maryland junior high, Lulu's peers had dressed to kill, starved themselves, debated her race as if it was their social history project and mimicked her accent. When Lulu moved from Louisiana, she missed scents and sounds she hadn't even realized she loved. Aromatic flowers, dependable as heat. The river. Music in the streets. They had departed suddenly after the storm and without her father, but at least they had fled that frightening friend of Rosa's. That was the beginning of her parents' official separation; figuring out how to provide, her mother became preoccupied during a rough transition. She hadn't any patience for Lulu's woes. "Life is no picnic. Don't ever forget," Rosa said.

Being at this school, it felt obvious. She could offer them solace. The kids would sustain her, too. Lulu watched from her seat, high in the bleachers, as Donna chalked plays on a mini blackboard, the team huddled close together as the crowd filed in.

"It's great the families come out for the games," Lulu said to Jeff, sitting beside her.

"Friends too. Fans from the visiting school. It's high stakes," he said.

She wondered if Monroe and Rosa would care to watch. She had taken Rosa to Doctor Kazanjian. Her mom had improved, but her respiratory capacity was compromised. Winters in the North were not a good idea. Rosa made noise about going back to Ocean Grove. Later, she sat on the phone with a buddy back in Jersey. Lulu thought Monroe was better off with Rosa in his house. Her sassy confrontations fired him up, kept him alert. He had fewer lonely times when he would forage for junk or take a bus to the off-track betting parlor. They were arguing about the plants and vegetables in the garden, when to harvest, what combinations thrived, how often to water, when to add fertilizer. Lulu noted the resemblance in their facial expressions as they bickered. She told them so.

"We're the product of confusion," Monroe said. "Our mama died young. Now Lulu, you and Rosa are alike. Maybe you don't realize."

She agreed they shared certain traits. Painful to admit now that she needed to pry something unspeakable out of Rosa. What did Monroe know about that man? Lulu had been busy setting up a meeting with the VA people to figure out additional benefits for Monroe (and for Rosa). She wanted to go home as soon as that was settled.

Mrs. Lady had invited Lulu to church for Sunday mass. Lulu agreed out of respect. "I don't recall how long it's been since I've set foot in a church," she said. "I've been to Buddhist ashrams, filled mostly with Jewish people."

"Count me out," Rosa added. The closest she had come to church was painting portraits of the Methodists.

"You'd best dwell in the Lord's temple once in a while," Monroe said. "If Lulu can and she's heathen, why not you?"

They got into an argument. Was Rosa acting like she was too good for church-going folks?

"Mind your own mind, brother," Rosa said.

The referee's shrill whistle brought Lulu back to the game.

Donna stood courtside: hand on her hip, eyes ablaze, muscular arms tensed when she removed her jacket. She reminded Lulu a little of Wendell, her Jamaican ex-husband from way back when. His wiry muscularity, no-nonsense talk and adoration attracted her, but he hadn't Donna's sensitivity. The coach's searchlight gaze honed in on Lulu, even all those rows up. Lulu waved. She hadn't experienced such lush attention from a woman in ages. She felt flattered, yet uneasy.

Little Smoke, the point guard, brought the ball down all the way, twisting and turning around defenders, eventually making a layup. Pretty to watch that small girl with braided hair fly. Jeff turned to Lulu with a gaze that flashed *I know what's hovering between you and Donna.*

Back and forth, teams scoring, missing, rebounding, fouling, parents cheering. Girls fell to the floor. Some tripped dramatically. A technical foul was called on one player from each team before the half ended. Donna threw up her hands. She paced. At some point, Lulu had to stretch, get up off the hard bleacher seat, walk off some agitation. She adjusted her skirt to cover more of her thighs.

At half time, she and Jeff bought sodas and Cajun chips. Jeff introduced her to a few people. "Yankee," she was labeled several times, invited over to at least one person's porch.

"Everyone has an opinion," Jeff said.

"I like that," Lulu said.

The rest of the game was a nail biter, as the lead kept changing. In the third quarter, the player known as "Swish" (for her light jumper that didn't jar the rim) got hurt and had to leave the game. They ran for ice; Lulu could discern that she seemed to be arguing to come back in, but Donna was pressing her into her seat.

"Donna won't cave," Jeff said. "These kids are tough…they want to win. She's going to have to sit out. There goes one of our best chances."

Donna's Eagles made a comeback of sorts, pulling within three—and with a chance to make it one—as Susie Cue stepped up to the free-throw line. To a mix of cheering and the words "shut up" from various parts of the crowd, Susie nervously bounced the ball. Donna shouted.

"Rebounders prepare."

The first shot bounced up, off the rim. The second, a bank shot, went in, so the Wolves had the ball. Threw it down court to their point guard, who spun past a defender for an easy layup. Eagles down by four. Lulu never realized kids' sports could be this nerve-wracking.

And then with two minutes to go, Little Smoke turned over the ball. A foul was called, with the Wolves making one of two free throws. The clock ran down. Donna let Swish come back in for the final possession. Her fans applauded, but you couldn't help but notice her limp. Lulu felt bad. The girl took a shot that fell short as the buzzer rang amid a chorus of groans and cheers. Some of the Eagle players outright bawled. Donna herded them to the center of the court to shake hands with the victors. They made a haphazard line, passing each other as the bleachers started to empty.

Lulu let out a sigh. "They were amazing." Donna's coaching inspired her.

"They have to deal," said Jeff. "That was the second close game they've lost. Hopefully Swish is okay."

Lulu and Jeff waited for Donna in the hallway. She finally emerged from the locker room with her team draped over her.

"What a tough one," said Donna. "I have to talk to Swish's aunt. They might have to get her x-rayed."

When Donna returned, she seemed tired yet calm. Outside they

Off the Yoga Mat

found Jeff's car.

Donna turned to Lulu. "Fine to have you here—what a game to witness. The Wolves were too vicious, the girls said." She clutched her gym bag. "It's a struggle."

"You wouldn't want it any other way," Jeff said. "Stay hungry."

Donna laughed. "I am famished. Lulu would you care to…join me for a bite?"

Lulu hesitated. "Sure." She could eat.

"Good night, ladies. I'm going to leave you to your own devices."

They exited his car.

Donna smiled at Lulu. She shut out all thoughts about getting back to Monroe's, rising early for church or of her besotted lover far away. She respected Donna, awaited her support.

The hot jock do-gooder cooked them omelets. Ran a hot bath infused with lavender oil. The distinct floral essence steamed the air throughout the house, a slowly floating aphrodisiac.

"Let me pamper you," said Donna.

"I don't know," Lulu said, jittery.

"I'm drawn to you. We can take it slow. It's essential that you feel comfortable."

In the past, Lulu used sex to validate her worth. Sometimes she succumbed to aggressive, abusive men. Other times, sex brought pleasure and connection. Lulu intended to honor the path towards mindful choices, including fidelity. What she and Nate had begun in New York felt like a blessing. Then Donna kissed her on the mouth.

"If you want me to stop, say so," said Donna, caressing her back and shoulders.

The coach was strong, impetuous. That frenetic game ignited something, as did Lulu's sense of honing in on the source of abuse. They clung to each other.

Donna's lips were soft, her fingers all knowing. Lulu quit thinking, felt sultry like the lingering sun. They ran their hands over each other's muscular limbs, kissed deeply. On fresh sheets with potpourri scent in the room, one thing led to another. They became a tangle of mouths and fingers, warm, wet. Moves made themselves. All the way to orgasm.

Donna named her tattoo. "She looks like a Gertrude," she said, stroking her.

"Gertrude Slime?" They cracked up.

Alluring, supportive. Donna understood. Oh no, thought Lulu. I've been carried away. Again.

June, 1999

Chapter Thirty-Five
Kiitos

(Nora)

Nora dreamed they wheeled her into a gray room. She clutched the metallic sides of a gurney, on her way to slip inside the belly of a tunnel-like machine. Her legs had been torn off at the knees. She rested on a sauna bench taking blasts of steam before being dipped in an ice-water bath. When she realized the horror of this vision, she sat up, fully awake, and reached for her legs. Thankfully they remained. Ever since she heard about her father's relapse, she dreamed like this.

She had fallen asleep before Ville came by with his car to help her purchase the final items for her party. It was time for the discussion of her imminent departure, their future. In June's never-ending days, the sun bled into night and then back to luxurious light. She couldn't delay the question.

They entered the car. "I hope you'll come visit me soon in New York," Nora said. "I'd like to give our relationship a shot."

Ville looked at her, his hands on the wheel. "Nora. I can't go to

America. I'm no traveler. I don't want to leave my son."

She took a breath. "Don't you want to see my city? Find out what might be next for us? Long distance romance is hard, but sometimes it works out." She had known of a few relationships destined to endure. "Bring Risto along."

Ville started the car. "I knew you'd be leaving." He pulled away from the curb. "You have been fantastic. I'm glad we had this block of time. I am the wrong guy for distance dating."

This was the famous Finnish honesty she had heard about, a direct answer mincing no words. He might have acted as if there was something worth fighting for. Couldn't he let her down easy?

They got out of the car, headed to *Alko*, the government-run liquor store. "Let's pick out some wine," Nora said, masking disappointment.

"Always the good planner, my Nora," Ville said, stroking her hair. He grabbed bottles from nearby shelves while Nora stepped away to the other side of the store. She felt used. To help him get over the shock of his wife's cheating. But I craved something too, she acknowledged, so in the end it was a fair exchange. She located wines from Spain and France and haphazardly chose a few.

Back at her place, she let him unpack and put everything away. "Will you make ice for the party, please? Leave it in the little freezer." She had seldom used the unit they bought for her.

What an icy, icy man, she thought. I see through him. How can we carry on for the next few weeks until I go?

When he approached her for a kiss, she barely met his lips. She was tired of relationships that got cut off at the knees, of men who stayed chained in their chairs while she lifted off. She'd miss his intense, dark humor, his down-to-earth directness, attentive caresses. She hadn't shared her desire to have a baby with him because of his shock over the separation with his wife (and his management of Risto). Now that proved a blessing. What about her chance of becoming a parent? Was it like pissing in the wind? Not by a long shot. Let them try to stop me, she thought.

When Ville left, Nora phoned Bethany, who was smack in the middle of arranging housing for new immigrants and sending others out to seek employment. "There's this orphan from Iraq," Bethany said. "She breaks my heart, clings to my leg. Wish I could take her home."

"I don't blame her for holding on," Nora said. "It must be so difficult for these children to lose their parents and be in a strange new place. I'm sorry to interrupt. Listen. I've just been dumped. Ville doesn't want to keep it going...I didn't let him see me get angry...I am about to cry."

Bethany sighed. "Go ahead and bawl. You had a pleasant interlude. Don't fret about your party. I'll bake a cake and make my mother-in-law's stew—reindeer meat with onions, fennel, carrots and a dollop of cream. The kids will bake cookies. Lilly and I will come early, clothe you in satin and lace, do your makeup and hair. I'll bring my treasure chest of sashes, tube tops, patterned tights...the works. He'll regret his decision," she said. "Of course, I'll sing."

"Thank you, Bethany. Do you know I love you? You've been an amazing friend." She felt a lightness inside her chest.

The night of Nora's party, her cheeks blushed, her eyes flicked with violet shadow and blue-black mascara. Bethany and Lilly dressed her in a see-through top over a camisole with a skimpy black-velvet skirt. Then they had her step into bird-patterned stockings. Nora stared into the glow of endless light outside.

When Jussi arrived, rings shining, wearing a leather vest, he looked her up and down. Then, he took control of the music, blasting Bowie's song "Scary Monsters," and tunes by Nightwish, a moody Finnish pop-metal band. Nora decided to act like a stage actress at a premier. She chatted with her teacher Mrs. Marakola and gave her a quick hug. The table overflowed with cold meats and cheeses, rye crackers, smoked salmon (but no bagels or New York schmear). Reindeer stew courtesy of Bethany, and Karl Fazer chocolates provided by Winn. A *pulla* cake and cardamom doughnuts from a bakery Nora liked. The crack of metal tops from beer cans, empties overflowing bags. Every window and door propped open, light streaming through.

Ville alternated between sympathetic glances at Nora and making phone calls. It didn't feel like a birthday party *or* a farewell gathering. She opened the apartment's logbook, the one she thumbed through when she arrived. "Sign it, please," Nora requested of her guests, planning to photocopy the pages. Their names would summarize her days.

This was it. She knew where she stood with Ville, but must get to the bottom of things with Jussi. Why had he rejected her? Jussi's silken hair hung down his back, his tight jeans reminding her of what she had been denied.

"Jussi," she raised her voice over the music. He stood behind a table in a corner of the living room. "I am leaving soon. Tell me something—when I kissed you...when I had you over, why'd you turn me down?"

His face remained expressionless as he plowed through a stack of CDs. "Nora, some things can't be explained."

"I'm not your type?" She treaded on thin ice. He pushed the button to play another song. She leaned on the wall.

"I don't have a type." He guzzled his beer, fiddled with the boom box.

"What am I then?" she asked. "Mymble in Moomin Valley? Pining for the object of her desire while he has other ideas?"

He smiled at her Moomin reference. "No. You are not Mymble. We are still talking, aren't we?"

"Meaning we wouldn't be if we had sex?"

"Sometimes it's like that. Besides, you're with that guy," he gestured in Ville's direction.

"I have been happy with him," Nora said. "But I thought about you."

He nodded. "Can I smoke in here?"

"No. Go in the backyard. Answer me. I wasn't even with Ville back then."

"I have a gift for you," he said.

She would have rather had him.

As Jussi dashed off to smoke, Bethany stood on the other side of the living room, chanting her scales. "People, we don't have to wait for cake to hear some tunes," she shouted as Lilly grabbed her hanging sleeve.

"Mummy. Antti is missing."

"He's what? Not now," Bethany hissed.

"I can't find him."

"That son of mine."

"He's not anywhere," Lilly whined.

"Ask your father," Bethany said.

"Father is smoking."

"I wish Mikko would give up those cigarettes. He's going to kill himself and take us with him."

Bethany and her rambunctious, disappearing son distracted Nora. She'd accept Jussi's response like a stone statue. She'd propelled herself further than she thought possible. Took calculated risks since the breakup with Nate. If only she might refine those instincts—Ville represented a step in the right direction. She'd focus on motherhood, certain to bring greater challenges than any she'd known.

Nora sought her co-workers, thanking them for their support. She wanted to sit with them, one-on-one. Ville came over, asked how she was doing.

"So-so," she told him.

"That is not bad."

"My son is hiding," Bethany interrupted. "Can I search in your bedroom? In the closets?"

"Search away. We will help you."

A search party went looking for Antti.

Nora knocked on the bathroom door. It was locked, but no one uttered a sound. Nora turned the handle.

"Are you in there, Antti?" she jiggled it. "Come out."

As she moved away from the door, it opened slowly. Out stepped her Nokia bosses, Alto and Aino, one then the other. She let out a snort; they were each married to others. He had recently separated. Who would have figured they'd be sneaking around? At work they behaved like professionals.

Nora gulped some beer, crept back into the kitchen to refill snack bowls. Something shifted under the low counter, covered with a table cloth. She knelt.

"Antti?" she whispered. She heard shallow breathing and drew her head under the cloth, came face-to-face with Bethany's son's freckled nose and smudged chocolate grin.

"I won't tell on you," she said. "You're a great hider…if you agree to come out. This is *my* party. You can't be the center of attention."

He shook his head. "I stay here." He clutched a half-eaten doughnut.

"Aren't you having fun? I'm upset if you're not. There's good food and music, and I put aside comics for you in my room. A *Tin Tin* and a *Donald Duck*. Okay?" she asked, tipping over, brushing against his folded legs.

He giggled. "I look at them later. Bring me some Coke."

"Sure," she said, thinking about what an operator he was. How would she parent a child full of such trickery? All she ever thought about were infants, swaddled, adorable in their little hats. Not a mischievous boy or a troubled teen. She hadn't been realistic.

We never comprehend all we conjure. She remembered a quote Nate mentioned from *Moby Dick*. "All visible objects are but as pasteboard masks." She was a fan of the pasteboard, also the mask. She had stolen her chance to arrive on this foreign stage and then she improvised. Her girlish aspirations to act hadn't gone by the wayside. She'd gained some chops. Adjusted to a foreign culture, formed new friendships, attracted a lover.

The night yielded more surprises. Bethany belted out "Proud Mary" with her son in hiding. Young Lilly danced with Mrs. Marakola. Mikko went round the corner to buy more beer. Aino confided to Nora there might be a job for her at Nokia if she decided to return to Finland.

"Maybe you can produce pastiche videos for us if everything goes well?" To Nora, that suggested an understanding between them that "mum's the word," as far Aino's tryst with Alto was concerned.

Soon, Winn and Bethany brought out a birthday cake with candles burning. Bethany led everyone in an English, and then Finnish, version of the Happy Birthday song.

"Blow out the candles, love," said Winn.

After Nora blew them out, Bethany bellowed. "Speech, Nora. How does it feel to be 40? I have a couple of years to go."

A little tipsy and red in the face, Nora looked at the flustered, expectant faces of her guests.

"It feels...freaking fabulous," she said, hiccuping. "Because you're all here."

Some clapping, "ahhhs," silent nods, Lilly applauding wildly. Bethany cut cake into slices that her daughter delivered to guests.

Ville came over and kissed Nora, then tried to feed her cake. She let him.

Soon after, Jussi handed her a wrapped gift. She tore it open to find a CD of Dylan's Greatest Hits and a *Moomin* paperback, along with a sealed note card she'd read later. She hugged Jussi. Planted a long kiss on his mouth, for closure.

"*Kiitos*," she said.

"*Kiitos* to you," he answered.

He'd remain her beautiful stranger.

Bethany made Nora promise she would come back to Tampere to try the smoke sauna in Pispala, the oldest one in town. Nora said she would. Try all of them, learn more about this land, these people, share her outsider insights. Had anybody written about Finnish saunas, their histories and mysteries? "Lingua Sauna" could be the phrase, how it was meant to play out. She'd focus on a subject that captivated her.

The party began to peter out. She gave away care packages of the food that remained. Out the open window, Nora noticed a hint of twilight at 3 a.m. Brightness dominated. She hugged or shook hands with each departing guest.

When everyone left, and after she sent Ville on his way, Nora sat on the front stoop, pulling off her tights, unhooking her bra. She watched revelers of the wee hours, staggering on sunlit streets, riding in vintage American cars, heading to the 24-hour kiosk for munchies. She became an honorary citizen of Tampere's nocturnal felicities, a product of extended light, beer saturating her gut. Here she had come to know the sky as three-quarters of earth's horizon, a lake down the hill in its own sky universe. She opened the flap of the envelope containing Jussi's card, slowly withdrawing it. It featured a Tove Janssen sketch of the character Little My with her hands on her hips, a scowl across her face. Inside he wrote in looped cursive:

Dear Nora: I lack eloquence with the English spoken word. I could never tell you how much I admire you, how special you are. As Dylan said don't admit you knew me when. I'm 28, living the free and easy student life, you are a serious older woman from far away, very smart, funny too. You flatter me. I thought it was best to keep the respect and conversation. I am sorry if I hurt your feelings. I hope we can remain friends. From the Finnish Bob Dylan, Jussi Mulaantu

She would remember him well.

Chapter Thirty-Six
DIY

(Nate)

Nate stood in the corner of the studio, on the second floor of a building that had been his second home. That creaky yoga room—empty, debased, holes in the plaster, crumbling paint— showed signs of returning to life. He had seen the manager's lackey, a tall, thin fellow with a scar on his cheek. The fellow babbled that if they didn't fix the damage, they would bill Lulu $2,500 and if it wasn't paid "someone might get hurt."

"That's outrageous," Nate said. "Lulu isn't even here to sort this out. Anyone could have done it."

"She'll have to pay one way or another," he said. "Should have vacated before."

With his credit card, Nate purchased paint, cleaning supplies, plaster. He pressured Gil to chip in. Some of the freegans (sans Mariel Day) and Fox Hole members, even Ginny, were restoring order to Lulu's studio.

"Nate. Why you going all DIY?" Gil queried. "You're Tom Sawyer. We're white-painting the place. If Lulu has insurance, they will compensate her. And if she has to get out, why bother? Don't assume my band trashed this place."

"You opened the floodgates," Nate said. "Don't know if Lulu has insurance. Haven't spoken to her about it."

"The front door was open. We didn't break in. Whazzup with you two? You're not merely her student. A disciple of love? A horny hanger-on? That's why Mariel is missing," he said, looking around. "You drank the Betancourt brew, took the full meal plan. I knew it. Finally succumbed, you dog." He smacked Nate in the chest.

Nate's cheeks burned; he resisted Gil's provocation.

"Let's figure out what to do about those holes." Nate gestured to the far corner of the room, where the old floor had caved in.

"If the colossal college is buying the building, why knock ourselves out?" Gil said. "You're not my boss."

Anita came over.

"Lulu should block the corporate university," she said. "We'll help her hold out. Fight this takeover. Maybe you and Lulu want to join us in Seattle for the protest?"

Gil gave Anita a peck on the lips. "You're hot when you spout propaganda."

"Stop thinking with your penis," Anita said.

Nate was vexed by their liaison. It was likely to blow up before the new moon. Her response was dead on. Maybe she'd make a dent in his armor.

"Fox Hole is donating all concert proceeds to the Seattle trip," Gil said. "We'll kick in something for Ginny and her homeless comrades." They had become part of the freegan brigade.

Nate found some delectable irony in the way this odd coalition had formed. He surveyed the place. Eerie, but showing signs of improvement. It was time to talk turkey.

Chapter Thirty-Seven
Deception

(Lulu)

Far away, Lulu blended into the heat of post-jazz-fest N'awlins, checking on the crop of vegetables and flowers Rosa was tending. Her mother's easel stood next to the backyard garden; Rosa painted in an oversized straw hat, swatted bugs. She hummed "Down by the Riverside." No one was permitted to view her canvas.

Lulu attended church with Monroe and Mrs. Lady. Her mind meandered from Christ the lamb, to the meek will inherit the earth, and finally to Donna. Gentle yoga poses on the bed. Baking scones, zydeco and blues out the boom box. Lulu shifted in her pew, meditating on sutras, while the minister's sermon addressed false piety. "If I speak in tongues of men and of angels, but have not love, I am only a resounding gong. If I have the gift of prophecy and fathom all mysteries, if I have a faith that moves mountains, but have not love, I am nothing," he piped.

She squirmed in the pew. She loved Nate. Loved Donna, too. Lulu acknowledged her bouts of deception. Loss of *shakti*, the subtle energy that's the true source of yoga. The sutras claim yoga liberates the mind…but what about hormones, and that porous boundary between pain and pleasure? What about trauma? The church organist pressed the keys. Lulu countered: Sutra 1.27, "God's voice is Om."

After church, she napped. In her dream, the stocky bald man stuck his fingers inside her vagina. Chatty Cathy pleaded when her string was pulled: "Change my dress." Lulu cried upon awakening, canceled plans with Donna. She pulled the cover over her head. When she got out of bed, she practiced more challenging *asanas,* like ramp. She inhaled, lifting her pelvis and groin upward, hands and fingers spread outwards. Then returned to *prana* breathing.

A few days later, she visited Donna's support group. But the stories they shared of abuse—in one case incest—depressed her. She wilted in her chair. "That's the process," Donna insisted. Lulu preferred to hang out at the school with the girls, demonstrating poses to complement their basketball jones. On their hands and knees, they enjoyed cat, and later, turning over, the bow. Three of them rocked in unison after she helped them grab their ankles, lifting their torsos.

"Cool, Miss Lulu," said Susie Cue. "I am my own rocking horse."

"Exactly," Lulu nodded.

Later, Donna said, "You are one hell of a hit with the girls," placing her arm around Lulu's shoulders. "You're healing even if you don't realize. You know, you could move here," she said, not realizing *this* Lulu was not the sum total, not a live-in type (and silent about her lover up North). If Lulu had raised the subject, she figured it would spoil the *je ne sais quoi* and trample their womanly bond.

Donna's buddy Jeff grasped Lulu's hesitancy. He sensed the muck of her deception. When he was around, Lulu avoided his gaze.

But Donna and Lulu planned to join Jeff and his date at a fundraiser party for subsidized housing in the lower ninth ward. Donna said it was about time funds were earmarked for locals. "There's so much need is the problem," she said. "Too much suffering and ignorance."

Monroe stood taller whenever Donna came around. She arrived to pick up Lulu for the block party/fundraiser. Lulu's uncle spouted Monroe-isms.

"I like it that you're with your own people—your business is *our* business." Donna listened attentively, questioned Monroe when he told her about Nam, how they became fighting machines. "We was dealing with dioxin. The Vietnamese breathed it. So did we." He went on about how his wife had turned away from him, that's why he divorced her (not that he was crazy). But his kids should forgive him, come back around. He wanted to die in his bed.

"Not in any of them hot spices," said Monroe. Lulu noticed Donna suppress a guffaw as she understood he meant "hospices." He then explained to Donna that Rosa had married a drunken sailor with the temper of a Simon Legree, and that's why his half-sister and niece moved away from Louisiana. From God.

Donna closed her eyes.

"My people came from Chicago. Originally, Tennessee. After Chicago, we lived in Texas," Donna said. "Harm was done, but I plan to stop the cycle."

"How you going to do that?" Monroe asked.

"It ain't easy. Learning from others, facing the truth, testifying in a supportive place," she said.

"Sounds like my church."

Monroe didn't ponder the nature of Lulu's connection to Donna. Rosa slowly realized the sexual component. Lulu wouldn't come back to sleep at Monroe's a few nights a week. As Donna chatted with Monroe, Rosa gave Donna the once over. She snorted and walked into the kitchen, where Lulu was putting away plates and glasses from the drain board.

"Donna's mannish," Rosa said. "Sleeping with her is an abomination. You're breaking my broken heart."

"Don't judge us, mama. You couldn't possibly understand."

"What's to understand?"

"She's helping me. Get through."

"With what?"

"Our troubles, the violence we experienced as children. I told you I've been having nightmares. About a balding white man, squat, with a mustache. Furious dark eyes. I dream he's chasing me, offering me candy and a jump rope, then forcing me to touch him…and I believe he spent time in our house when daddy went on one of his benders. I want to know what you know about him."

Rosa stood still. Rubbed her stomach. "Let me be." She folded her arms, stood over the sink.

"Try to remember, Mama. I found a photo," Lulu pressed her. "I'll show you."

"You're mixing things up. You're bent on distraction. You a worse hussy than your grandmother in her day," uttered Rosa.

"Who was he?" Lulu shouted. "You owe me an explanation."

Rosa turned on the faucet, let the water run to fill a glass, but the water ran over the top. She backed away from Lulu. The flow continued.

"Shut it off. I'm not going to stop asking." Lulu decided she'd see what Monroe had to say about the photo when she had a minute. In the living room she found Donna. Pulled her from the chair in the middle of a Monroe story.

"Aren't we late for that fundraiser? Let's get out of here."

"Sorry Monroe. Tell me another time," Donna said graciously.

"You are leaving us to our own devices?"

"Yes sir." They kissed Monroe goodbye. Donna invited him to a basketball game at her school.

"Can I make a small wager on the outcome?" he asked.

They were silent in the car. Donna drove a mile out past Esplanade Street into the Bywater district, where revelers filled a small cul-de-sac with hanging light bulbs. The crowd danced with abandon, their clothes kaleidoscopic shapes in warm air. After downing a shot of bourbon and listening to the blues band tear it up, Donna undulated in the shape of a parabola: diving down, spiking high, rolling low. Her well-chiseled biceps seeped out of her t-shirt. Hair cropped close and tight—fierce, thought Lulu. Rosa's criticism and prejudice, her silence about what happened, surrounded Lulu like humidity.

Later on, back at Donna's, when her lover started to massage her shoulders, Lulu said, "I don't want to be touched."

"I get it," said Donna. "Want to talk?"

"No. Let's zone out."

They watched an episode of *Law and Order*. Familiar scenes of New York City evoked the restless pull of her other life. Warm sensations of an East Village summer approaching. Heat reflecting off concrete. Punks hanging by the benches. A fountain and hydrants spraying cool water on sticky city kids. Gay, lesbian and trans folks ruling Tompkins Square Park leading up to the fabulous Wig Stock festival. She used to run into Allen Ginsberg and Peter Orlovksy at De Robertis, a tiny Italian bakery near her studio and hold one-on-one yoga sessions with Ellen Stewart, the experimental theatre queen of La Mama. Those were special times. She considered the melancholy tone in Nate's voice when they had spoken. She missed him more than she admitted. Her yoga students, too. She woke up in fits and starts in Donna's bed, understanding she disappointed everyone. Rationalizing her appetite, her need. Like Gerty the frog, I'm catching another fly on my flickering tongue. Lulu tried to suppress her negative thoughts about the way that she loved. It didn't work.

Just as she speculated why Evelyn, the substitute yoga teacher in New York, hadn't responded to her calls—thinking she had better contact the manager to discuss eviction—Nate telephoned. She listened as he spoke in clipped, fraught words.

He described what went down, how he was attempting to take care of it. Transfixed by his story of destruction and rebirth for 2 Squared, she felt the stalks of her life shorn at the root. Not only was her emotional life unraveling, but the yoga studio on Second Avenue—her livelihood, her pride—was a smattered remnant. Nate spoke in an empathetic monotone:

"The studio was trashed; homeless folks, musicians and freakgans moved in...cops shut it down; there might have been looting," he said. "The university is engulfing the East Village, ordering everyone out of your building—threatening to sue."

She took in the reality. Those developers wanted to smoke her out of her small yoga farm, a stalwart in the community, welcoming everyone. Most folks felt appreciatively better after singing *Om Shanti* with Lulu. That place was gone; she hadn't fought to keep it. Am I being punished for my contradictions, my lack of constancy? Those thoughts raced through her head.

"Nate. What should I do? I can't start over."

Silence on the phone line. Then he spoke. "Yes, you can. Visualize the sun as you salute it, streaking across the window. It finds you. Again."

Chapter Thirty-Eight
Dismay

(Nate)

Listening to Lulu's response to the news, Nate grasped her raw pain. "I wish I knew who broke in and trashed it," she had said. "I tried to improve the situation here and find out about my past. Now there's nothing left."

When he said he'd help her find another space, she hadn't listened. Went on about how she had tried to check in with Evelyn, a yoga teacher she hadn't known but decided to trust. In hindsight, that woman proved irresponsible. Lulu said she wanted to consult a tenants' rights group. From what they pieced together, Evelyn may have forgotten to lock the door…that had been the beginning of the end.

"I should have tracked down Bina, who's been with me for years. I got caught up with stuff here," Lulu said. "My regulars must have moved on."

"Don't worry about them." Nate tried to calm her, absorbing her dismay.

When he told her that Gil and his band had been using the space for rehearsal, and that Ginny had settled in, Lulu let out a nervous laugh. "They took advantage, didn't they?"

"I believe so."

She mentioned setting up veteran's benefits for her mother and uncle, dealing with unresolved violence from childhood. More nightmares. Photographs. If only he could hold her.

Nate admitted he hadn't pieced it all together until the past week; he apologized for waiting. "We started to make repairs."

After a half minute of silence, she responded.

"Thanks for salvaging the wreck," she said, her voice heavy. "Nate, you came through, you took it upon yourself. I have insurance against personal injury for students. But not for destruction caused by negligence. And about the university taking over the building, we'll let them, I suppose. But where can I teach?"

"Other tenants were offered cash," he said. "You must find out what you're entitled to."

"I'll come up by the end of the week," she said, sounding exhausted.

Nate feared for the worst. Lulu helped him find his center. When he located it, somewhere between the floor and the ceiling, she gave him a sense of purpose. Later, he realized he loved her. I have been the catalyst for some of her troubles, he thought. Maybe someone down in New Orleans played music to her. Lined up outside her tent, vying for access. He knew of her reputation, recalled how she had been fooling around with that guy in the studio. Then came my turn, incredible, but for how long?

He hated the way certain men ignored women of substance, focused on their looks, appeared threatened by the whole person. He would never let himself turn into such a prick. But what if she was through with him? His temples throbbed. Jealousy released its spell. He imagined Lulu making it with a Southern man. They had never discussed exclusivity; there hadn't been time. For him, there could be no one else. He swallowed his panic.

He had no inclination to write about *his* jealousy. What made Monica think he'd jot this stuff down?

Chapter Thirty-Nine
Verdant

(Nora)

Nora would immerse her body into the large and glistening beauty of Näsijärvi, where the temperature was in the range of 55 degrees Fahrenheit. After packing her suitcases, she took a solo journey to bid farewell, riding the bus to the lake and hiking down a dirt path shaded by leafy white birch and placid firs. At the water's edge, she began to count out loud in Finnish.

"*Yksi, kaksi, kolme,* nobody told me," she chanted, dipping her feet in the cold, clean water up to her ankles. Water's rhythm, never shy.

"*Neljä, viisi,* feeling dizzy," she continued. At this point, some of the children in the shallow water stared. She inched forward slowly until she reached up to her knees. Freezing indeed, numbness you must withstand.

"*Kuusi, seitsemän, kahdeksän,* no one here to hold my hand." She waded in up to her tummy, shaking, wanting to cling to one of the children, anything to distract her and make it easier to acclimate. Bethany's son Antti would have squealed, darted away. At her party, he had finally come out of hiding, consented to let her hug him. He liked the comic books, even shared them with Lilly. She imagined how she'd take her own little one into the water, offer piggy-back rides. She and her brother Ben frolicked in the community pool while growing up, jumping into their parents' arms when the adults ceased playing bridge. Her dad taught her how to swim. He'd hold her on the surface of the water's sheen, and she'd kick while rotating her arms. He showed her how to turn her head and take a breath, never letting go until she insisted. It took practice and frustration to coordinate those movements. She thought about her dad's chemo, imagined being with him, remembering this lake, telling him of its size and stark beauty.

A shiver descended like the trill of a flute. The sauna nearby could ease discomfort. That was its job. She strolled over to the heated room, joining a small group of men and women. This time it was her who poured water on the rocks so it sizzled with rolling steam, *löyly*. That's when she noticed the small bundles of tied-up birch sticks and leaves that bathers used to smack themselves and others for stimulation. The leaves released a scent that was fresh and verdant, infusing the air. She found a bundle tied with string and mimicked the motions of the others, thwacking the plants lightly against her skin until they almost adhered. A brisk awakening, releasing a sublime scent. One organism speaking to another. She followed a couple out the door. Submerged again into the clear gentle waves, warm meeting cold, opposites conjoining.

In the all-knowing water, she bobbed between elemental forces. Ready to go back. Be with family and friends. Leave Secanor if it came to that. Time to prioritize motherhood. Winn's offer was not her only option. Before leaving for Finland, realizing the futility of conceiving with Nate and in the wake of her boss Jeremy's predatory behavior, she had ordered a selection of sperm-donor profiles from a cryobank in California. She heard about an organization of single women considering solo parenting via insemination and by adoption. She would attend one of their meetings, figure out her next move. As her heated body merged with the cool lake, compromise met premonition.

Chapter Forty
Coming Clean

(Lulu)

After Lulu picked vegetables from the garden with Rosa, they stood over the sink, washing lettuce and dandelion greens. "I'm flying to New York in a few days to take care of some trouble with my yoga studio," said Lulu. "I'll come back as soon as I can."

"Can I go too? Then head to the shore?"

"Not now. Get Mrs. Lady to assist you. I am leaving you the number for Veteran's Affairs. I will bring you up North when I settle things. You should spend at least half a year here from now on. I found out you're entitled to some of daddy's benefits you hadn't claimed."

Rosa shook her head—a refusal.

Lulu made the arrangements to fly to New York. Before she took off, she must ask Monroe about the photo that included the stout bald man. Do it before she changed her mind.

She shut off the TV set and sat down next to Monroe. Placed the picture in his hand. He studied it, holding it far away then squinting at it real close.

"Where'd you find that? My, my," he said, "I put him out of my mind." He blinked, fanned the air with the photo. "I saw this fellow," he said, "once or twice—demonic spirit. Your mama found something in him. They're in my house in that shot—see? I recognize the curtains." He pointed to the drapes. "Same, but faded."

"Was Mama involved with him?"

"A terrible man. I suspected he harmed you. You cried something awful."

"I don't know," Lulu said, sadness welling up. "I am trying to figure it out. How do you know he hurt me?"

"Rosa. Back then she tried to keep him away…from you. They was over at my house a few times. I remember visiting your house with Helene, my wife at the time. She gave you a big hug, tried to cheer you up."

"I'm going to get Rosa in here now. She's got to say something."

When she entered, Monroe stood up and handed her the photo.

"Your daughter wants answers," he shouted. "You brought that awful man here—remember? Helene took this picture."

"You neglected your wife," said Rosa.

"What has that got to do with it?"

Lulu and Monroe stared at Rosa. She sighed.

"Not much to say, really. That's Ridley. With your father gone, I was looking to keep company, I was lively. Then I couldn't get him to leave. He didn't go to bars like Maximilian; he stuck around. He called you 'pretty one.' Said you as sweet as a lollipop."

"He was mean," Monroe said.

"What happened?" Lulu inquired, trembling. "You've been covering it up."

"Listen. I got even! He hurt me too," Rosa raised her voice. "The timing was right for that storm," she nodded, eyes bulging.

It didn't all fit. "What did he do?" Lulu asked. "Tell me everything, Mama."

Rosa stood still, folded her arms into her chest. Took a deep breath. "I don't know," she said. "It's dead and buried."

"No. It's not…that's why I'm messed up with memories in bits and pieces."

"I don't know the extent of it. You cried, you didn't keep quiet, said you hated him. You said he took your doll. I ordered him to stay away. 'Leave the child alone.' I made you lock your door from the inside. But I couldn't stop him," her voice cracked. "I had you sleep in my bed.

We'd sing 'Michael Row your Boat Ashore.' Remember?"

"I don't remember singing. He made me touch him, didn't he?"

Rosa hesitated.

"Mama, you have to tell me," Lulu yelled.

"Yes! You said he made you pull on his thing," she said, then paused. Her face crinkled. "I was at my wit's end. I said to stop or I'd call the cops. It was so long ago. I put it out of my mind." Rosa shriveled as she spoke.

"Is that all? I bet there's more," said Lulu, her voice a piercing cry. "You owe it to me."

"How awful, making me speak of it!" Rosa pursed her lips. "You said he hurt you in your privates." She spoke low, barely above a whisper. Then she grew animated. "He died, you know. Two years after we moved to Maryland—from a stroke. I heard from someone. Before that I kept thinking he'd find us, cause he was threatening. Imagine living with that! I kept waiting for him to show up." She put her hand on her heart. Sat down on the ottoman. A wisp of a woman.

"Mama." Lulu bent down and shouted in Rosa's face. "Why didn't you protect me? Why didn't you call the cops?"

"I wanted to," Rosa said.

Screams from the inside, bloody arrows. "I knew it." Lulu scream-cried. Who could find words? The point of the arrow in her chest, trying to exit out the back.

"You kept silent all these years, you lied…almost as bad as what he did." A lump constricted Lulu's throat. A monsoon of tears. "All these nightmares." She knew for certain Ridley made her fondle him. And he raped her. A small child. More than once. Pushed himself into her.

"Monster," Monroe said, his eyes bulging. "See what he did to an innocent child!" he shouted. "You and Ridley will burn in hell."

"Shut up! I was terrified," Rosa said. "Don't put it all on me. He hit me." One colossal tear streamed down Rosa's right cheek as she stood up and leaned against the wing chair.

Lulu sobbed in a steady rhythm. She wanted to pummel her mother. She raised her hand, approaching, but Monroe grabbed her.

"Don't hit your mama," he said. "I would strike her down. Won't change a thing."

"I told you I fixed him," Rosa shouted, wide-eyed. "Listen. That storm came, protected us."

"What did you do?" Monroe asked. He threw his arm around his niece, held her. "Let me get you tissues."

"I stabbed Ridley," Rosa proclaimed. "More than once. With a big kitchen knife—in the arm and stomach. He bled across the bed, couldn't believe a small frightened woman could cut like that. We boarded up the house, evacuated. I rammed in the knife. I told him to go ahead and die. I wanted it. He fled to his people—or he would have taken revenge right then. I got him best I could."

Lulu had more questions, but she withheld them, thinking of her petite mother attacking that monster with a knife. She sobbed into the box of tissues. Monroe closed his eyes. Started to hum a church hymn. Eventually she and her mother moved closer to Monroe into a tentative, stiff circle.

"Amen," whispered Monroe. "Pray to Jesus for forgiveness. Pray for cleansing."

The weight of despair, of recognition, crushed Lulu. She touched her mother's matted hair, held in place by a single bobby pin. Rosa looked winded from release. Did she cry when I was violated, Lulu wondered. I can't recall her tears. Why can't she sob now? Or apologize?

Soon after, a black knot of revulsion expanded in Lulu's stomach. Her head felt swollen and she wanted to sleep. As a girl she planned to wrestle with that man. Did her best to keep him at arm's length, kicking, throwing Chatty Cathy at him as a last resort. Persistent, bringing gifts, taking the doll away. She had never felt safe. Conjured a fantasy to explain the unexplainable: that's when she landed on her pleasant island, the one that gave her peace, with gentle grass and sand, blue water, orange sunsets. She longed for solace now.

After a long period of silence and some centering breaths, she knew she must share these truths with Donna. And so much more.

Soon, it came to her. I'm coming clean, Lulu thought. Donna

needs to know everything I've been hiding. Nate does too. I can't harbor these lies.

***

Lulu tried to enter a state of consciousness that would make it easier to face Donna (as well as the challenges waiting in New York). She headed outside. Walked north into the Garden District, with its pastel-colored mansions, gold-plated porticos, Ionic columns, sculpted angels, cooling birdbaths. Cypress and palmetto trees abutted high gates. Hushed-up old money. She spun on her heels, did an about-face. Walking, trying to stop her mind from reeling.

Downtown, thick and funky, streetcar rattling past…gold, red and green Mardi Gras beads jangling from branches. A man and a woman in Saints' jerseys arguing outside a grocery store so intensely she thought they'd come to blows. Impulsively, Lulu entered a unisex hair salon as if willed by an invisible agent.

She was tired of dyeing her hair, brushing it off her face, straightening it. That old arrangement didn't capture who she had become. She wanted short, natural hair. I'm going to let myself grow older and grayer, she thought. Accept what I've learned. Shed this troubled skin.

"Lop it off," Lulu told the young stylist. Clippers buzzed, scissors snipped. Hair fell away in clumps. Her slender neck grew bare and red. She would face what trials followed. Her abuser harmed a small girl whose mother had lacked common sense. Rosa was a victim and a perpetrator. Everything that happened remained distorted and grotesque. Lulu watched as the stylist turned her locks into a boyish pixie cut. She could never be that person again, the one from before, in the dark. It was time to find Donna.

Lulu entered Donna's house without ringing the bell, without knocking. Donna's mouth formed an "O" shape. Lulu began with what came easiest.

"They destroyed my studio while I was away. Not sure who or why. But it's wrecked."

Donna comforted her. "Don't let that stop you. You can begin those classes for young people, maybe seniors too, keep the business going. And get some therapy," she said, taking her hand, then touching Lulu's head. "You cut your hair, my dear. You're letting go."

Lulu took refuge in Donna's arms, summoning the courage to continue. "I found out my nightmares are real," she said. "My mother had an abusive boyfriend—it was that husky bald man who fondled me, made me touch him…he raped me, Donna. There, I said it. Rosa admitted he was violent. Claimed she couldn't stop him. She fought back afterwards, cut him with a kitchen knife."

"Oh, Lulu," Donna held her tight, "poor child, go ahead and wail. It's better that you know."

"I'm numb. And angry. And…I have to go back to New York."

"Now?" Donna brushed the fine hairs from Lulu's clothes, gathered them. Her brushing motion was hard, almost painful.

"I can come along if you want. I love you, sweetheart."

"I know you do, Donna. That's what makes this next part difficult, even cruel." Lulu wiped her tears with her sleeve.

"I have to tell you. There's…a guy back in New York. Nate. He started out as my student. It blossomed into something deeper, something beautiful. He's been cleaning up my studio, god bless him."

"Oh," Donna said, "really."

Lulu placed her hand over her heart. "I should have told you sooner. I couldn't. I'm so sorry," Lulu said. "Thing is, I love you, too. You give me courage."

Donna let go of Lulu's hand. "If I had known," she said, "it might not have stopped me. I'm glad we became close. One never knows what's going to happen, that's for sure. But I can't deny that it pierces my heart." She stood up, stepped away from Lulu.

"I'm so sorry," Lulu said. "I've been selfish."

Donna looked in her eyes. "Damn right. But you know what? I'll do something for you. For us, anyway. I'll take these stray hairs I gathered from your clothes to the Esoterica voodoo shop, order two mojo bags and mix the hair with herbs and spices. Jasmine, basil, something from the bayou, something from the garden, a little bit of me, and more of you," Donna said. "For protection. To keep us close."

"Thank you, Donna. One of these days, maybe you'll forgive me."

"I don't know."

Donna said she'd keep one bag and give one bag to Lulu as a parting gift, letting the magical alchemy bless and unite them during their separation. She claimed it would ward off evil.

"It'll go on my altar," said Lulu. "My source."

She figured it was best if she didn't linger.

***

Lulu flew to New York in a meditative haze. She tried to keep her mind off her family, off the harrowing revelations. She did not think of Ridley, but sometimes flashes of Rosa's knife appeared and of herself as a child, perpetually lost, wondering what she did to deserve that evil presence. In the airplane, while staring at the take-out sushi rolls on her tray, which she hadn't touched, Lulu filled imaginary compartments in her mind. She saw blank boxes, corners, containers. Squares and rectangles in the re-circulated air. After a while she realized it was a Japanese bento box she was imagining, with ginger and wasabi mustard in the center of the box. Green salad in peanut dressing was sitting next to steamed rice, sometimes mixing with it. Sometimes she picked up a little of both with her chopsticks. Separate but tangential. Yin-yang, symmetry of stretching then releasing, bending it back the other way.

She envisioned a studio bento. Hatha classes, yes, but also a training program for aspiring instructors. A class for at-risk youth from the nearby projects. Another for seniors and women from shelters and soup kitchens, even women from the streets. A special class supporting victims of domestic abuse and trauma. She'd rebirth her studio—offer yoga to make a difference for those who needed it most, like Donna did with basketball. Connect the dots of her speckled life. She wanted to tell Nate.

She touched her mojo-bag potpourri. It would be activated, powerfully magic with the new moon. Donna promised.

How would she explain her connection with Donna to Nate? And how might they proceed? Could she integrate their lives with hers? A relationship bento seemed unlikely. Might she serve everyone's needs and keep her commitment to mindfulness? I would love the chance to try, she thought.

When she got home, entering her apartment for the first time in quite a while, the sun streamed onto her carpet and sofa. She clutched her back. She needed to stretch out from all that sitting. She put down her bags to do her planks and a plow. Then a bow: folding her legs behind her back while on her stomach, holding them over her head, rocking so as to stretch her muscles, backwards and forwards. She was hoping to shake away collapsing structures of her life. A body could be pliable if trained—taught lovingly how to bend without breaking.

Chapter Forty-One
Jealousy

(Nate)

Nate found Lulu more splendid than ever; he was floored by her boyish haircut, tanned skin, sinuous grace. When she arrived, he showed her the repairs underway. She surveyed the scene. He even handed her *The Village Voice* commercial real estate section so they could look at potential spaces.

She ran her hand over the dusty windowsills with busted blinds, bent to examine the hole in the floor, temporarily boarded, surveyed the spots where they had plastered damaged walls. A few mats (some torn) and two yoga blocks rested disjointedly in one corner. He thought she might burst into tears.

"What happened to the rest of the mats and blocks?"

"I don't know," he answered, taking her hand.

"I guess I'll buy new props. Let's get out of here…it's depressing. So many years of my life come down to this."

As they crossed from the studio to the outer vestibule, Nate embraced Lulu and kissed her with bottled up fervor. But she pulled back.

"I need to talk to you," she said.

He braced himself, the vertebrate in his neck and back contracting.

"Let's head to my place," he suggested. "We can warm up leftovers."

They walked silently through the rowdy streets. He belabored each step.

At his place, he methodically took out leftover noodles from Dojo's restaurant, placing them in the microwave and removing papers and books from the tiny table. Better to keep his hands busy. Steam from the food curled into their faces.

Lulu spoke haltingly. "Nate. It's wonderful to be with you again. I am forever indebted to you for taking charge of the craziness. But listen," her voice dropped. "I haven't been honest with you."

He looked away.

"I met someone in New Orleans. Donna. A gym teacher who coaches girls' basketball. She helped me...find my way. To accept the abuse in my childhood I hadn't realized, some terrible things."

Donna? Terrible things? His mind began to spin.

Lulu drummed a chopstick on the table. "Donna and I...well, we became lovers."

What? It sank in. He had intuited she would betray him. Except it was not with a man, but a woman. Was that any different? He didn't know, couldn't ponder it. When he realized how much he wanted Lulu, he made love to her with unprecedented clarity. In a heartbeat, she had gone and found someone else. He *knew* he was nobody. Jealous rage, a noxious gas in his system. He pounded the table, rattled the steaming bowls. One toppled over.

She stepped back.

He wanted to crush her. He stared at the noodles.

Her wailing started like a crack in the wall and then it spread through his apartment. Peaked sobs reddened her eyes; her face grew engorged.

"I'm so sorry I hurt you," she pleaded. "It was difficult being around my mother and uncle, close to the source of my abuse. I forced my mother to tell me...terrible details, Nate, what that man did to me. Donna went through something like that too. She understood."

Anger lodged in his throat, even as he was moved by her words and tears. He shouted in the tenor of a mad man. "Something wasn't right. I suspected you *were* fooling around." His premonition paled in comparison to this.

"It's not like that, Nate. It'll…take some time to digest," she said, attempting to restore her calm but she was still trembling. "I should have told you. I'm bisexual. I have been mostly non-monogamous. I never met anyone like Donna. She enabled me to process what happened when I was a child. It's not easy to explain. I wasn't looking for anyone. I never stopped caring for you."

He looked at her blankly—she was right. He didn't get it. He had zero experience with an adventurous, bisexual woman. Didn't want to hear about Donna or how she soothed Lulu. Couldn't fathom her abuse. His mind flew to the shame of being jilted many times…how his cousin always got the girl they both wanted, how he was abandoned by Nora when he needed her. He felt brutish, unsophisticated.

"Why am I not enough for you?" he asked.

Lulu stared at him through bloodshot eyes. She groped for his hand. He withdrew it.

"You are enough," she said. She moved over to where he stood. "I'm in love with you," she said softly.

Those words should have thrilled him, but they grazed his ears like a shot whizzing past. He couldn't absorb her emotions. He shrank from her, pushing away her arms.

He upended the rickety table. Noodles and bowls crashed to the floor, cups of water spilled and seeped into his frayed rug. He kicked a bowl across the floor and it skidded into a wall. He needed to hurt himself, inflict physical pain. He reflected on how long he had suppressed this jealous rage, naked, cold hate, emptiness.

Lulu got up. Walked over to him. "Let me hold you," she said. "Please."

"No, Lulu. Get out."

Tears cascaded down her face and into her shirt; she slipped away without another word.

Chapter Forty-Two
Millennial

(Nora)

Back in New York City, the crowds, noise and the intensity disturbed Nora. She walked like a stranger, out of step with everyone brushing past her. When you live in it all the time, you don't realize you've become a creature of fragmented hysteria. Nora missed the relative stillness of her early morning walks to the office in Tampere: cars and buses passing on a much smaller scale, young children heading to school, magpies hopping amid leaves, lush pink and purple lilacs. She thought of the massive lakes—one mere blocks from her apartment and the other across town—and the river, snaking through downtown with its own waterfall. Here she had the Hudson River, with its gray lulling waves, giant cruise ships, sailboats, ferries and Lady Liberty at the mouth to the sea. An occasional kayaker or whale sighting made her smile. She almost forgot the city belonged to nature, too. She vowed to saunter in Central and Riverside Parks, to check out Van Cortlandt, Pelham Bay, Inwood Hill, and Prospect Park.

Her parents opened the door to their house, and then lit candles on a belated birthday cake for Nora. All her tension and guilt evaporated that weekend in Bethesda, as Nora regaled them of her life overseas. Her mom kept linking her arm through Nora's; her dad seemed frailer than she remembered, but high in spirits. His first round of treatment was over. He needed to rest, but he and the doctor were optimistic. Zelda waited on him with an attentiveness Nora had never seen. "What do you want to drink, dear?" she asked her husband. Zelda had put on a few pounds, yet she didn't gripe about it.

"We want to hear your stories," her mother said, "but we can't process them all at once. You said you'd visit us more often?"

"Nora let me look at you," said her dad, sitting in his favorite recliner chair. "Whatever they fed you, whatever you've been drinking, it agrees with you."

After they ate cake, he showed her a device he had been building. It charged multiple electronic products at once. "Dad," Nora said, "keep away from electromagnetic fields. When the Y2K bug hits in a few months, your devices are going to crash, so back them up." He listened as she spoke of Bethany, Winn and Ville, and her work at Nokia—how they celebrated her final presentation. She shared about spiritual and emotional cleanses in the saunas. She neglected to mention heavy drinking in bars, her encounter with Nate's cousins or her travails with Jussi.

She went back into the kitchen where her mom cleaned up. "I have something for you." She handed her a box that contained a necklace of silver swans, facing each other and forming a heart-shape. "A symbol of Finland," Nora said.

Her mom asked Nora to close the clasp around her neck. She beamed.

Nora presented her dad with a box of dark Fazer chocolates, a tie clip with the Finnish flag and a book about Finnish history (that included a long chapter on Nokia). She also left behind a poster by the artist Harro and a Nightwish CD for Ben, who would be visiting soon. She wished he was there to complete their family unit. She wanted to inform them all at once. For the time being, she withheld her significant pronouncement.

Back in Manhattan, Nora had no crew. Like a glass marble rolling down a toy ramp with byways and openings, she crossed a bedazzling array of loops indeterminately. The city as maze, with so many choices…a mass of humanity from all over the world. She had finally figured out her niche in Tampere; now she was back, waiting on the right ramp to begin her next foray.

While they ate breakfast at their favorite diner, Nora listened to

Off the Yoga Mat

Lonnie gab about the final preparations for her upcoming nuptials.

"You won't believe the amazing mansion in the Hamptons my great aunt offered for the ceremony and reception," she said. "Right out of *Gatsby*"

It's my turn to be supportive, Nora thought. I can't bomb her with statistics on sperm donors and inseminations. Nora believed Lonnie's role as her personal sounding board and sympathetic advisor would take shelter in an inconvenient limbo. As the bride-to-be, Lonnie was like a Jane Austen heroine—one who advised others with decency and charm—about to receive her due. Nora felt like a weary traveler, opening her logbook of experience. No interpreter could fathom the richness of her sojourn.

When she got back to her apartment, she took out a catalogue of sperm donors she had sent for before departing for Finland. She punched holes in the side of some pages, placed them in a binder and circled three. Potential for Nora meant a good education, few health problems and well-rounded pursuits for a young man, such as tennis playing, art-loving and a penchant for travel. She knew there was a random messiness to the idea of creating a well-curated baby for the new century. After a few days, she called to order more detailed profiles of the donors. These included health histories and lists of personality traits of a few of the entrants, who were known by only their numbers. She chose a Texan scientist, who was a mix of African-American, Native American, and Irish-American; a soccer player/musician of Dutch and East Indian descent, and a Jewish philosopher from Berkeley, whose favorite sport was ping pong. Donors with complex heritage for the new, more tolerant century. She sent an email to Winn, asking him to discuss with Doris his offer to donate sperm.

Nora didn't let shame or fear stop her from attending the meeting. Run by a group of women who were single or divorced, and mostly in her age group; some were adopting while others were trying to get pregnant via anonymous donor insemination. A few had chosen a friend, or someone with whom they made an arrangement to be a "known" donor. One woman found her sperm donor in *The Village Voice* personal ads. Someday we'll laugh or consider these choices no big deal, Nora thought. She wouldn't tell Lonnie about this project until after the wedding.

When she entered the conference room, located within a foundation office, where the group held their meetings, she felt overwhelmed. The women spoke of doctors, sperm banks, fertility pills, injections, hormones and ovulation. What economic and emotional support they'd rely on. One older woman who had a small child handed Nora the group's bible, a thumbed-through paperback explaining the steps to take in choosing single motherhood, starting with checking hormone levels—the first milestone in acknowledging declining fertility. Nora seemed ahead of the learning curve. The reality of having a baby moved her. It didn't matter how this child would be conceived.

Chapter Forty-Three
Shame is Pride's Cloak

(Nate)

Nate powered through his jealousy and depression by writing the rest of his dissertation in a few weeks. It was as if his dissertation was penned by a hotshot scholar on speed who eyeballed pithy statements and burdensome jargon and slashed them away. He was Offendorf's and Heddy's man, fingers clacking on keys, channeling torrid rage into words and footnotes, smoking out bullshit. He couldn't believe it when he read over the whole thing—nothing stood out to him as hideous or jumbled. He thought: did I actually write that? *Finito! Dénouement!* He wanted to celebrate, but if he let himself feel anything, it would unleash the compartment where he stored despair. All he could manage was to smoke a joint, listen to bebop on his radio and take himself to a red-sauce Italian restaurant a few blocks away with no nostalgic memories attached to it.

He set a defense date in less than a month with Offendorf, who congratulated him and then complained that Raul Zazūk had been forced onto Nate's committee by the English Department chair. The thesis mother-lode was about to lift; Nate couldn't be distracted by academic turf wars. What a change to feel a pleasant breeze while writing versus a chill, thinking about Lulu.

Nate's back and neck ached; twinges coursed through his arms. Sciatica ravished his hip like an old man. He half-heartedly tried to find another yoga class because any yoga reminded him of Lulu and his still smoldering passion; he recognized he *would* have been even more outraged had she slept with another man. If that made him a sexist homophobe, so be it. He knew from scientific research that love and jealousy were addictions, embedded in the reptilian core of the brain. Sexual infidelity by a woman he perceived as "his" came as a blow to his primordial male ego. That information didn't deaden his pain. The fact that she cheated on him with a woman made him feel inadequate. Lulu and Donna's pact wiped him off the earth, and he returned to his cowering adolescent self. He couldn't help envisioning Lulu making it with others, too. Imagination met indignation.

He resorted to long sullen evening walks in Alphabet City and the Lower East Side, predicting with harsh resentment which couples he passed would deceive one another. As he approached a pair waiting for the light to change, Nate almost shouted, "Might as well call it off, buddy, before she cheats on you!"

He prowled like a lone wolf outside the pack, hoping some hunter would pick him off.

He trolled deserted streets and those rocking with nightlife. He imagined he saw Lulu whenever he passed near her apartment or studio, even though that building was padlocked. Any glint of upper-body tattoo art on a woman, any pixie-haired buxom gal strolling or on the arm of a date, any near whiff of jasmine disassembled what remained of his peace of mind. Fear fed his demons. He wanted to hide from but also re-encounter her.

When he calmed down, he remembered. She had spoken of love. The jealous man believes in love more than he believes in life. She had found something tragic from her past; he should have shown her some compassion.

Gil asked him to get together. He didn't want to, but he decided it would distract him from the full throttle of his obsession.

"You look like a hungover werewolf," Gil remarked, over cheap beers at Holiday Lounge. "Do me a favor—take a shower. Shave." They started to play a game of pool, but when Nate leaned across the table to attempt a tough shot, he swore he spotted Lulu passing outside from the corner of his eye.

"Gotta go," Nate shouted, the cue thudding to the floor.

It was her! He knew to keep his distance. She carried heavy bags, appeared thin and fatigued. He couldn't read her face. He wanted to grab her packages, accompany her home, collapse into her arms. He needed to know if she planned any rendezvous. So, he followed. As her building's outer gate slammed shut, he couldn't assume there'd be no one waiting upstairs. He stuck around outside the building for an hour before staggering home, smoking a wad of hash Gil had gifted him. Cockroaches scurried across the floor. Moths multiplied. He wished he could be interred inside the walls, like one of Edgar Allan Poe's madmen.

His mom called for their customary weekend chat. He shouldn't have picked up the phone. He mumbled hello, then grunted.

"What's the matter?" Audrey asked.

"Everything. I'm not discussing it," he said, with a sarcasm resembling his father's. "Don't try to cheer me up."

"Can't be all bad," Audrey said.

"It's worse."

"I know you're on some kind of substance that exaggerates your feelings," she said. "You've got to stop smoking pot...or whatever it is. I'll pay for therapy. This has to be about that woman you've been seeing. Nothing gets you so worked up."

"Yes. It's that woman. She...."

"Take it easy. Don't be a fatalist, or sexist. Trust me. There are lots of women. Is Nora still single?"

"Stop. I have to go."

"Before I forget," she added, "Danny's wedding is the Saturday after July 4th. Shortly after your defense. Write it down. Come to our house. We'll drive over together."

That's right, Danny boy, whose achievements stood as a counterpoint to Nate's history of fucking up. A wedding was the last event he'd willingly attend. His cousin's run as a hot shot lawyer and loving groom would be on full display. Nate planned to get heavily sedated.

He got off the phone with a gruff goodbye. Didn't get out of bed.

Later, he took refuge in a volume of William Blake that Monica had mailed him, along with a few other books, as a fortieth birthday gift. The visionary English romantic poet and artist, with prophetic aspirations in "The Marriage of Heaven and Hell." Nate read these words: "*Without constraint, no progression…shame is pride's cloak…you never know what is enough unless you know what is more than enough. What is now proved was only once imagined; to the Devourer it seems as if the producer was in his chains; but it is not so, he only takes portions of existence and fancies that the whole. Opposition is true friendship.*" They provided some perspective. Quieted his frantic judgmental self for a time. This rift with Lulu created realizations and deep reflection, portions of the whole. He cleared some space on his torn carpet to stretch, execute a warrior pose. With one foot turned, the other straight and his arms taut, he folded over. He shut off the stream of invective. Then, he supported his legs and arms on the floor as he moved into plank and downward-facing dog.

***

With more free time, he started to hang around again with the freegans, listening as they discussed the agenda to disrupt the global summit in September. He agreed on principle. They felt optimistic about the year 2000 (as long as they took action and didn't sit back).

"I'm not signing up for anything," he told Anita.

It was inevitable he'd run into Mariel Day. Now he knew what it felt like to have someone you trust pull the rug out from under you. He apologized again, his voice cracking, his eyes downcast. She accepted but kept her distance. Seeing Mariel, he recalled his inability to acknowledge Nora's desire for a child; he pushed her away because it was easier than considering such a commitment.

His old friend Gil had become embedded in the freegan scene to be around Anita. Gil philosophized to heartsick Nate.

"Too much suffering, my friend. No woman is worth it. Let's plan a blowout party for when you've kissed off the dissertation."

Nate couldn't envision such a party. "I'm bad company."

"No worse than usual," Gil said, lightly pounding Nate in the gut.

Nate could barely tolerate Gil's antics. He summoned the strength to deal with him.

Nate got used to sifting through garbage bags and dumpsters with aplomb. They were experts at cooking spicy stews with what they found; Nate took solace in the way hot chilies burned through him. He had also agreed to provide some office work for the activists, zipping off a press release and a few solicitation letters to raise funds and publicize their movement. During those moments, he didn't focus on betrayal and loss but on changing society from the grass roots—the place to begin. The freegans provided a sustainable fortress of hope. There were so many others in the city and the world with worse problems than his. He should be grateful for all he had. He began to feel lighter, guilty about his privilege and the gift of luck.

Something inside him broke down, internal composting. One evening he ended up next to Gil inside a larger dumpster. They flung scraps at each other, mischievous boys hauling the baggage of deranged men.

"Make believe I'm Lulu," Gil egged him on. "Go ahead. Speak your mind."

Nate threw a hard, bitten bagel at Gil's head.

Gil ducked. "Missed me! Nate Dart—sulky baby." He picked up a random handful of garbage, tossed it hard at Nate's back. "Get over it," Gil shouted. "You're not some great catch. We've all been burned. Yet we survive."

"Never said I was a catch," Nate replied, falling into the pile. It was true. Why did he think he had a real shot with Lulu Betancourt? So, it turned out that monogamy was not her strong suit. But then again, he hadn't realized he wanted commitment, a love that might last. Assumptions hang over us. Jealousy contains the word lousy. Lulu said that she loved him even as he shunned her. He lay down quietly in the refuse pile, *savasana* in hell. Blake would have approved.

Gil lobbed over a hunk of rotten meat that left a stain on Nate's chest. He removed it.

"I'm done," Nate shouted. "Finished with all of this."

"Surrendering?" Gil said, out of breath, waving. "We're filthy, foolish and ready to roll, my friend."

"Is everything alright in there?" Some freegans called to them from outside the dumpster.

"Yes and no," Gil responded. "But we didn't spoil anything edible if that's what concerns you."

"Listen, Gil," Nate said, moving closer. "You think you're helping me, slogging it out, playing games, saying women aren't worth much. Look at us. We're grown men. Middle-aged. Not those losers from high school."

"Speak for yourself," Gil said.

"Something has to give," Nate said. "Let's grow up—dissing women isn't the way to go. No more games and delusions. We've got to move on."

"Oh yeah?" Gil said, shoving his hand into a bag, feeling around. "Why so serious?"

"I don't have the answers," said Nate. "But for starters, we can behave less like Bart Simpson. I'm going now. I don't think you're capable of understanding."

Gil started to laugh.

"You forced yourself on Lulu. I can't be your friend."

Before Gil could defend himself or make light of it, Nate climbed out of the dumpster and headed home.

After cleaning up, he did a three-part breath to aerate his system. He thought of Lulu. She had said she was devastated over what she learned in New Orleans. If she really loved him…why should he even attempt to control her? Mariel hadn't guilt tripped him. Nora wanted to have a baby *with him*. Terrifying. Beautiful, too.

Donna lived far away. During rational moments, it did not make sense to worry about what he could not control. He didn't know Lulu's plans for another yoga studio…for her life. There were people who preferred open relationships, and he hadn't judged them. Most of his relationships had been casual or short-term. It was time to admit he was a great traditionalist who hadn't been ready. Until now. When he loved, he grew possessive and jealous. He wanted to try on something shiny—no longer wear victim drab. It might not work out with Lulu Betancourt. But it wasn't over.

***

Nate's realization boosted his confidence as he traveled to Maryland to defend his dissertation in late June, before everyone left campus for summer. He had been told by others who went through the process that a Ph.D. defense was a mere "formality." Offendorf and the other two members of his committee would ask obvious questions about the manuscript, possibly query how he would go about seeking publication. Audrey and Albert drove him down to Maryland State University. They waited in the lounge, dressed in their summer finest, while he stepped into the small conference room. His parents were going to join the committee afterwards for a celebratory meal.

Offendorf's face appeared flushed, his hair uncombed, as he walked into the seminar room. Nate noticed a shirt button popped open against the prof's belly. Why did his advisor look even more lackluster and disheveled than usual? Raul Zazŭk, a product of the Yale School, stood lean and oh-so-cool in leather pants; his mechanical arm was covered mostly by his suit jacket. A late addition to the committee, he had never returned Nate's calls or emails. The third member of the defense was Dr. Celeste Cordero, a professor from comparative lit who had chaired Monica's committee. Nate had only spoken to her once about a few of his chapters. Monica assured him she'd be fabulous.

Offendorf banged his fist on the table. "Here, here. Let us commence so it won't be long before we get a stiff drink. We've all read Nathaniel Dart's dissertation. We know he's been focused on writing for many a year. We can ask for clarifications or give him feedback so that he can make minor adjustments before depositing his copy for binding. I shall start by saying I was quite pleased with the revisions he made since I last perused these pages. I'm especially fond of the chapter on *King*

Lear and sibling rivalry. I suggest you send that chapter out as an article, Nate."

"I liked that one too," said Professor Cordero. "There are a few minor revisions I'd suggest. I can recommend a couple of journals that might be interested."

Zazŭk cleared his throat. "Excuse me. I was asked to join this defense quite late as a favor to the chair; I must say that for me, Darwin is an interloper in this project. Mr. Dart needs to refer to Lacanian psychoanalysis to analyze jealousy in Shakespeare, not refer to stereotypes based on animals in the wild. I cannot support this dissertation in its current form."

"What?" Nate asked, amazed. Could this professor really object? His heart started to pound like a hammer. "But Dr. Zazŭk, I examine human gender and sex roles in relation to Darwin's species-based theories."

"I am sorry," Zazŭk continued. "In my book *Post-Nomad Uncanny,* which you should have read, I discuss dread and perception as praxis in literary texts, scientific discourse and art. With your reliance on Darwin, you merge unconscious processes into some predetermined biological miasma, like fitness or the behavior of renegade finches. If I'm to sign off, you must revise."

Offendorf and Cordero sat in stunned silence. Nate threw up his hands.

"Professor Offendorf went over his objections six months ago; Professor Cordero didn't ask me to edit much." Nate struggled to control an inclination to erupt.

He kept talking, hoping his chatter would soften the blow. "I added a section on the commodification of human intimacy, how we are influenced in late capitalism to objectify and fear each other's differences. That was…kind of personal. Monica Portman recommended I take the work in that direction," Nate said.

"Monica Portman," said Professor Cordero. "I am pleased that you consulted her."

Offendorf coughed. He rose from his low chair. "Don't you worry, Nate," he said, staring at his colleague. "I will take care of this. Zazŭk, it's too late for you. Nate will NOT go back over his work to fulfill your masturbatory desires. His Darwin is rendered non-essentialist due to his use of feminists like Kristeva and Donna Haraway. His knowledge is situated, partial, as is all of ours. Since I am retiring at the end of the month for reasons I can't legally disclose, I say cease and desist. Fuck off. Case closed."

And so, to Nate's astonishment and by some incredible piece of luck, it was.

Chapter Forty-Four
Compensation

(Lulu)

Lulu struggled to accept the hurt she had inflicted and the losses that followed. She stayed locked in her apartment, stretched across her unmade bed, unable to exert herself or even shower. She barely slept. As the yogis say, desire that hurts another is destructive…her desire engulfed surrounding islands. She wouldn't claim trauma as an excuse, but she believed the abuse she suffered had affected everything else.

Seeing Nate jealous and hurt reinforced love's frightening grip. She had avoided commitments over the years, except to her students and her practice. Nate touched her deeply when he opened up and revealed himself; he cleaned up her studio after it was ransacked—no small favor. Like Rosa's love, hers was tinged with allowances, denials, silences. And she had deceived Donna, used her as a means to heal, then took off. Triangular love might seem solid, but not in this case. She had gotten away with narcissistic relationships, surface connections, dalliances. Truthfully, she had enjoyed some of them. Her erotic life followed a proud, if troubled, trajectory. She wanted to enter a new phase. The good news, she supposed, was that neither Nate nor Donna fit the old categories. They were ripe and round connections. She had wanted to drink the red and the white. She heard about non-monogamous liaisons, called "polyamory," where three or more linked lovers resided together, or took multiple partners by consent, an arrangement like the open marriages of yore. It sounded temping, but inconsistent with her desire to practice self-restraint and develop stronger boundaries.

She couldn't reach out to anyone. There were no classes to hold, nothing to do but to wallow. But after a week of brooding, barely eating or sleeping, Lulu phoned Donna. Calmly, she told her she planned to make a quick trip to New Orleans soon. She would move Rosa back north to the shore. In a shaky voice, she shared some of what had transpired when she informed Nate about them, but she didn't get into his jealous rage or how he had thrown her out.

"You've been through a lot in a short time," Donna said. "You're raw. Find another place to teach yoga. And get a good therapist."

"Sound advice," Lulu said. "I don't have the strength."

"You do. I know you."

"Thanks for tolerating me," Lulu said.

Lulu found pro-bono legal advice. She entered into negotiations to reach a settlement with the building management and the university. They charged her for some of the damages—still, she ended up with $50,000. But it was hard to get excited over money. Therapy was the right move, so she began to try to find someone.

While searching for space to open her bento box-inspired studio, she almost walked into the pole of a street light. One evening during June's late dusk, on East Sixth Street, she saw Nate among the freegans, packing up supplies for the day. He blended into their funk with his messy clothes, straggly hair and intense concentration. He bent over a low kettle. A pang of anger and envy rose in her—she wanted to jump into the dumpster, too, if that's what it took. Then she noticed Gil, and Mariel, so she walked off.

A realtor showed her commercial spaces. Room after room with resigned stillness, blank walls and floors like Lulu's empty plate. The future unfolded, not fixed or mechanical—influenced by yesterday, precipitating today. Some people were counting down what remained of 1999, anticipating failures in all digital clocks, a blackout, the erasure of essential data everywhere. No more "business as usual" incited panic. Lulu knew time could not be contained in any system; it consisted of small units of action and contemplation. The nines of 1999 would soon become living, breathing zeros. Uncertainty could be expressed in numbers and signs. She hoped Nate and Donna would suspend their expectations. Her time with each of them had been precious, and it enabled her to reassess what might come next. In Lulu's mind, they worked it out, she could stay with both of them. But that required a stretch.

Would Nate truly desert her? She had met his lower self: jealous and defensive, full of repressed rage, unable to accept weakness or forgive. Where was sweet, determined Nate? Could she encounter him again? They were good together. She would always love Donna, considered her kindred.

One evening, out of the corner of her eye, she saw Nate following her as she hauled groceries to her apartment. It was tempting to let on that she noticed, but she decided not to. Something inside of her accepted that creepy Nate cared for her.

In time, Lulu practiced postures in her apartment and chanted extra-long. Kneeling at her altar, she made a request to her spiritual guides: *Deliver loving kindness. Let Nate and Donna forgive me. Let me absolve Rosa and the others, living and dead, who violated us. Help me temper my impulsive desires.* She chanted *lo-ca-sama-stah-sukhi-no-Bhavantu. Om Shanti.* She tried to do a headstand (*sirsasana*) against the wall. She failed to stay centered; her legs buckled.

July, 1999

Chapter Forty-Five
The Wedding Reunion

(Nate)

Shortly after Independence Day, Nate Dart, Ph.D., stood in an opulent banquet hall in Southampton, the elegant Long Island beach town known for its celebrities, artists and upscale decadence. He was wearing a white linen suit. Outside, tents stood on the sprawling, manicured lawn and a platform dance floor baked in the sun. Indoors, the air conditioning blasted icicles. Out of the corner of his eye, Nate spotted Nora. At the nuptials of his cousin Daniel! He felt a chill up his legs and his brain hit pause. What was *she* doing here? He crossed his eyes trying to figure it out. A throng of guests anticipated the grand entrance of the bride, Lonnie.

Nate's disoriented response to the discovery of his ex-girlfriend at the affair, coupled with his cloying parents, made him cringe. With new credentials he could stand tall, claim authority. But, as it turned out, he had encountered Lulu only yesterday. They came to a halt on a crowded section of St. Mark's Place near Second Avenue. Hasty pedestrians clogged the sidewalk as they stood figuring out what to say.

"How are you, Nate?" she murmured. "I'm late for an appointment."

She checked her watch. Someone bumped into her.

"Are you okay?" He almost pulled her into his arms.

"I'm fine, thanks." She shifted her purse from her arm to her shoulder.

He could tell by the tone of her voice. She's not even close to fine.

"I've been to Maryland again," he said. "And I came back."

She blinked. "Your dissertation defense? Can I say hurrah?"

"You can. I was hoping we could…I don't know." Celebrate? Talk? He wasn't sure what he wanted.

"Listen. I've got to run." She scanned the crowds down the street. But then she gazed at him, expressing sympathetic affirmation, her wide eyes projecting tenderness. That's how he interpreted it. Did it matter that neither of them could use words? He knew what he knew. Her pride wouldn't let her admit she missed him.

Now, here stood Nora. Dolled up, about to go off for some photographs with the rest of the wedding party. Then he realized it. Lonnie—a close friend of Nora's whom he had forgotten about. She's marrying his cousin! He felt lightheaded. He'd inquire about that trip Nora took to Finland, a safe subject. He wondered if she knew he defended his dissertation—contentious baggage that had marred their relationship.

Nate watched the bridesmaids, engaged in chit-chat as the photographer made them pose, alone and then with the groomsmen. In an off-the-shoulder mauve gown, Nora appeared strikingly Grecian. He recalled she once worshiped him like an emperor.

When the bridesmaids and groomsmen broke up their coffee klatch, he approached Nora.

"It's only me," he mumbled, fighting the sun's glare and his feelings of queasiness.

"Well hello, Nate." She pinched the lapel of his jacket. "Have I seen you in this suit?"

"Probably," he answered. As it was a gift from his mother for graduation, she had not. "How did it go in Finland?"

"I had an amazing time," she said, flipping her hair. "Guess what? I interviewed your mom's cousin for my Nokia phone surveys. Great folks! You should meet them."

"Really?" He smiled. "Strange coincidence. How did you know I had family there?

"My great memory. And guess what? There's a chance Nokia might offer me a job."

"No kidding. You'd move back?"

"I don't know. I'm definitely planning to return. To do research. Maybe write a book."

Did she say *book*? "What kind of a book?"

"About Finnish saunas. They are a deep cultural expression of spirit and nature, a kind of social therapy. By the way, they pronounce it sow-na. With an 'ow' sound."

"I had no idea." In fact, it struck him as quite whimsical, even scholarly (in a pop culture way). Maybe Nora's stories about Finland would carry him through the day.

"Tell me," she said, moving under a tent where bartenders poured drinks. "Is it true you've finished your dissertation? Defended it? Massive congratulations!" She patted his shoulder, pressed herself lightly into his chest while holding a drink in one hand.

"Yup. It's over," he exclaimed, dabbing the sweat from his forehead, surprised she half embraced him. "Despite a near setback. One of the committee members wanted me to read his book, take a totally different approach. Offendorf overrode him," Nate said, grasping the miracle of closure for the umpteenth time. "Can you believe Offendorf *defended* my use of Darwin and feminism? He's retiring. Before him and his favorite grad student are investigated for some grading scam." He assumed Monica had a hand in that development.

"Sounds like a complicated situation. You made it out alive." Nora looked him up and down. "By the way, your hair needs attention. Haven't you found anyone besides me who has a way with scissors?"

"I like it long," he said, frowning.

"You're sulking? I assumed you'd be intolerably arrogant."

He nodded. "You know how when you solve one problem, another appears? It's like that." He let out a shallow breath. "I didn't realize my cousin Daniel was dating your friend Lonnie."

"I didn't put two and two together, either," she said. "It happened in a flash, mostly while I was away. I didn't know who she was dating…let alone marrying. They met at a little gathering we organized."

"*You* organized," he said. "I got in the way."

He wouldn't have paid attention. Yet, if they had been the ones who prompted Daniel and Lonnie's courtship, perhaps he could forge a less-than-bitter association with that know-it-all relative.

"We may have unwittingly greased the wheel," she nodded. "Anyway, based on what Lonnie tells me, they're well suited. I was preoccupied. Had my share of misadventures while I was away."

"You dumped me to go on a quest. What happened?"

She fanned herself with a droopy napkin. "I didn't dump you. As I recall, you pushed me away, and I left town. I did think about you. A few times."

How about that? Ironic, even flattering. What could he say? "I'm getting another drink. Excuse me, Nora."

"Catch you later," she said, fanning harder. "I'm melting."

***

His mother gestured with her head. He moved inside the door where she stood.

"What's up mother?"

"Don't be angry," she said. "I've got to say something. Nora makes a stunning maid of honor. Imagine her as your bride, if you worked it out. Bring her over. I'd like to say hello."

"She's busy," Nate said haltingly. He didn't want to get into a blow up over his mom's meddling. "Neither of us knew Daniel had fallen for her friend. Nora's been away. Working abroad." He failed to mention the meeting with Audrey's relatives.

He hadn't disclosed any details of his affair with Lulu, or the reason for their break up. His parents were basking in the glow of his doctorate. He inhaled his mother's aspirations, overlaid with piquant bouquets. He grabbed another high ball.

Everyone was told to come indoors, take their seats. After a few unsettling minutes, a booming voice announced: "Mr. and Mrs. Daniel Moss!" The pair entered to wild cheers and applause. His cousin, fit and tall in his gray and white tux, bowed to the adorning crowd. Some folks whistled after each move. Someone yelled "Hey, Danny Boy! You the man!" Lonnie, with her long train pinned up, let out a whoop and pumped her fist. She ran a victory lap around her groom as disco music boomed.

After toasts and a foxtrot (featuring dangerously low dips by the bridal couple), loud rock alternating with R&B erupted from massive speakers. There were flutes of champagne and finger foods served on trays. A buffet and full bar materialized inside, while a mellow two-piece band played outside on the patio. Nate had no appetite for revelry or food. He wished he could shrink inside his suit, appear as a headless specter. He leaned against a Doric column and stared as Nora eased a little out of her frock, dancing the twist. That bare shoulder of hers, that cleavage! Next, Nora sashayed to "Billie Jean" with his dad. Nate forced a grin. Nora owned her sensuality in a way she hadn't before. He stirred his drink with a swizzle stick. Why hadn't he appreciated her?

His mother stood next to him, applauding her husband's snazzy moves. Finally, Nora came by. Embraced his mother.

"I'm returning your husband."

"You wore him out."

"He's energetic. How have you been? Such great news—your nephew's marriage to Lonnie. And Nate is a Ph.D.!"

"I can't quite wrap my mind around it. We are thrilled." She grabbed Nora's arm and spoke softly into her ear. When her voice raised several registers, Nate could hear most of it.

"Give my son another…chance. He's lost without you."

Livid, Nate turned away.

Then Nora said something to his mom that he couldn't make out. Whatever it was, Audrey smiled, but then grew silent. Her lips curved downward. Nora hadn't taken the bait. She gazed at Nate with sullen brown eyes and pulpy mascara, a full-on nostalgic vibe.

"Wanna dance?" she queried. He shook his head, no. He couldn't.

But he wondered what it would be like to get close to her *now*. He downed his drink in two gulps. He'd wizened up. What transpired in Finland that breathed controlled fire into her? She seemed less high-strung. The cloying odor of mums, dahlias, forsythias tickled his nose; he still pined for Lulu's earthy jasmine. He envisioned an odd introduction: *Lulu, meet Nora. Glorious and tender, she tolerated this tousled soul. Prepared me for you. Nora, behold Lulu. She betrayed me, has me tied up in knots, but stokes my heart's and cock's desire.* These dangerous beltway beauties, he mused, these women from metro Washington, D.C. Sirens lined the Potomac.

Chapter Forty-Six
Belatedness

(Nora)

"Where are we going?" Nora queried, stumbling in her heels and spilling her drink, reluctantly dragged off by Nate in white linen. She thought he'd consented to a waltz. For old times. He jerked her arm.

"I have a surprise," he said. She stopped resisting. She liked surprises. "It's noisy here. Sweltering outside. With my parents flitting about, we can't have a conversation. I found a quieter place."

Before the wedding dinner was served, the exes climbed a spiral staircase to the second floor of the mansion. Nate escorted her down the hallway into a suite with a dressing table and mirrored-lights, a full-length mirror, long fuchsia sofa, plush chairs and thick cranberry drapes. Long-stemmed roses stood in slender vases around the room. A ceiling fan spun. Lonnie's ready room. Nora knew better than to sneak in, but Nate insisted. She wondered what he wanted to say after months of silence.

She picked up the bouquet on the dressing table, sniffed it, felt the unforgiving pinch of her gown's waistband. Too many *hors d'oeuvres* out of stress, out of habit. She hadn't had time to tell Audrey about meeting her relatives. She thought of how his mom urged her to reconnect with Nate.

"Sit," he gestured. She sank into the plush cushion.

"So," said Nate, sitting beside her. "What happened in Finland? Tell me something substantial."

Strains of Prince's song "Let's Go Crazy" filtered in from downstairs.

"Nothing much," she said. It felt like old times, but lighter. Fine to catch up, but she'd already released him. "Why do you want to know?"

"Making polite conversation," he said.

"I'll boil it down. A lot happened in a short time. For starters, I let go of you—I had to. And I escaped my lecherous boss. Then came a few painful crushes, and I made wonderful friends. I learned about Finnish culture...how they plan to handle a Y2K meltdown. And the sauna culture, it's religious, really," she said, uncrossing her leg. "I even had a Finnish boyfriend. But, listen Nate. There's a serious consequence of the trip."

"What?" he asked, leaning closer.

"Towards the end I realized it, and when I got home, it became even more obvious," she said. "I am going to get inseminated. Next week. With an anonymous donor's sperm. I want to raise a child."

He gulped his vodka tonic and squeezed his eyes shut. "I know you do. But that's extreme. A child needs two parents." Nate stood up, walked to the dressing table, put down his empty glass. "Too hard to handle alone."

He looked angry; perhaps he felt remorse. Nora took a breath. "I know it's not easy. But I can't wait at my age. It's not like I haven't tried," she said. "With you. With others, too."

"Okay. I get it." He paced between the mirror and the door. Then he stood in front of her. "Good luck," he pronounced. The percussive rhythms of Talking Heads' "Burning Down the House" vibrated through the floor.

Nora intuited his jealously, and her plan appeared to challenge men's role in parenting. But Nate had thrown away his chance to join her.

He stared where her gown dipped low—her shoulders, one of their favorite erogenous zones. Perhaps she evoked that famous, unravished bride of quietness depicted in John Keats' famous ode, a poem Nate had recited to her. Nora stood up and preened in front of the full-length mirror.

"You look hot," Nate muttered. "I should have complimented you...more," he said, slurring his words. "I was preoccupied. Immature."

She couldn't believe what she was hearing.

"I appreciate you saying that. Sometimes you *were* unreason-able." She'd never get over how powerfully she had loved him, despite his childish, narcissistic antics. "I didn't handle certain things very well either. I'm sorry it ended the way it did. Something's different about you, Nate. I shared my secret. What's yours?"

He walked to the sofa. Planted himself there. Nora leaned towards the vanity mirrors where Lonnie had gussied up, primped her hair, applied make-up. She beheld her own face, thinking, not bad at all.

"You'll enjoy this," Nate said. "I...actually got really jealous. Hid-eous. Blew up, wanted to commit violent acts, self-flagellation, stalking her. Still haven't flushed it out of my system. But I suppose it's brought about some insight."

"Nate Dart! Wish I was wearing a wire to record your confession. What happened?"

"I started seeing my yoga teacher," he said. "She two-timed me. It's tearing me apart."

Nora threw back her head, absorbed his words. Her waistband pinched callously. This woman who provoked his jealous passion...who was she? Nora fished for appropriate words in her confused state. His yoga teacher? Good grief.

"It's terrible to experience rage and frustration, Nate," she said. "Welcome to the human race." Nora plopped down next to him, patted his thigh. "It will get better—you'll see," she said. "You stuck with yoga?" She felt woozy. She might have to lie down.

"Yes. I try to practice regularly. Lulu spent a lot of time helping me because, well, you know my back problems, my lack of flexibility," he said. In the flush of his cheeks and the glow of his eyes, Nora discerned his tender feelings for the woman in question.

"We have to go downstairs," she said. "We're trespassing."

"Thanks for loitering with me." He gave her a generous hug, held her as they stood there. Her eyes teared up.

"Nora," he said, "I'm sorry I didn't treat you right. I couldn't help it. I hope you find success...with the baby thing. And the Finland proj-ects."

He found some tissues and took one, dabbing her eyes. "Your mascara is running."

"Thanks, Nate. Best of luck to you, too." She searched for the right words. "Get a handle on your jealousy. The forgiveness part...will be amazing. Experience all your emotions." She touched his chest where the jacket lapels fell away. That woman was lucky—Nate found her at this ripe juncture in his life.

"Just a minute," Nora said, pressing against him again for old time's sake. She planted a small kiss on Nate's cheek, then withdrew. He seemed surprised. He put his arm around her neck and kissed her back, on the lips. Nora's heart-beat crested.

Nate's hand ran up her leg and under her dress, searching, probing. His lips were all over the curve of her shoulder, and he pushed her down on the sofa, her pulse rushing into her ears. It felt amazing. Fast, no time for rational thought. He pulled down his fancy trousers, his erection pushing out. She surrendered to wildness as he stroked her wetness and then entered her. Like their early times together, wordless want and delirium.

After their hot, quick tryst left them out of breath, Nora and Nate eyed each other like thieves escaping with treasure.

"We needed that," he said, swallowing air.

"Lightning strikes," said Nora, sweaty, pleasantly disheveled. She straightened her dress, ran her fingers through her tousled hair. "Were you evening the score?"

He didn't answer.

They headed towards the spiral stairs, returning to the wedding feast, shaken, titillated, semi-composed. Audrey spotted them. She grinned.

The classical spiral staircase, long and curved, turned a corner, like time in the final summer of the twentieth century. Nora and Nate descended in slow motion.

Off the Yoga Mat

Chapter Forty-Seven
White Walls

(Lulu)

As Lulu readied Betancourt's Bento, her deluxe, spacious new studio on Allen Street—not many blocks from the old one on East Second (although it seemed like a world away)—she formally requested Nate's presence. No use leaving their next meeting to chance or prolonging any wounded indecisiveness.

Through a hand-decorated invitation, perfumed with jasmine, she summoned him by mail:

Dear Nate: my new studio bento is open but empty.
Come visit. Help me envision ways to fill it.
Lulu

She figured it was his move now.

She had settled Rosa back at Mary's place in Ocean Grove, the alcohol-free Mecca on the Jersey shore where Mary said she could stay until winter. During a brief visit to New Orleans, Lulu had handed Mrs. Lady some cash to supplement Monroe's veteran's benefits. She had also persuaded Monroe's daughter, her cousin Anne in Baton Rouge, to look in on her father. Lulu signed Monroe up for a creative writing workshop for veterans at a local community center. Mrs. Lady said she'd remind him to attend. "Monroe is a natural poet," she said, hinting at the possibility that she might tag along and try her hand at writing, too.

Lulu went to see Donna. She missed her company but felt it best to speak plainly.

"For the unforeseeable future, I'll be busy in my new studio," said Lulu. "I couldn't have done it without you." They worked in the small garden in front of Donna's cottage. Lulu's nightmares came and went with less intensity; she found she could intervene in certain dreams, will herself to swim to her island away from Ridley's demands. Lucid dreaming, they called it. Naming the demon and knowing the circumstances had diminished his strength.

Lulu pulled weeds as Donna watered flowers. She turned to face Lulu.

"Do what you have to," Donna said, pressing on the spigot. Then, she shut it off.

Lulu attempted to upend stalks that wouldn't give. "I'm really sorry we couldn't make it work."

"Me, too," said Donna.

Lulu knew of Donna's rich life, fueled by her job at the school, her hours coaching the girls, her support group and volunteering at the art gallery with Jeff. No promises or platitudes needed. Kneeling, they pruned weeds. When they stood, and it was time for Lulu to go, they hugged rather formally.

Two weeks after she had sent Nate the note, Lulu paced the empty bento studio. Then she stood still, giving herself time to drink it in before pacing again. Nate phoned to say he'd drop by. She surveyed the two large rooms set aside for yoga. A small room for training or conferences. Every footstep on the floor echoed off the walls. Time warped, a special effect of blankness in empty space.

When Nate showed up, they stood miles apart.

"Whoa," said Nate. "This place is huge."

"I know. Thank you for coming. How are you doing?"

"Well."

She found herself pitching to him like a real-estate agent. "This room is 900 square feet, and the one over there is even bigger. Where I'll hold hatha, pre-natal and gentle yoga depends on enrollment," she said.

"I'll hire someone to work with local children, recruited from schools and housing projects." It occurred to her that Donna would have been the perfect teacher, but it was not meant to be.

Nate nodded.

"See the large kitchen? I envision three tables, accommodating lunch once a week for the homeless and hungry...with help from the freegans, volunteers, and donations. Ginny and Anita are on board."

"It's ambitious. Your energy will be pulled away from teaching."

"True. But I'm ready for change," she said, conscious of avoiding the "you and I" conversation. Blank walls multiplied their withholding. Neither Lulu nor Nate perused the other. They stood at right angles.

Lulu kept talking. "In time, the upstairs room will be sound-proofed. We'll rent it out as a rehearsal space for musicians. To generate income. Eventually, I might open a small café, serving vegetarian sushi, noodles and smoothies." Lulu gnawed at the nail on her little finger.

"Quite an enterprise," he said. "Not a replica of the old studio."

"I miss the spirit of that place. Terribly. It's time to take this leap." She paused for a second, exhaling, clearing her throat. She was unsure of what to say—hoped that he'd jump in. Although standing apart, they eyeballed each other. He appeared taller and thinner. His hair neat, shorter. Sensual brown eyes, with their undercurrent of sorrow. He wore a clean white t-shirt, form-fitting jeans. What a far cry from the scraggly pothead who had stumbled into her life last winter.

"I've got to move to the next phase," she said. "Listen, Nate. I'll make you an offer. Of peace, reconciliation. If you'll allow me," she lightly skimmed his arm. "I am very sorry that I hurt you. And that I wasn't honest."

"Thank you for saying it again. I went berserk," he said. "I stalked you. I'm basically a jealous brute."

She looked him over. He had shaved. "One sexy brute."

He looked pleased. "I have to ask you something," he said. "I won't make assumptions, but here goes: If you and I...consider getting back together, do you plan to have anything on the side?"

"You don't mean mashed potatoes?"

He grinned. "No potatoes. No pasta. I'm serious. I don't fancy sharing when it comes to your affection."

"I don't plan to be with anyone else, Nate. But I'm far from perfect."

"Me either," he said. He touched Lulu's shoulder. "Maybe it's best to take it slow."

That was the Nate who couldn't reach his toes when he bent over. He needed coaxing. He put his hand on her shoulder. Doubt and hurt lessened in this pristine space, on the cusp of a new century.

"We can progress bit-by-bit, like we do with difficult yoga stretches," Lulu said. "You know, build trust again."

He flashed a gauzy look, his upper body relaxing. She believed he had let go of most of his rage against her. She sensed an unfamiliar openness. Pointed to the skylight above.

"My favorite feature of this place," she said. "We can lie down and watch the clouds. Please trust me, Nate."

"You should trust me too," Nate said. "I'm…willing…to give it a try."

Lulu moved closer to him. "Caution doesn't suit us, does it? Your mind is working with its fears. Mine does that too. Can we push past?"

"I hear the subway," Nate said. "The F train. Do you know how much I've missed you?" He pressed his body against Lulu's, then brushed his lips along her neck.

She leaned into it—a vibrant current up and down her shoulders and arms. "You've touched off my third rail," she said.

His kisses grew bold, more ardent. How dizzying to feel his lips against her skin. Desire—blessed relief, flaring in circles.

There were many sparkling surfaces in the new studio to housewarm with their lovemaking. First, let them lay their bodies down, admire the sky.

December, 1999

Chapter Forty-Eight
A New Millennium

(Nora)

Nora read the report from Secanor's parent firm: the Y2K virus appeared dormant in mainframe computers, but their desktop machines would go haywire and stop functioning if they didn't take charge. Jeremy had appointed her to head the committee—his form of revenge for the way she masterminded the Finland trip. He stayed on after RMC returned, but he had found a girlfriend so serial flirting and come-ons ceased (for the time being).

Naysayers believed the Y2K problem could be the electronic equivalent of the El Niño weather system, disrupting temperature patterns. To conspiracy theorists, it signified the end of the world. The U.S. spent billions to prevent any disasters; more was being budgeted. Nora recalled how Finland faced the two-digit problem. After the year 2000, they planned to change their National Identification System. Instead of entering numbers, they'd put "A" for those born in the 21st century, solving that pesky numerical conundrum.

She wondered what would happen if her unborn child (now in

its fourth month of gestation) failed to be accounted for, obliterated into a desktop gone AWOL, records erased. Finns worried about nuclear fallout from plants in the former Soviet Union, something equivalent to Chernobyl's meltdown, which spread toxic clouds over Scandinavia and required the slaughter of reindeer herds. As preparation for Y2K, Finns purchased iodine in droves to counter a radiation emergency.

Nora recommended that Secanor spend several hundred thousand dollars to monitor the situation and secure back-up systems set to operate after New Year's Day. She couldn't allot all her energy to Y2K because of the impending birth of her baby. A child of a new generation, blessed with a mother's unconditional love. Her family accepted it joyfully. When Nora walked into her parents' house, she sensed their relief—no more talk about cancer or the wait for the next scan to learn if her father had stayed in remission.

Nora planned another trip to Finland using vacation days. She would go sometime in the next couple of months, before her final trimester. Her child would not arrive there, but she needed to research her book on saunas (she wouldn't use them while expecting) and find out if a job offer from Nokia might be forthcoming. Or perhaps she'd wait. Everyone warned her life would change in ways she couldn't envision, so why make concrete plans? She weighed "before" and "after" options when thinking about travel and career path. Nora tuned into her body's rapidly changing prerogatives, measured time in the span of a fetus's developing limbs.

Nora refuted scaremongering and paranoia; she believed Y2K terror displaced the real issue, or "event horizon," the arrival of January 1, 2000. That milestone provoked anxieties including technological glitches: *deus ex machina*. The earth and its living creatures were facing pain and glory, on the edge of possibility and extinction.

She used to dread New Year's Eve, a high-pressure excuse to procure the hottest of hot dates, to mark time, watch balls drop and make feckless resolutions. In actuality, you could pursue them on your own timeline, as life dictated. Her mind flashed to Prince's anthem "1999." We were dreaming when he wrote this, she thought.

Off the Yoga Mat

The outgoing year had proven a watershed for Nora Jane Lester. In funk and soul, she trusted. Two thousand? Party, no, not over…just beginning?

Hormonally, Nora could only conjecture so much regarding clocks. She headed out to take a prenatal yoga class on the Lower East Side, recommended by none other than bossy-boss Rebecca Magum-Chin, who was a big Nora fan now that she was about to become a single mum (by choice). Nora guessed her pregnancy had revealed a defiant streak, one that had been previously unfathomable in kiss-ass Nora. If only RMC knew that Nora had drunkenly made love with her ex-boyfriend at her best friend's wedding the week before her first insemination, stressing over which shot of sperm would do the deed—only to get her period three-tense-weeks later. That led her to change donors for the next insemination. In the future, she and her boss might share working-mommy anecdotes, breastfeeding challenges, daycare options and sleep-deprivation complaints. Bodies support other bodies, animal-human's nurture. In the long view, she and her boss would minimize Nora's embrace of assisted reproductive technology by focusing on their children.

"Betancourt's Bento." Strange new-millennium title for a yoga studio…sounded like a Japanese maze that included lunch. When Nora heard the name, it struck her as uncanny. She knew Nate's girlfriend was a yoga teacher in the East Village, her name was Lulu. She had done her research, and she figured out Betancourt was possibly run by Lulu. So, Nora called. Asked if Lulu worked there; the person who answered said, "She owns the place." Nora's heart skipped a beat. She'd catch a glimpse of that woman Nate had fallen for.

She entered the large space on Allen Street, found it humming: a small city of classes, services and rooms. Close to where Nate used to live. She couldn't help but think of him now, how he might have fathered her child and come back full-force into her life. Daniel was the one who heard that his cousin Nate had left the city, and Lonnie passed the news to Nora. She couldn't imagine her ex in the cold isolation of a small upstate college town, where he knew not a soul. But at least he finally

Cheryl J. Fish   263

procured that long elusive job. He had to contend with a long-distance relationship. How was that going? She wished he would have contacted her directly with his news, and she would have given him hers.

Her plan B had moved on its own trajectory; Nora invited Lonnie to tag along for insemination (round two). On the bus, they carried the heavy tank containing the frozen sperm from the storage lab to her reproductive endocrinologist's office. Lonnie sat in the examination room as Nora reclined on the table—fifteen minutes of what she called "post-insemination afterglow," pantomiming drags on a cigarette. Lonnie said she and Daniel weren't sure if they wanted kids—a relief for Nora, who figured maybe they wouldn't move away. That time proved to be the charm. Nora had help from gonadotropin, a fertility drug Lonnie had injected into her buttocks at the precise hour prescribed. Two weeks later, she tested positive for pregnancy. After peeing on a stick in the crowded bathroom during a free Patti Smith concert in Central Park, she thundered into the bleachers where her friends sat squished together: "Guess who's having a baby!"

Soon after, Nora informed Winn that his services weren't needed. "If it doesn't work out for some reason, I'm still available," he said. "I can be baby's Uncle Winn."

Inside the Bento, a harried elderly woman at the front desk directed Nora to Ms. Lulu herself. The yogini sat surrounded by Hindu art, depicting couples in the sexual embrace. On the carpet, a large stone Buddha presided over a fountain spouting water. Nora thought, how weird. I can't imagine Nate accepting new age drivel.

Nora filled out a form and answered a few questions, confirming that she was past her first trimester, which was necessary to take the class. She noticed a head of a frog inked below Lulu's shoulder blade. Her hair was shiny and two-toned beneath a head scarf. I get it, Nora acknowledged. She's enticing, calm...not a nag. Nora glanced at one painting, confounded by the pretzel logistics of a couple's sexual congress. How did they manage? Why were they on the wall? Did Lulu and Nate attempt such positions?

"I want to ensure you're in the right class," said Lulu. "You'll stop if you feel any discomfort or pain. There is a changing room. Bask in the experience. If you have questions, see me afterwards."

Nora felt pampered. She tried to stop thinking of carnal Hindus, Nate and Lulu's coitus, Y2K glitches. I'll partake of deep breathing and stretches with my limb-budding, gestating child. Amen.

Chapter Forty-Nine
Matter Over Mindfulness

(Lulu)

To Lulu, Nora was one of many newcomers that she showered with a personal touch: her way of doing business on and off the yoga mat in the dark days of December '99, performing *seva* and running from there to here. When she saw that name written on the consent form, a switch turned on. This must be Nate's ex-lover, Nora Jane. The one whose attentions and instigations helped shape the man she knew. What was she doing here, pregnant? Lulu recalled a story from Nate about his cousin Daniel's wedding—he and Nora had spoken privately in a room upstairs, patching things up somewhat drunkenly, with tears and poignant expressions of what-might-have-been. Nate didn't exactly confess to banging Nora, but Lulu had sensed it; they had been estranged. At that point, he was crazy jealous, ripe for revenge. Lulu started to sweat.

She imagined him cheating to get back at her...and fathering Nora's baby. Was he even aware Nora was expecting? She held her breath. Probably not. She tried to calculate the likelihood the child was his. She must inquire discreetly: piqued fear would not leave. Since she still taught one or two classes a week to keep her instructional skills, she decided to lead the prenatal session that Nate's former flame was attending. She would shift the regular teacher elsewhere.

Lulu entered the room and asked the students to begin with light stretches in a seated position. Then, she instructed the small group to gently roll their knees to the side, turning their heads in the opposite direction. Nora struggled. It reminded Lulu of Nate's initial awkwardness and hesitancy. Lulu kneeled at Nora's side. Adjusted her back and knees so they relaxed. Then she placed her hand on Nora's wrist. "You're on the path. Don't try so hard. Curl your knees into the air. I've got them." She gripped Nora's knees solidly.

"Thank you," Nora said, as tension eased from her brow. "I've never done this before. I've had a tiring work day."

"Let go of it all," said Lulu. Do for her what I'd do for anyone, she told herself.

Later, Nora let out an unfettered groan (something that had taken Nate weeks to accomplish). Turned out she had a cramp in her foot. So, Lulu took it gently into her hands and rubbed it thinking, we probably share many connections beyond our affection for Dr. Dart. She must find out who the baby's father was. She held her breath as she continued the session.

Afterwards, Nora, still on the mat, said "I feel more comfortable and centered. Thank you."

"You're very welcome," said Lulu. "Come back soon. Develop a routine, and everything will flow easier. You'll gain flexibility even as your belly grows."

"I will," said Nora.

"Partners can participate and be supportive," she said, creating this scenario on the spot.

"I'm doing this on my own," Nora said.

"Good for you."

Okay, she thought. But that did not fully address her worry.

***

Lulu realized Nate would be back in the city before she knew it, over Christmas break. They'd usher in the new century together. She kept busy planning a volunteer-run event for the holidays. They would feed festive meals to the homeless and the needy; freegan-in-chief Anita Willis helped, back from a triumphant protest against the World Trade Organization Ministerial conference in Seattle. They hoped the New

Year would bring mindfulness, peace and justice.

Lulu had received a call from Donna, who told her she visited Monroe. The gym teacher had met someone new. "She's a homegirl and a runner. Monroe's getting into his writing, so I'll send you some of his poems. Read them and give him a call. Mrs. Lady is asking after you, too." Lulu hoped her connection with Donna would endure.

As the winter solstice approached, new challenges appeared. One lover out of the picture, the other a weekend visitor. Temptations mostly slinked away with her old studio; she was channeling her libido into tasks and management decisions. She flirted casually with a few students that passed through her door but kept it light. A long-distance relationship became matter over mindfulness: heart always on the line. But Nate's exile stoked her protective, loving nature. She pampered him when he visited, staging everything from breakfast in bed to a burlesque act; she had him play-acting for her entertainment too. Her *shakti* energy spilled over into their lovemaking. He brought her books on every visit. An encyclopedia of feminist mythology, works by Robert Graves, H.D., Maryse Condé, and Toni Morrison. They liked to read from them out loud. Together, they found affordable housing for Ginny.

***

Nora returned to the yoga bento to take another pre-natal class. This time she brought along a friend she'd met in her single-mothers-by-choice group. While they grabbed their mats and blocks, Lulu heard them speak of catalogue numbers and sperm donors.

Lulu felt deliriously happy knowing Nora's baby was not likely conceived with Nate. Her shoulders relaxed, her smile radiated. Later that evening, as she meditated by her altar, she felt as if some master clock or hovering ancestor had pinged her in the waning days of the twentieth century. Might she choose to raise a child, conceived biologically or via adoption? With Nate perhaps, if their partnership thrived?

Chapter Fifty
Along the Path

(Nate)

Nate Dart snapped out of lunkheaded inertia when Janice Donovan phoned in desperation. One week into the Fall 1999 semester, she offered him the teaching position at the upstate New York college where he had blown his stack.

"We made a mistake," Janice dished humble pie over the line. "If you want the job, get here on the next bus."

He found out from Offendorf that the woman they had initially hired received a better offer elsewhere. Nate said yes to Donovan. He must accept. He was fired up about teaching, becoming gainfully employed at age 40, finally earning a steady salary with benefits. That pleased his father to no end. But the downside (realizing he would be living a three-and-a-half-hour car ride or five-hour bus trip from Lulu) gave him the gumption to ask for more money than they initially offered. He mentioned he had loans to repay. Janice cowered, saying she'd check with the dean.

"But don't worry, I'll insist," she promised.

"I'll be there," Nate answered.

He had left in a rush the second week of September. After settling in, he could even see himself staying on beyond the year of his contract. A small college town turned out to be a fitting setting for droll Dr. Dart, who became a favorite among English majors (if not the institutional rabble-rouser he had imagined). Armand enrolled in his Shakespeare course. Carrie Joan stopped by to discuss feminism and queer theory. Nate ran a study group for students who procrastinated or failed to complete their papers. He'd meet one-on-one with each person, listen to their specific struggles and encourage them by setting up a list of actions written in a planner. He required them to go to counseling and check in via email. On his door, he posted aphorisms, like this one from Emerson: "Always do what you are afraid to do."

"It works, most of the time," he told his group. "It took me too long to realize, so don't wait."

Nate had lured Lulu upstate only once since taking the position; in his fantasy, she'd hand over or sell her yoga Bento Box before too long (or establish a smaller version near his campus). He hadn't mentioned it, and felt a bit daft and sexist for such retrograde thinking—setting Lulu on a trajectory like his mother's, following Albert, downsizing her career.

As he sat, reading dense theory books and staring out the window at bare branches in the yard of his rented house, Nate wondered if Lulu would consent to settle down and marry him. He envisioned them together in a luxurious bed, his-and-her altars. But rather than spend more time gazing into the future, he looked forward to the Christmas break. She'd attend his family's holiday dinner; Audrey and Albert would finally meet Lulu. Rosa had been invited, but they weren't sure she'd make it. Lulu spoke of bringing her to Monroe's early in the year 2000. Since Nate would be on break, he planned to accompany her to New Orleans. How he looked forward to hearing jazz in clubs and on the streets and visiting the place of Louis Armstrong's birth, the city of the first family of jazz, the Marsalis's.

One day in mid-December, Audrey pulled up to his place for a short visit, presenting him with his swivel chair, which had been broken into two sections and packed inside the trunk. It was the sole piece of furniture from his studio apartment he had wanted to keep. He told her he was grading papers and chipping away at an essay on jealousy and love triangles in Shakespeare and contemporary film.

"Read me your draft," she said. "I'll give you feedback."

"After dinner, Mom. I'm taking you out."

The next morning, when it was time for her drive back, Nate had a flash of genius. "Can you drop me off in the city?"

"Sure, dear." He sat in silence during the ride, visualizing Lulu in her legendary orange-and-pink spandex top, replaying their initial coupling. Imagining the best way to sneak up and surprise her.

As he entered the Bento Box on Allen Street, he saw Ginny at the front desk, thumbing through a book on the sutras. He asked to see Lulu.

"She's teaching pre-natal in room three," said Ginny. "Don't interrupt."

"I'm just going to peer in," he said. There were small fiberglass panels on each side of the studio doors. He walked down the hall.

He looked inside. Lulu crouched to tend to someone's foot. She never rubbed mine, he thought. When she moved to the front of the room, he almost lost his lunch. There was Nora! Struggling to stand from a seated pose, looking lost but determined. He made out a rolling hill of a belly. Feeling flushed and weak, Nate's throat grew as course as sand paper, his legs turning into Jell-O.

What was happening? Lulu and Nora knew each other? Were they conspiring? His mind made desperate throw-back calculations to his wedding tryst with Nora. He leaned against the wall. What if she was carrying his child? As terror surged through his body, his breathing accelerated. Was this a panic attack? He was about to burst into the yoga room when Lulu turned around, likely noting his sallow, troubled face. Her lovely mouth upturned into a smile. She spoke some words to the class. Slipped out, shutting the door softly.

"Nate!" she threw her arms around his neck. "I wasn't expecting you for two more weeks."

He was too flustered to move or speak.

"Your skin is clammy," she said. "Are you ill?"

"What…is Nora doing in there?"

Lulu giggled. "Yes. Strange, isn't it? She showed up to take a class a couple of weeks ago, came back for more, just like you did. When

I read her name on the release form, I realized who she was."

"So…you recently met?"

"Yes. She knows who I am. We haven't acknowledged it, or discussed you."

He bit his lip.

"I have to get back inside," she said. "You look like you were hit by a truck."

"Feels like it."

He failed to mention any pregnancy. Lulu could read the fear in his eyes.

"Don't stress, Natey," she grabbed his arm. "It's not yours."

He stroked her shoulders.

"Of course, it's not mine," he shouted. How did she know? He would not ask. His stomach began to settle. He realized the cadence of such a coincidence. Quite a hoot!

"Go back inside," he said, in a near-normal voice. "Guide those sweet mamas. I'll be waiting."

Nate found a mat. He rolled it open in the hallway. He reached down, came within an inch of touching his toes…damn close. Might get there eventually. He kneeled on all fours and rose up, then flowed to the floor, going from downward-facing dog to cobra, then child's pose, kneeling, head tucked into his chest, arms close to his sides. Snuggled, soft. Finally, he rested: a splayed-in-the-hallway *savasana*.

He could sustain postures for longer intervals than before, with some backpedaling. With all that tensing and releasing over the past year, his jealousy and forgiveness muscles had acquired new grooves, like compartments inside a queen bee's hive. As he came to realize that he'd struggle and adjust as best as he could, and he'd collapse too, his convictions soared. He stood up slowly, treading lighter along the path.

THE END

ACKNOWLEDGMENTS

OFF THE YOGA MAT in its current form took many years, set-asides, and revisions to complete. I am filled with gratitude for the many readers and supporters who contributed to the novel's development and changes over time.

Jackie Cangro and Suman Sridhar read first-draft chapters; their comments and enthusiastic support made a huge impact. Beta readers of early drafts included Margaret Barrow, Karie Parker-Davidson, Jane Weiss, and Suzanne Louis; Jane Cousins read the manuscript during the COVID-19 pandemic and provided thoughtful feedback. Help with Finnish language and historical accuracy came from Annika Lindman and Suzanne Louis. Yoga teachers Renee Simon and Kendra Mylnechuk Potter affirmed the accuracy of descriptions and terminology of yoga *asanas,* and yogi/writer Stefanie Lipsey published an excerpt on her blog *Writing Yoga.* My two prose-writing groups helped me work out significant details: Thanks to Jonathan Vatner, Kathleen Crisci, Carol Bartold, Judith Padow, Pitchaya Sudbanthad, Sujata Shekar, Mark Prins. Workshop sessions with Roxanna Robinson, Whitney Otto, Lisa Garrigues, and the Writers Hotel pre-conference feedback from Scott Wolven and Shanna McNair proved invaluable. Sam Hiyate helped with pacing and development; Sabrina Lightstone provided feedback and enthusiasm. *L Magazine* (no longer publishing) named an excerpt from the manuscript a finalist in their fiction contest. Thanks to Bonnie Jo Campbell, Sheryl St. Germain, Linda Cutting, Deborah Chiel, Lila Fish, Christine Youngberg, Kathryn Paulsen, Karen E. Bender, Marlene Barr, Angie Pohja, Liselotte Wajstedt, Liisa Holmberg, Toni Lahtinen, Fulbright Finland, University of Tampere, University of Helsinki, and US Fulbright Foundation for support, feedback, opportunity, and inspiration. Residencies at Wellspring House, Drop, Forge and Tool, Kulttuurikauppila, Atlantic Center for the Arts, and a desk at The Writer's Room near Astor Place provided time and community for writing. Thanks to Katelyn Peters for editing the final manuscript, Sasha Berry and Marjorie Shaffer for helping with page proofs, Alexia Howell for her perceptive reading on delicate issues. Finally, I'm grateful to Joe Taylor at Livingston Press for believing in this book.

Cheryl J. Fish grew up in Flushing, NY. She is a poet, fiction writer and environmental justice scholar. Her recent books of poetry include CRATER & TOWER, on trauma and ecology after the Mount St. Helens volcanic eruption and the terrorist attack of 9/11/01, and THE SAUNA IS FULL OF MAIDS, poems and photographs celebrating Finnish sauna culture, the natural world, and friendships. Her poems have appeared in journals and anthologies, including *Poetics-for-the-More-than-Human-World, New American Writing, Newtown Literary, Terrain.org, Reed, and Hanging Loose.* Her short fiction has been published in *Iron Horse Literary Review, CheapPop, Spank the Carp,* and *Liar's League.* Fish's essays on films and photography by Sami artists challenging mining and extraction have appeared in the books ARCTIC CINEMAS; NORDIC NARRATIVES OF NATURE AND THE ENVIRON-MENT; AND CRITICAL NORTHS: SPACE, NATURE, THEORY. She is the author of two books and essays on African-American travel writing, June Jordan's environmental justice poetics, and women's travel literature. Fish has been a Fulbright professor in Finland and visiting professor at Mt. Holyoke College; she teaches at BMCC/City University of New York, and is a docent lecturer in the Dept. of Cultures at University of Helsinki.